Warden of Time

Books in the *After Cilmeri* Series:
Daughter of Time (prequel)
Footsteps in Time (Book One)
Winds of Time
Prince of Time (Book Two)
Crossroads in Time (Book Three)
Children of Time (Book Four)
Exiles in Time
Castaways in Time
Ashes of Time
Warden of Time
Guardians of Time
Masters of Time
Outpost in Time
Shades of Time
Champions of Time

The Gareth and Gwen Medieval Mysteries:
The Bard's Daughter
The Good Knight
The Uninvited Guest
The Fourth Horseman
The Fallen Princess
The Unlikely Spy
The Lost Brother
The Renegade Merchant
The Unexpected Ally

The Lion of Wales Series:
Cold My Heart
The Oaken Door
Of Men and Dragons
A Long Cloud
Frost Against the Hilt

A Novel from the *After Cilmeri* Series

WARDEN OF TIME

by

SARAH WOODBURY

Warden of Time

Cover image by Christine DeMaio-Rice at Flip City Books

To Deb, Tom, and Jon
... who've been in this with me
from the start

A Brief Guide to Welsh Pronunciation

c a hard 'c' sound (Cadfael)

ch a non-English sound as in Scottish 'ch' in 'loch' (Fychan)

dd a buzzy 'th' sound, as in 'there' (Ddu; Gwynedd)

f as in 'of' (Cadfael)

ff as in 'off' (Gruffydd)

g a hard 'g' sound, as in 'gas' (Goronwy)

l as in 'lamp' (Llywelyn)

ll a breathy /sh/ sound that does not occur in English (Llywelyn)

rh a breathy mix between 'r' and 'rh' that does not occur in English (Rhys)

th a softer sound than for 'dd,' as in 'thick' (Arthur)

u a short 'ih' sound (Gruffydd), or a long 'ee' sound (Cymru—pronounced 'kumree')

w as a consonant, it's an English 'w' (Llywelyn); as a vowel, an 'oo' sound (Bwlch)

y the only letter in which Welsh is not phonetic. It can be an 'ih' sound, as in 'Gwyn,' is often an 'uh' sound (Cymru), and at the end of the word is an 'ee' sound (thus, both Cymru—the modern word for Wales—and Cymry—the word for Wales in the Dark Ages—are pronounced 'kumree')

CAST OF CHARACTERS

David (Dafydd)—Time-traveler, King of England
Lili—Queen of England, Ieuan's sister
Callum—Time-traveler, Earl of Shrewsbury
Cassie—Time-traveler, Callum's wife
Ieuan—Welsh knight, one of David's men
Bronwen—Time-traveler, married to Ieuan
Arthur—son of David and Lili (born June 1289)
Catrin—daughter of Ieuan and Bronwen (born Nov. 1288)

Nicholas de Carew—Norman/Welsh lord
William de Bohun—David's squire
Justin—David's captain
Bevyn—David's adviser
Huw—Member of the Order of the Pendragon
Darren Jeffries—time traveler (bus passenger)
Peter Cobb—time traveler (bus passenger)
Rachel Wolff—time traveler (bus passenger)

1

September 1292

David

The courtyard of Canterbury Castle was full of men and horses when Carew and I entered it. I was already late for my meeting with the emissary from the pope at the Archbishop's palace, and my guard had been gathering in preparation for accompanying me.

It was true that the King of England came and went as he pleased, and even a papal legate couldn't complain if I blew him off, but it might get our meeting off on the wrong foot. I didn't want the legate to read anything untoward into my lateness or think me petty, but it probably couldn't be helped that he would. It wasn't as if I was going to explain what had held me up.

Looking for Callum, I put one foot in the stirrup and boosted myself to a standing position so I could look over the heads of everyone else, but I didn't see him. He and Carew were supposed to be coming with me. I was about to drop to the ground again when Peter Cobb, lately of Avalon, led his horse underneath the gatehouse. He stopped to speak to the guard at the gate before continuing through it. As I watched, the guard pointed towards the castle steps. Peter looked in that direction, his brow furrowing, and I waved a hand to draw his attention. His expression cleared, and he hurried toward me.

"What's up?" I said, settling into my saddle as he reached me.

"Callum asked that I report to you," Peter said, speaking in a variation of medieval English so Carew could understand him. "We've found Noah and Mike."

"Where?" Carew stood nearby, about to mount his horse.

"In an alley outside an inn," Peter said.

I looked at Peter warily, thinking this could not be the good news it seemed at first. Lee, Mike, and Noah, my three most discontented time traveling bus passengers, had been missing since earlier that morning. At first I'd thought nothing of it—they'd been carousing and womanizing since they'd arrived in the Middle Ages ten months ago—but then my old captain, Bevyn, had arrived in Canterbury, having traveled all the way from Wales, to tell me the bad news.

These three weren't just discontented. They were traitors. And it was dealing with the consequences of their treachery that had made me late for my meeting.

Peter sighed. "They're both dead. Noah was stabbed and Mike's throat was cut."

"Oh, wow." The exclamation came out before I could modify it to something more appropriate to the moment.

"That means murder," Carew said. "Did you return just to tell us that or does Callum want King David to come to him?"

"Please, sire." Peter took in a breath. "Lee left a message Callum thinks you ought to see."

"You'd better lead the way," I said.

Peter mounted and headed back towards the gate.

Justin, the captain of my guard, had been talking to several other soldiers. At the sight of me following Peter to the gate, he quickly organized a phalanx of knights and men-at-arms to accompany me. I wouldn't have left the castle with just Peter and Carew—I knew better than to do that—but a small, evil, and unworthy part of me had been amused to see Justin sweat about it. It was better than thinking about what faced me in that alley.

I wasn't squeamish. I'd killed men myself too many times. It wasn't something I was proud of, but it was a fact of my life, going back to that first fight against King Edward's forces at the Conwy River when I was fourteen. Murder, however, was different from battles, even if it made no material sense that it should be. It was a crime not only against the people who died, but against their families and the state as well.

"Where are we going, sire?" Justin said as he pulled up beside me.

"Callum has found Mike and Noah," I said. "Dead."

Justin's mouth formed a silent 'O', and then he waved a hand to his men to form a tighter grouping around me. Two guards rode in front, with Peter ahead of them leading the way. The main street of Canterbury was wide enough for four men to ride abreast, and we ended up in something of a diamond formation, with Carew and me in the middle.

The people of Canterbury were out in force since it was barely noon, and they scurried to get out of the way, gawking and bowing as we passed.

Peter didn't take us far—we could have walked, though I generally didn't walk anywhere. It was a matter of a few turnings among progressively narrower streets until he arrived in an alleyway between an inn and a row of two-story houses built one against the other. The alley had been blocked off by a wooden sawhorse, and a crowd of people six or seven deep pressed against the barrier.

Peter elbowed his way through them, and Justin got his men to clear a path for me. I dismounted just outside the alleyway and handed my reins to an eight-year-old boy who stood watching. I hoped he hadn't seen the dead men, but this being the Middle Ages, he probably had. "Take care of my horse for me, will you, son?"

His eyes widened when he realized who I was, and he ducked his head and bowed. "Yes, sire."

Carew and the others followed me as I sidled between the barrier and the wall. Several guardsmen stood facing outward, shielding the dead men on the ground from the onlookers' view. Each bent his head to me as I moved through them, and then I stopped short as soon as I saw what lay beyond their circle: Noah and Mike, just as Peter had said.

Blood soaked the front of Mike's gray tunic, having flowed from a terrible wound in his throat. It looked as if Noah had been harder to kill—perhaps having come through the doorway of the inn into the alley with more wariness than Mike. He'd been stabbed in the midsection, and from the amount of blood coating his shirt, he'd bled out after having been settled against the wall. More blood pooled underneath both men.

Dr. Rachel Wolff, another bus passenger, crouched before Noah's body. She took notes on a piece of paper, her eyes flicking from the bodies to her medieval version of a clipboard. She looked over at me and grimaced but then went back to her work. I was glad I hadn't eaten anything since breakfast. I didn't think I would have lost the contents of my stomach on the ground, but my meal would have sat like a rock in my clenched belly.

Callum stood with one arm folded across his chest and his fist to his chin. He acknowledged me with a nod of his head as I came to stand beside him. "Thank you for coming."

"Of course." I consciously steadied my breathing. It wasn't that I was feeling light-headed exactly, but it was best to pre-empt any possibility that I might. "What do we know?"

Callum gestured towards Mike and Noah. "They're dead, as you can see. I have men questioning the neighbors and the owner of the inn to see if anyone saw or heard anything. Jeffries is heading up that task as he has the most experience. It seems Mike and Noah trusted Lee when they shouldn't have." Then Callum pointed to the alley wall.

Up until that point, I'd had eyes only for the bodies, but now I allowed my gaze to roam upward. An image of a fist had been painted in the middle of the wall, in what I thought (sickeningly) might be blood. I really hoped it wasn't. Below the drawing were the words: *Tiocfaidh ár lá.*

"I'm not sure what I'm looking at," I said.

Callum glanced at me in surprise, and then he dropped his arms and turned to look at me more fully. "I apologize, my lord. I forgot where you grew up. It means, 'our day will come', in Irish Gaelic. That's a slogan of the Irish resistance to English rule."

"Lee did this?" I said.

"Who else could have drawn that fist?" Callum said. "It isn't as if we might possibly entertain the idea that Noah and Mike were jumped by street thieves."

"I suppose not."

I rubbed my chin, more befuddled than I could articulate by this turn of events. While I dithered beside Callum, two of my men covered both bodies with cloths so they were no longer exposed to sight. Rachel had straightened to talk to Peter, and Callum gestured that they should come closer. "Do you know the time of death?" he said.

"The bodies are warm, but they're stiffening," she said.

"So, they've been dead a few hours," Callum said.

"More than three, but fewer than twelve. I don't have the equipment to say better than that," she said. "The alley is used to store refuse, and the killer scattered straw over the bodies, so they weren't found immediately. But you're right, it couldn't have been long."

"Mike and Noah were seen in the castle shortly after dawn," I said, "but not since then."

Rachel checked the sky with a quick glance. "It's noon now? So, that puts time of death within six hours." She nodded. "That makes sense."

Footfalls came from behind me, and Bevyn's gruff voice said, "Sire, we have a cart available. Can we move the bodies?"

I turned to look at my old captain, not actually knowing the answer, but Callum nodded. While Rachel and Peter moved off with Bevyn to supervise the work, Callum and I shifted to one side to allow room for the cart to maneuver in the narrow alley.

Cassie, another fellow time-traveler and Callum's wife, had been standing a few feet away, studying the writing, and now she joined us too. "Why would Lee write that on the wall?"

I let out a breath I hadn't realized I'd been holding. "I'm standing here, aren't I? It's a message from Lee to me."

2

The day had started out so well, too. It had begun like most of my days, with me rising at dawn, having woken beside my beautiful wife. Pregnant again, Lili was past the worst of the nausea and radiated health. Although Lili's overall serenity was hard to undermine, she and I shared a mutual panic that in a few short months we were going to have to meet the emotional needs of *two* children. Without disturbing her, I'd slipped out of bed to find my three-year-old son wide awake in the adjacent room. We'd breakfasted together, Arthur talking non-stop the whole time.

He'd then played at my feet for the next hour as I'd signed documents, made plans, and overseen the many divisions within my government. It was laborious work, often tedious and frustrating, but it was also necessary for the running of the country. My routine was the same whether I was staying in Westminster Palace, York, or here, at Canterbury, sixty miles east of London, and would have been even if I hadn't been trying to drag England towards a future it probably wasn't ready for.

Other daily appointments included hearing grievances in the great hall and conferring with a larger group of men—essentially my cabinet, consisting of any officers of state and representatives from Parliament who'd come to my court that day. Politics had become my life. No wonder King Edward, my predecessor, had spent so much time making war. It was easier than keeping the peace.

Then had come the bad news: Bevyn had stormed through the door of the expansive room that I was using as my office, my brother-in-law, Ieuan, on his heels, and announced that not only had Lee, Mike, and Noah fled the castle together with their belongings, but that Lee, in particular, had spent the last ten months working against me and my father, the King of Wales.

We hadn't known then that Mike and Noah were already lying dead in the alley, so we hadn't yet made the Irish connection, but what Bevyn had turned up was daunting enough: Lee had taken money my father had given him as an allowance and used it to charm those he could befriend and bribe those he couldn't into becoming his allies, in preparation for a possible rebellion against my father. The list of people involved ranged from high lords within the Kingdom of Wales to men-at-arms to lowly serving maids.

"I thought Lee had become something of a friend," I said, more than a little nonplussed to learn I'd harbored a snake in my court.

Bevyn's face had been devoid of all expression. "I know."

Years of acquaintance with Bevyn had taught me to listen when he spoke, even if I didn't like the words he said. He and I had gone through a rough patch in the aftermath of my crowning as King of England, but my fundamental trust in his loyalty—and my need for his wisdom—had pushed me to move past my occasional concerns about his methods.

More often than not, when Bevyn and I were together, we fell easily into old patterns of master and apprentice. I didn't begrudge Bevyn his role. He'd been my first teacher in Wales. He'd give his life for me, as would Carew, Callum, and Ieuan. And I'd give mine for them. Sometimes, when I hated being king a little too much, I felt like I already had.

"He must have been prepared to leave at a moment's notice." Ieuan's blue eyes had flashed with annoyance, and his black hair had been mussed as if he'd run his hands through it several times. He was wearing it long these days, pulled back and tied at the base of his neck with a leather cord. Lili, his sister and my wife, thought he looked particularly dashing that way.

I wasn't one to judge another man's style, but I'd resolutely kept my own sandy brown hair cropped close to my head, the better to manage the wearing of a helmet. Or a crown. Lili complained that it was really that I was too lazy to be bothered with doing anything else with it.

Bevyn grimaced. "I wouldn't be surprised if he had a contact in Wales or London who warned him I was coming. He could have been ready for the day when I learned the truth about

what he's been doing all these months and acted against him."
Bevyn was a legend among the Welsh soldiers and spoken of
almost like the bogey-man among the English ones. He'd been my
first captain and was now castellan of Llanfaes Castle on Anglesey.
He was also one of the leaders—if not *the* leader—of the very
secretive Order of the Pendragon, whose purpose was to protect
me and my interests.

I kept my gaze steady on Bevyn's face and resisted the urge
to lift my eyes to the painted and carved ceiling above my head,
struggling against my frustration and anger, and trying not to
direct either at Bevyn, who was only the bearer of bad news.

"If I may." Callum looked at me warily, as if he knew what
could have been coming from my lips and wasn't convinced it
wouldn't at any second, "that could be the good news. We could
have forced them to run before they were ready."

"I hope you're right about that, but you may need to
reexamine your use of the word *good*," I said.

Bevyn pounded a gloved fist into the palm of his other
hand. "I failed you, sire."

"No, Bevyn," I said. "It is I who should have been smarter."

Up until May, Lee had been lumped in among the
malcontents who'd vexed my mother so severely she'd come to me
for an intervention. Mike, in particular, had been nothing but
trouble from the first moment he'd arrived in the medieval world.
For most of the past year, the three men had lived at Caerphilly

Castle in Wales with a number of other bus passengers who'd banded together in their disgruntlement.

Not that I could really blame them. Through no fault of their own, they'd found themselves in the Middle Ages, simply because they'd happened to be on the same bus as my mother and sister at a moment when Mom's and Anna's lives were in danger. What happened to them wasn't their fault.

What was their fault was how they responded to the adversity. Being on that bus may have ensured their survival, since the bombing of Cardiff's city hall and courthouse must have killed quite a few people inside the buildings and on the road, but these disgruntled few didn't necessarily see it that way. Nor were they in any way thankful for the help they'd received once here. They resented their need to forge new lives and refused to even try to make the best of it.

During the time these discontented passengers had spent under my mother's watchful eye, Lee, for the most part, had been an enigma to her. With every day that passed, however, Mike had grown more combative. He was a large man, taller than I, and he outweighed me by forty pounds, which made him dangerous when he was drunk. In turn, Noah, Mike's partner in crime, had spent those same six months at Mike's right hand, drinking him under the table despite being one-third smaller. Noah had a narrow face and pointed chin—and a wolfish way of looking at a man like he was assessing whether or not to eat him for dinner—or like a rat inspecting a particularly dubious piece of cheese.

Their drinking and carousing had reached a point where my mother demanded that I either throw them into a dungeon, as my father wanted, or try to make something of them. Last May, I'd chosen the latter, in hopes that seeing more of this new world they lived in might assuage their discontent. In truth, I felt guilty about their continued presence in the Middle Ages, knowing that I could take them back to the modern world if I was willing to risk all of our lives to make that transition one more time.

But it was a risk I wasn't willing to take. It might be the one time it didn't work. And I certainly wasn't willing to risk my mother or sister on that chance. What made my decision all the harder was that they all knew it—from the very beginning we'd been honest about who we were and what we were capable of—and it was an honesty we all had to live with, Mike, Noah, and Lee included.

Thus, also at my mother's urging, I'd taken Lee, the only other single, male bus passenger staying at Caerphilly, into my court too. Within a day of the trio's arrival in London, however, Mike's and Noah's behavior had reached an epic low. In a drunken stupor, the pair had climbed onto the wall-walk and peed off it onto the head of the captain of the garrison. They'd spent two nights in a cell simply to sober them up.

On the third day of their incarceration, with me showing no signs of letting them out, Lee had come to me to speak for both of them. Mike had only ever given me bravado and monosyllabic answers, and the less volatile Noah had risen to a certain degree of sullenness, still without much in the way of forthcomingness. But that day, Lee showed himself to be perfectly polite, sharply intelligent, and in possession of a keen sense of humor. He didn't smile often, but when he did, it lit his pale face. He'd reminded me of Callum's friend and confidant, Mark Jones—not in looks, since Lee was six feet tall and thinly muscular—but in attitude.

Lee had sworn to me that from that day forward Mike and Noah would live a reformed life, and if they didn't, I could conscript them into my newly-established navy. So I'd given the pair one more chance and been rewarded because they *had* reformed. Or so it had appeared. I couldn't help thinking now that Mike, Noah, and Lee, like the Three Stooges, had been running rings around me the whole time. Except these three weren't funny.

Instead of rescuing Mike and Noah from my (and the garrison captain's) wrath out of the goodness of his heart, Lee had made himself the ringleader of the three men, and their reformation had been only on the surface.

To my credit, I hadn't entirely bought the idea that they were completely reformed. I'd brought all three with me on this journey to Canterbury out of a growing belief that something wasn't quite right about them. There had been an innate brutality about Mike and a slyness in Noah that had worried me, and I'd been afraid to leave them alone in London under less watchful eyes. My intuition, unfortunately, hadn't revealed to me any specifics, or that it was Lee I had to be most wary of, not the other two.

It looked as if my father's suggestion to toss the trio into the Tower of London would have been the better choice. But even though I'd often wished that Mike and Noah hadn't been on that bus, I would never in a million years have wanted them dead.

3

"What message is that?" Cassie said. "Free Ireland?"

I shrugged. "That's what it looks like to me."

Ireland was an ongoing problem. Portions of it had been conquered by Norman barons over a hundred years ago, and the English king had ruled it ever since, taking the title of Lord of Ireland. I'd reluctantly inherited that authority four years ago when I'd become King of England and had been trying to negotiate a graceful way out of ruling it ever since.

"What sucks is that my sympathies are entirely with the Irish," I said. "I just haven't figured out how to leave."

"It would be easier if you didn't mind your barons rising up against you," Cassie said.

"And even if I were willing to risk that—which quite frankly I am—I won't be able to change anything if I'm not the king."

"Catch-22," Cassie said.

"To Lee, that might be a pathetic excuse for inaction," I said. "After my crowning, I put off dealing with rights for women because discrimination seemed too culturally ingrained and difficult to change. It was easier not to address it. This is the same."

"As always, you're too hard on yourself." Callum said. "You have so much on your plate already."

"That may be, but when will I have less?" I said.

The answer, of course, was *never*.

Cassie studied the wall, her brow furrowed. "I still don't get it. How does that symbol on the wall, and that writing, which only Callum understands, free Ireland? Why kill Mike and Noah? What's the point of any of this?"

"We won't know until we find him, though it occurs to me that I may know something about Lee that could help us," I said.

"That's more than I can say," Callum said.

"That reminds me—" I gestured to the wall, "—of something Lee said a while back. Several times since he came to London, Lee mentioned the Troubles in Ireland, the ones with a capital 'T'. When he mentioned them, I made sympathetic noises, but I didn't want to talk about Ireland with him since it's a sore point, as you know. I do remember him mentioning some talks that were due to start around the time you left Avalon in the bus." I glanced from Cassie to Callum. "Do you guys know anything about that?"

Callum frowned. "I do. Cardiff was to be neutral ground for a meeting of representatives from the Republic of Ireland, Northern Ireland, and England, as well as the EU. The economic crisis had brought some problems to the forefront that needed to be resolved. The negotiations were to begin the week after we left."

"Maybe that's why Lee was in Cardiff that day," I said.

"Are you wondering if he was there as a demonstrator?" Callum said.

"He could have been. It's clear he doesn't think much of English control of Ireland," I said.

"There's a big difference between demonstrating in front of city hall and murder," And then Cassie gave a gasp as she realized what she'd said.

A wintry chill settled in my chest, and my breath caught in my throat too. "City Hall."

Cassie looked from me to Callum. "He couldn't have—" She broke off.

Callum put up both hands. "Can we put anything past him, given that he murdered Mike and Noah?"

"But if he had something to do with the bombing—" Cassie closed her eyes for a second. "I have never met an angrier man than Lee."

"Before we get too far ahead of ourselves with this, are we sure that the murders are his doing?" I said, and then at the incredulous looks on my friends' faces, grimaced. "Yeah, you're right. I'd be stupid to think otherwise."

"We must be very careful," Cassie said. "Armed and dangerous doesn't quite cover it."

"We already know about his activities in Wales," Callum said. "If his anger is directed at David, and if it's about Ireland, that's where we start our inquiries."

"David, he could be gunning for you," Cassie said.

"He hasn't tried to murder me yet. He's had opportunities before. You know he has." I chewed on my lower lip as I thought. "I'm more worried about my father."

"You sent a pigeon to Cardiff to warn him that Lee is missing," Callum said. "You've done what you can. Your father will be prepared in case Lee returns to Wales to renew his mischief there. But I think he won't. He's up to something else."

"If that's true, why murder Mike and Noah? Why now?" Cassie said. "What are we missing?"

"A lot," I said. "Not even Bevyn saw this coming."

"Lee could have other plans for you," Cassie said. "It's only you, your sister, and your mother who can return him to Avalon. Maybe Lee wants you alive so you can take him back when he's ready."

"After he's wreaked havoc here, you mean," Callum said dryly.

"It's odd," I said. "He never once talked in my presence about returning to Avalon."

"Mike did," Cassie said. "He talked about it all the time. It was annoying."

"But not Lee," I said. "What if he was glad to find himself here because this is where the conquest of Ireland started? What if he thinks he can change things now so the future never happens?"

Cassie frowned. "He does realize this is a different universe, right? We think of ourselves as time travelers, but we're really not."

"He knows," Callum said.

I ran a hand through my hair, my eyes going automatically to the bloodstained ground where the bodies had lain. I forced myself to turn away. "As important as Lee may be, he must take a back seat to my current and very pressing dispute with the Church. I was due at the Archbishop's palace an hour ago."

"I would agree that the dispute with the Church is more important—unless Lee's sudden departure and your disagreement with the pope have something to do with one another," Callum said.

"I can't see how that could be," I said.

Callum made a rueful face, and I returned my eyes to the ground, silently nodding in acknowledgement that it usually paid to keep an open mind when it came to affairs of state. I looked up again in time to see the identical apprehensive look cross both Cassie's and Callum's faces, which would have been comical if the situation hadn't been so serious.

With the bodies loaded into its bed, the cart headed down the alley towards the cross street. Mike and Noah would lie in a room off the barracks awaiting a more thorough examination by

Rachel. It wasn't a task I envied her. She'd already mounted her horse in preparation for returning to the castle, and Cassie left us to join her. Beyond them, the crowd had moved aside to let the cart pass by, and then Justin replaced the barricade.

"Who found the bodies in the first place?" I asked Callum. Now that everyone else had dispersed to their various duties, he, Carew, and Bevyn were my only remaining companions.

"Jeffries," Bevyn said, butchering Darren's name into something barely recognizable. Bevyn's English was functional, but he hadn't ever gotten a handle on English names, which he considered bizarre and unnatural. "He and Cobb together."

Darren Jeffries and Peter Cobb had also been on that bus. While Darren had worked at MI-5 with Callum and stuck close to my mom and sister, even knowing they were time travelers, Peter had been in the wrong place at the wrong time. Fortunately for Peter, he fit right in. He hadn't worked for the intelligence services, but he'd served in the military in Afghanistan, even doing a stint in the military police. Both men were now part of Callum's personal retinue.

"Keep them at it." I put my hand on Callum's shoulder. "Whatever you're doing, however this hunt progresses, they are from Avalon and need to be involved. My family brought Lee here. I included him in my court. He is *my* responsibility."

"I don't agree, but I hear what you're saying," Callum said. None of the others even blinked any more at my use of the word *Avalon* as a way to talk about the modern world. We all used it now, time travelers and medieval people alike. With the arrival of the bus, a portion of the truth had literally fallen front and center into everyone's laps, and there was no more denial: we were from a different world. Fortunately, accusations of witchcraft hadn't yet been leveled at any of us.

For all that it had always been a fear of ours, that fear arose more from media representations of the Middle Ages than actual fact. While the burning of heretics was common practice in this time, the witch trials that had spread throughout Europe were still over a hundred years in the future. The Spanish Inquisition, which was responsible for tens of thousands of deaths, was another hundred more.

"I should have acted against Lee sooner," Callum said.

"You did more than I," I said.

What I didn't say, because Callum already knew it, was that the best thing about the arrival of the bus last year was that it had brought forty potential friends from the modern world to medieval Wales to share this life with us. The simple fact that we were all stuck here together gave us a feeling of camaraderie. It was natural—and maybe even necessary, given how hard this life could be—to assume the best until someone proved him or herself untrustworthy. I had viewed my three malcontents as an irritation, not a threat, and now my fingers were well and truly burned.

I was reminded again why monarchies were a bad idea. Too much depended upon the whims of a single man—in this case, me—who sometimes didn't listen as closely to his advisers as he should or listened to the wrong people.

Nicholas de Carew, who'd so far said nothing and wore a noncommittal expression on his face, made a dismissive motion with one hand. "It's everyone's fault. We've long known about Mike's and Noah's discontent. Lee held himself apart at Caerphilly, but we should have been keeping a closer eye on all of them before this."

Half-Welsh and half-English, Carew maintained a double life in this new world order I'd created. Upon the execution of William de Valence, my father had installed Carew as the Lord of Pembroke, which had been Valence's title under King Edward. In England, Carew was the Earl of Winchester, with most of his lands in the south and west of the country. Not quite forty years old, he cut a fine figure—tall and broad shouldered—and always wore the latest clothing styles. Today he wore a blue tunic and tight brown breeches tucked into high black boots. To his regret, however, his blond hair was both graying and balding.

Some of my barons had accused me of favoring my Welsh advisers over my English ones, but for all their complaints, only Ieuan and Bevyn were truly Welsh, and they'd earned their place beside me. I relied on their wisdom every day, and I was pretty sure I wouldn't have had a kingdom to govern at all without their help.

During the two years that Callum had been stuck in the modern world, I'd missed him more than I could say. Not only was he well-educated, smart, and capable, but I valued his ability to see situations clearly. Although he'd taken up the mantle of the Earl of Shrewsbury upon his return to the Middle Ages, he spent most of his time in my court.

As with Carew, I tried not to feel guilty about making him neglect his lands and people—they were by definition my lands and people too—but Callum had a capable steward in our mutual friend, Samuel. And I *needed* Callum, especially today—and that was before I'd learned about what Lee had been up to during the ten months he'd lived in the Middle Ages.

I looked away, sifting through the interactions I'd had with Lee for anything I might have told him that he could use against me. I hadn't involved Lee in any confidential plans, but by the simple fact of living at my court, Lee knew more about me and my rule than I would want an enemy to know. He'd been part of my entourage for months, and it seemed he'd been working against me the whole time, just as he'd been working against my father while in Wales. I could only hope that by removing him from my father's court, I'd short-circuited whatever insurrection he'd been planning there. It may be that we'd inadvertently been just in time.

Unfortunately, even with the Irish fist on the wall, we didn't know what he intended here in England. Any time over the last three months, he and I could have talked about something that was of lesser importance to me, which I'd since forgotten, but was vital to him.

I closed my eyes, sickened through and through and fighting to put aside my personal resentment so I could deal with what was before me. Controlling my expression was something I'd been practicing. I didn't need to hide my feelings from these close companions. They would have known I felt betrayed even if I didn't say anything.

I was already facing the greatest challenge of my reign so far in this confrontation with the papal legate, over what the pope saw as an excess of religious freedom in England. When I saw the legate, I needed to make sure that the only emotions that showed on my face were ones I wanted him to see.

Then, as if the weather knew what a crappy day this had already been, the clouds let loose their rain. We all took a step back into the relative shelter of the alley wall. Within a minute, the bloody image across from me began to run, and I studied it morosely. Though the dark clouds mirrored my low mood, that mood hadn't, in fact, begun this morning, but at the moment the Archbishop of Canterbury had asked me to travel to his seat.

He'd done so because the papal legate, Cardinal Acquasparta, had fallen ill on the journey across the English Channel. Once he'd reached land, it had become clear that he wasn't suffering from the usual seasickness. He'd managed to make it to Canterbury, but so far had been too ill to complete the journey to London, to the point of being bedridden and near death.

I would have been happy to wait to meet him until he recovered. In fact, I'd been avoiding for months (if not years) what I was sure would be a disagreeable conversation. But a papal legate, and the pope's concerns about my rule of England, could be put off for only so long.

In addition to not wanting to talk about religious matters with Acquasparta, I was worried about the precedent it set. Delegations presented themselves to the King of England, not the other way around. I wasn't normally one to stand on ceremony, but I was very aware of my precarious position. I didn't want to appear as a supplicant, especially not to this pope, especially not when everybody (me included) knew my stance on the freedom of religion was so at odds with his.

On the positive side, the papal legate hadn't rejected my offer to have Aaron, my physician and friend, examine him to see if he could put him on the road to recovery. Aaron was Jewish, one of many members of his religion whom I'd welcomed into England, and a good doctor besides. To send him away because of his religion would have been cutting off the legate's nose to spite his face. This bit of practical acceptance gave me hope that our meeting wouldn't be as contentious as I'd initially feared.

The time had come, however, to find out.

4

Leaving the investigation of Lee to the experts, namely Darren, Peter, and Bevyn, I took Callum and Carew to ride the short distance with me to the Archbishop's palace. We were accompanied by a portion of my usual entourage, led by Justin, deeming it unnecessary to descend on the Archbishop's palace with more than thirty men.

Those of us who would enter the Archbishop's precincts weren't armed either, and it was strange not to feel the familiar weight of my sword at my side. But John Peckham was a man of God, genuinely loathing war, and he had asked that we leave our weapons behind when we entered his domain. Though he was very frail now, the Archbishop of Canterbury was still the most powerful churchman in England, and I'd bowed to his request.

With Lee on the loose, I hoped I wouldn't regret my decision. Still, it was only a half-mile to the palace from the castle, and the route was as secure as Justin could make it. My hand-picked company of Welsh archers watched from the tops of buildings and the city walls. I was surrounded by those men of my own guard who could be spared from the task of hunting Lee, while the city's regular garrison patrolled the streets. All in all, I thought both the attention to detail and security were impressive and had said as much to Justin.

The rain had continued to fall as rain in England tended to do, and my horse picked his way through the muddy street. I kept to the exact middle, careful to avoid the wheel tracks where water had pooled. The roads weren't cobbled, so the dirt had turned to mud, mixing with the muck created by ten thousand people living too closely together without modern sanitation. Up ahead, in fact, was a garbage collector, loading his cart with what looked like soiled straw from a barn.

I gave the cart a wide birth and held my breath as I passed it. He was doing an important—if not crucial—job, though not one I would ever have wanted. Worse would have been a night soil collector with his cart; *night soil* being the medieval term for human waste.

Many people lined the edges of the street and bowed to me, undeterred by the weather. Above me on both sides, windows opened, and spectators shouted, 'The king! The king!' as I passed. I lifted one hand to them briefly before using it to tuck my cloak and hood more tightly around myself. This wasn't so much because I was cold, but because I wasn't in the mood to smile right now and didn't want my people to know it.

Thomas Becket had been murdered in Canterbury, and it was because of that murder that Canterbury had become a place of pilgrimage as well as a thriving merchant town. It was near enough to the English Channel to be a waypoint for commerce between London and Europe, as well as a market fair for the whole region around it in eastern Kent. At one time, before the Norman conquest of England, Canterbury may have been bigger than London.

The city itself, oval in shape and running from southwest to northeast, was protected by a town wall. It had been built initially by the Romans and then refortified by the Saxons when they came to Kent. Unfortunately, the walls hadn't prevented the Vikings from sacking the city at least twice, nor the Normans from taking it when they came. Over the last hundred years, as peace had come to England, the walls had been allowed to fall into disrepair. Since I'd become king, I'd authorized Peckham to see to their improvement, and over the patter of the rain, I could hear the distant tapping of stone masons working.

Although some businesses were located outside the walls—a meat market and a few houses—those same walls constrained Canterbury's growth. Buildings were two or three stories high, pressed up against neighboring houses in groups of a half-dozen or so, with narrow alleys between the blocks. Canterbury Castle protected the southwestern part of the oval, with the castle walls forming part of the city's defenses in that area. We were riding to the cathedral, which took up a whole sector in the northeastern part of the city.

"We're fortunate that the legate fell ill, you know," Callum said from where he was riding on my right side.

"How so?" I pushed back my hood and turned my head towards him. The wind was coming from behind us, so the rain pattered on the back of my head and shoulders, soaking my hair. But the rain was cooling my temper and felt cleansing after the sights and smells in the alley.

"Whatever the outcome of this conversation you're about to have with the legate and Peckham, it might be some time before he is able to get word back to Pope Boniface of the extent of your disagreement with him," he said.

"That's supposed to cheer me up?" Yet even as I spoke, I laughed, glad that Callum had stirred me out of my melancholy. I was tired of it myself, which meant my advisers had probably been throwing up their hands in frustration with me. "You do realize that this meeting is probably going to end in my excommunication. The legate being ill is only putting off the inevitable."

Carew spoke from my other side. "You could reconsider your present course of action."

"I have considered it and reconsidered it," I said, a hard edge returning momentarily to my voice. "You know my reasoning, and you also know why I will not back down from my stance on this issue."

Carew bowed his head, admitting defeat. "Yes, my lord." Then he looked at me sideways and said, sounding more like himself, "You don't have to be so cheerful about it."

I reached out a hand and clapped him on the shoulder. "Don't give up on me just yet."

"Never, sire," Carew said.

The issue before us was freedom of religion. To say I was in favor of it was to grossly understate the case. I'd been fighting a rearguard action for years against the prejudices of this time. Having talked my father into admitting the Jews into Wales back in 1284, I'd lifted all restrictions on their activities and fields of employment once I'd become King of England.

Unlike previous kings—in England and in most countries on the Continent—I also didn't require anything different from the Jewish community than from the Christian one in terms of behavior or distinguishing clothing. For example, Jews no longer had to wear a badge on the outside of their coats as King Edward had required.

My position towards Jews had been taken quietly by Archbishop Peckham and the Church up until now. Even better, in the eight years since my father's edict had welcomed Jews into Wales, I was even beginning to think that the level of distrust among the general populace had lessened. Canterbury—as well as London, York, and Chester—had become more diverse in recent years, as people from across Europe had come to take part in our prosperity. It was harder to be prejudiced against people who were your neighbors.

Plus, it wasn't just Jews whose lives had changed. Women could vote for representatives to Parliament now, as could people who didn't own land. A Jewish man had even been elected by the Christian majority in Shrewsbury. Maybe I was fooling myself into thinking the culture here had changed. Maybe anti-Semitism remained just below the surface, and Canterbury could explode into violence tomorrow if the economy crashed. It had happened before. Still, even if I was naïve, the job of a king was to *lead*, and the decision to treat people of all faiths equally had been, quite frankly, one of the easier decisions I'd made.

The real issue before me at this hour, however, wasn't the status of Jews in England. It was heresy, which could be defined as beliefs that were at variance with Church doctrine or customs.

I understood the Church's problem—really, I did. Because there was only *one* church at this time, many heretics were setting up mini-churches inside the Catholic Church and declaring they had the *real* truth. It was like camping out in the middle of the nave during a priest's sermon and telling everyone not to listen to the guy in the black robes near the altar.

The pope was free to kick out people in his church who didn't believe the doctrine. His house, his rules. I was cool with that part—but only as long as the people were free to make their own choice about it. They could believe ... or leave.

But as this was the Middle Ages, the choice tended to be more along the lines of *believe ... or die.*

Recent heresies had been laid at the feet of such diverse groups as the Cathars, with their dual gods and focus on sin, and the Waldensians, who preached poverty and strict adherence to the Bible. Both groups had taken root in southern France, and both insisted that the current Church was corrupt, a claim with which I couldn't disagree.

To counter these schismatic beliefs, the Papal Inquisition had been in full swing throughout this century, mostly in southern France and Italy. To be fair, its initial intent had been to provide a forum for accusations of heresy, as a counter to mobs of townspeople murdering fellow citizens without a trial. Particularly since the middle of this century, however, the tribunals had grown more powerful and harder to control—and I wanted no part of them in England.

Nicholas IV, the previous pope, and I had come to an understanding on the matter out of necessity and pragmatism. He'd turned a blind eye to the fact that I was welcoming believers of every stripe into England, and I allowed him to catalog and tax the churches in England that were under his jurisdiction. I even snagged ten percent of his take.

Unfortunately, Nicholas had died in April of this year, and the new pope, Boniface VIII, believed that all humans on the planet should be subject to him for their salvation. Heretics, then, were a big deal because, in his eyes, *it wasn't possible to separate yourself from the Church.* Everyone was Catholic. Period. So, everyone had to believe what the Church told them to believe.

In addition, he believed that his word was the final authority over not only the church but the state as well. While Carew may not have fully understood my position regarding freedom of religion, even if he accepted that I was willing to stake my throne on my belief in it, he was all for me standing up to the pope on matters of state. If I let the pope dictate national policy, even in small things, that was a slippery slope that neither I—nor my barons—wanted to go down. All of my barons could understand and support my refusal to accede to Boniface's assertion that his word superseded mine in secular matters too.

Mom had suggested that, having saved Dad's life and changed history ten years ago, we had started moving further and further away from the historical trajectory that she knew. Most of the time I thought that could be a good thing, though not if the change meant I was about to get my head handed to me on a silver platter by the papal legate.

Boniface had been in office for only a few months, but it was a difficult time for Christendom. He was under pressure from the rest of the clergy to increase the reach of the Church. Their power and wealth depended on his actions in the same way my barons' power and wealth depended upon mine. A year ago, Acre had fallen to the Muslims, and with it had gone the Kingdom of Jerusalem. It was a painful loss for the Church.

I couldn't help feeling that the Pope's focus had turned northward because he sought to compensate for the loss by tightening his control on the Christian nations in Europe. To send a legate to me at this early stage of his rule meant Pope Boniface was interested in testing the limits of his power—and mine.

5

The Archbishop's palace lay adjacent to Canterbury cathedral, and my company halted in front of the iron-barred gate, which resembled a portcullis, though without the murder holes above it through which to pour oil on attackers, or the sturdy drawbridge in front of it. I could see through the gate into the courtyard of the palace, which had a well in the center of it. The bucket hung suspended from its rope and was protected from the elements by a little roof with a bell on top.

At our approach, the gate swung open, allowing us to halt in the shelter of the stone gatehouse. My horse stamped his feet and shook out his mane, and I leaned forward to pat his neck before dismounting.

The Archbishop of York, John le Romeyn, was waiting for us in the porch, protected from the rain by an overhanging roof. Born illegitimate (to a churchman!), he had degrees from Oxford and the University of Paris, and in my few interactions with him, I'd found him to be a reasonable man. All things being equal, I wasn't sorry to see him today. Like Peckham, he concerned himself mostly with the behavior of the priests, monks, and nuns within his purview, and was less concerned about the individual beliefs of the common folk.

Though Romeyn started towards me, I gestured that he should stay where he was, calling out to him. "There's no point in both of us getting wet."

A Welsh soldier took the bridle of my horse, even as the young monks who doubled as stable boys ran towards us from the shelter of the adjacent stable. It wasn't large enough to house all thirty horses, but at least their gear could be removed and kept dry while I was speaking with Acquasparta.

I set off across the courtyard, Callum and Carew in tow.

"Sire." Romeyn bowed when I reached him. "If it pleases you, Archbishop Peckham is prepared to receive you."

"Thank you, Romeyn."

My castle at Canterbury was one of the oldest in England, built by William I shortly after the Norman Conquest and later expanded by King Henry I. The main keep alone was over eighty feet high, with a foundation that was nearly a hundred feet wide on each side. And that was just the keep. The Archbishop's palace was equally enormous, but it was less well fortified, which made it a more comfortable place to live. Men of the Church liked their luxuries. If nothing else, the palace had bigger windows because nobody was worried about trebuchet missiles coming through them.

Once inside, I openly admired the decorations—the ornate tapestries on the walls, the carvings on the cornices, and the painted ceilings—rather than focusing on what lay ahead of me. It was better not to wind myself up about this meeting any more than I already had, because I didn't know what Cardinal Acquasparta was going to say. Until I did, there wasn't much point in speculating about it. I was here. I would find out what he wanted in a minute.

Carew paced beside Archbishop Romeyn, and Callum walked a little behind me to the left. It seemed to me that his breathing was coming more easily than mine.

I was expecting to meet first with Peckham, since the whole reason I'd come to Canterbury in the first place was because Acquasparta was on his deathbed, but we entered the reception room to find both men drinking wine before a roaring fire. The legate was dressed in rich red robes, and I almost laughed at the contrast, since I had dripped water and left muddy boot prints all the way down the fine hallway behind me. Still, I'd dressed well underneath the black outer cloak that swathed me from head to foot. Serving temporarily as my squire, Carew helped me remove it to reveal a gold-embroidered mantle and blue tunic.

Once I was clear of the threshold, Peckham moved towards me, his arm outstretched, and when he came within hailing distance, he bowed his head. "Sire! Thank you for coming. You honor us with your presence today." I didn't kiss Archbishop Peckham's ring (nor he mine), as it wasn't customary between us. We would see in a moment if Acquasparta thought it should have been.

I allowed Peckham to gesture me towards the fireplace, at which point he introduced me to Acquasparta, who inclined his head in greeting. Acquasparta was a thin man in his fifties, tall, with a full head of dark hair and a patrician nose.

I'd grown used to the pomp by now, and even if it didn't come naturally to me, I'd learned to read meaning into every bent waist and bowed head. Acquasparta was showing me the proper amount of respect, and I extended an olive branch too, pretending I hadn't noticed Acquasparta's frown at my approach. He either didn't like playing diplomat or was objecting to something more mundane, like my unavoidably muddy boots or my age. I was twenty-three. The word from Aaron was that Acquasparta thought I was a hothead.

"I apologize for my lateness. Something came up at the last moment that could not be deferred," I said, not wanting to get into the ongoing drama surrounding Lee, Mike, and Noah.

"Such is the way of kingship, or so I understand," Acquasparta said. "I am grateful that you came at all."

"Your health has improved, I see," I said.

Acquasparta wobbled a hand to say *comme çi, comme ça* as the French do, though he was Italian. "Today is better, but fever strikes me when I least expect it."

"There were many times I feared he would not live through the night, to tell you the truth," Peckham said, "and yet, here he is."

"I thank you for the assistance of your household physician," Acquasparta said to me. "Between him, my dear Archbishop, and God, I am in good hands."

I tipped my head regally, suppressing my suspicion that I was being played, though Aaron had reported on how ill the legate was when we'd arrived three days ago. Our meeting had been postponed twice, in fact, because of it. Aaron wouldn't lie to me, so I had to accept that this meeting was taking place only now because of how ill the legate had been earlier. I was comforted, too, that the cardinal had taken the opportunity to mention Aaron, implying that my policy of providing a refuge for the Jewish population of Europe wasn't one of Pope Boniface's concerns today.

"You are most welcome," I said. "Aaron has cured many difficult cases since he came to us." Out of the corner of my eye, I caught sight of the man himself, standing in the shadows of a far doorway. I lifted a finger to him without looking directly at him. He saw the gesture, however, as I hoped he might, and acknowledged it with a nod before disappearing back into the darkness of the corridor behind him. He would know now to seek me out before I left the palace.

Aaron was a physician first, but his loyalty to me was unquestioned, making him an intelligent and capable spy as well. Given what was at stake, I'd felt I needed as much information as I could acquire about the goings on between Peckham and the papal legate, and Acquasparta's illness had provided me with an excellent means to insert someone I trusted into Peckham's household.

"May I offer you wine, my lord king?" Peckham said.

"Thank you." I went with Acquasparta to two chairs placed across from one another in front of the fireplace. All the other advisers who'd occupied the room before I'd arrived took Peckham's offer of wine as their cue to leave. Only Archbishop Romeyn, Carew, and Callum remained. Callum stood with his hands behind his back, close to the door. His job, like Carew's, was to listen and advise if I needed him. Romeyn poured himself a goblet of wine from the carafe after Peckham poured mine. The two men were all but equals, and they exchanged a nod so minute I wasn't sure I'd seen it, indicating they were comfortably in accord. I hoped that was a good thing.

Acquasparta, for his part, needed no assistant. In a moment, the six of us were alone, and the legate and I seated ourselves on red silk pillows that cushioned the chairs. I was hardly able to believe the contrast in my surroundings between now and an hour before. It was as if the murder of Mike and Noah hadn't happened.

Romeyn and Peckham found seats a little farther away, but still within easy speaking distance. I was sure my medieval advisers would have wanted my rear to hit the chair a second before Acquasparta's, because as with everything else in this dance I was currently doing with the cardinal, appearances were everything.

Or so they would have said.

I wasn't convinced. Pope Boniface—and Acquasparta as well—had too much at stake here to worry about who sat first. It was my submission they wanted. English kings had bent to the wishes of the pope in the past, and if they were dealing with only an English king, they might have gotten what they wanted. But I wasn't like any English king they'd ever dealt with.

That wasn't arrogance talking either (or only a little). It wasn't that I was smarter than everyone else in the room. Callum had a degree from Cambridge; I didn't even have a high school diploma. But what I had that they didn't were radically different tools to think with.

I accepted the goblet of wine Peckham handed me and took a sip. Carew moved to stand behind my chair.

Acquasparta wasted no time getting to the point. "I have come to you from his Holiness Pope Boniface VIII with many concerns, my lord king."

I swallowed my sip of wine, not so much stalling for time but so I could order my thoughts before I spoke. "Such was my understanding and why I am here, Cardinal Acquasparta. Perhaps you could take this moment to elaborate?"

Acquasparta made a small gesture with one hand. I'd been warned that, as an Italian, he spoke with his hands as well as his mouth, but this was a motion I couldn't interpret. "My lord king, it has come to his Holiness's attention that you have not only allowed into England those who preach doctrines that run counter to the Church, but have openly welcomed them. This is troubling to him."

So heresy *was* to be the first order of business.

Out of the corner of my eye, I saw Romeyn's own hand twitch in Acquasparta's direction, but he stilled it without speaking. Perhaps Romeyn was objecting to how straightforwardly Acquasparta had spoken, though for my part, I welcomed it. Better to lay the cards on the table right off and deal with what was before us, than do some arcane diplomatic dance where nobody spoke the truth. Then Callum, Carew, and I would have to spend the next three days sifting through the lies and evasions.

"I would appreciate an explanation of why this action troubles His Holiness," I said, which *was* pure evasion, and I gave Acquasparta a small smile to further validate the idea that the query was innocent.

Acquasparta appeared unfazed. "Many men are weak minded and cannot tell the difference between true teachings and heretical ones. They become confused. It is our responsibility to keep the people on the correct course."

This, in broad strokes, was the reason for the Inquisition and the root of my disagreement with the authority of the Church. "We—" I hesitated, knowing that what I was about to say was far too straightforward and would probably give members of my inner circle a heart attack, "—don't agree."

The faces of Peckham and Romeyn went completely blank. I couldn't see Carew, since he was behind me, but Callum shot me a small smile from his place by the door.

Acquasparta *knew* now that I was, in fact, a hothead. He leaned forward. "Heresy is dangerous, my lord. It must be dug out of the soil before it can take root."

I studied him, many thoughts running through my head, not the least of which had to do with what I saw as the real problem here. It was the pope's fear that if people believed something different from what the Church taught he would lose his power over them. And money. The whole structure of the Church could crumble.

I believed without a doubt that many men of the church were truly good and genuinely devoted to God and what they believed to be His divinely ordained Church. But I'd been raised in Oregon, where a man's beliefs were between him and God. Certainly the intricacies of doctrine were lost on me. I didn't care whether the blessing of communion turned plain bread and wine into the body and blood of Christ, and I certainly saw no reason to go to war over it.

I didn't say any of that, even though I really wanted to. I could feel Carew behind me, his body tense as a bow string. He was probably sure that at any moment I was going to say something utterly irretrievable. For example, I could have said, *by the way, I'm a heretic too.* I amused myself with the idea for a second, but I'd never had any intention of destroying in a single day everything I'd worked so hard to build by making a few unwise comments to the papal legate.

Instead, it was Romeyn who said what I couldn't: "The common folk may be easily led, your Holiness, which, on one hand, means they can wander astray."

Acquasparta nodded, believing at first that Romeyn had made his point for him.

But then Romeyn proceeded to reveal how arrogant I'd been to think these men hadn't the wherewithal to match me. "But on the other hand, Cardinal Acquasparta, it means their mistaken ideas can be refuted with a few well-chosen words. A heretic in his own home is no threat to the Church. It is our duty, rather, to gently guide him to the straight path."

—not burn him at the stake. Romeyn had sense enough, however, not to add the last bit.

And I had enough sense not to look at Romeyn or allow even a hint of astonishment to cross my face. Romeyn, the Archbishop of York and a true believer in the Church, had just shot the first volley of the Reformation across the Church's bow.

Acquasparta's face paled instead of flushing. I couldn't tell if he was so upset he was going to pass out, or if his health had taken a sudden turn for the worse. I leaned forward. "The Archbishop of York speaks plainly, but I agree that if your beliefs are the true ones, they are built on solid rock. The buffets of the waves far below can not harm you, and you can ignore them."

"Until, over time, the waves undermine the rock, leaving it perched precariously over the sea," Acquasparta said.

I sat back, canting my head in acknowledgement of Acquasparta's rejoinder. "Perhaps my metaphor leaves something to be desired. I suspect it would be better if I left the discussion of theology to more able men." I tapped my fingers on the arm of my chair. "What other concerns does Pope Boniface care to bring to my attention?"

Acquasparta blinked, surprised at the change of subject. Carew, on the other hand, gave an audible sigh of relief and his hand dropped away from where he'd been gripping the top rail of my chair.

"His Holiness would like to discuss the *taxatio* conducted under his predecessor," Acquasparta said. "It gave ten percent of the monies acquired to you. His Holiness feels that money should have stayed with the Church."

Peckham cleared his throat. "If I may—"

Acquasparta turned his gaze on him, and Peckham's mouth snapped shut as his face reddened. The cardinal's face held a look of such disdain that it was a wonder Peckham didn't collapse into a puddle on the floor in his mortification, for the crime of interrupting our conversation. Acquasparta had succeeded Peckham in his position as a teacher at the papal curia when Peckham had been promoted to Archbishop of Canterbury, and Peckham was also a papal legate, of equal standing to

Acquasparta, so it was a little rich of Acquasparta to treat him so poorly.

"Please speak, Archbishop," I said, cutting through Acquasparta's glower and delighted to displease the cardinal a little more, "I would be happy to hear you."

"The charter between Pope Nicholas and King David for the *taxatio* was signed, witnessed, and sealed," Peckham said.

Acquasparta inclined his head, not disagreeing, though he eyed the two English churchmen with extreme disfavor. Perhaps before the meeting he'd thought them on his side, whereas before five minutes ago, I hadn't realized the extent of their support for *my* side.

"Does the Holy Father deny the validity of that agreement?" I said, trying to distract Acquasparta from Peckham and return his attention to me.

"No." The word came out in a short, very Italian staccato. "He simply requests your consideration in this matter."

I rubbed my chin. Pope Boniface thought giving church money to the crown set a bad precedent, which it did, so I couldn't blame him for not liking the agreement. It was incredibly bold of him to ask for the money back, though. Acquasparta gave a small smile.

"I will think about it." I paused, listening to the rain patter on the large window to my left. The earlier torrent had abated and was no longer the hard drumming it had been. Perhaps our ride home wouldn't be as wet. I could hardly wait to get out of here. "And the third matter?"

Acquasparta looked directly into my eyes. "His Holiness asks that I speak to you on the matter of Aquitaine."

I raised my eyebrows. This time he had surprised me. "What is the supreme pontiff's concern with Aquitaine?"

"He asks that you withdraw your claim to it," Acquasparta said.

The rule of the Duchy of Aquitaine had been in dispute since the death of King Edward and his younger brother, Edmund, in 1285. The duchy had no clear male heir, but there were many claims, the most valid coming from Thomas, Earl of Lancaster, Edmund's eldest son. For seven years, various barons had put in their claim, including King Philip IV of France, who sought to bring all of what the modern world called 'France' under his control.

At the moment, Philip controlled roughly half the country, most of it in the north and east. He and I were the same age, both born in 1268. Thanks to my mother's Ph.D. in medieval history, I knew a lot more about him than he did about me.

This was the man who expelled all the Jews from his country in 1306. This was the man who on Friday the 13th, 1307, moved against the Knights Templar in France, arresting many and torturing confessions of heresy out of them, and then burned them at the stake, in large part to free himself from his indebtedness to them. Back in Avalon's history, in ten years' time, Philip also arranged for the arrest and eventual death of Pope Boniface himself. I really wished I could mention it to Acquasparta, but of course I couldn't.

At one time, I'd supported Thomas's claim, but he was only fourteen, without the political strength to overcome Philip. And since his half-sister was the queen of France—Philip's wife—things had gotten complicated really fast. I'd put in my own claim because I could, and because not to do so would be viewed abroad as showing weakness. My claim was through my mother, whom everyone believed to be the illegitimate daughter of King Henry III (who'd also been Duke of Aquitaine).

"Why would the pope concern himself with such temporal matters as my claim to the duchy?" I said.

"He wishes to avoid the war that would be inevitable if you pursued your claim," Acquasparta said.

"Has he said anything to Philip?" I said, and when Acquasparta didn't answer, I looked at him carefully. "The pontiff supports Philip's claims over mine?"

"He supports peace."

"What right does Philip have to Aquitaine?" I said.

Again, Acquasparta didn't answer, but this time the delay was only because he was searching for the right words. "The duchy sits in fief to the King of France. If the dukedom is vacant, it is his right to take it back."

Behind me, Carew cleared his throat. "Your eminence, may I ask what King David might expect in return for these sacrifices?"

Acquasparta gave a wolfish smile that reminded me suddenly of Noah, the other problem of the day which I'd completely forgotten about since my conversation with Acquasparta began. "The Holy Father's gratitude."

Wow. I sat back in my chair, and this time it was I who didn't respond, since my head was spinning with the injustice of it all. Fortunately, it wasn't necessary to answer just yet. This conversation was only the first of many we would have. Acquasparta had laid out his objectives, none of which left any wiggle room for me. If I did everything he wanted, I got nothing in return. The question I wanted answered was what would happen if I *didn't* do them.

My own smile turned wintry. "I will need to think about these matters and consult with my advisers."

"Of course," Acquasparta said. "I have no plans to travel for at least a fortnight. Your physician does not believe I could possibly be completely well before then."

That meant I had two weeks to find a diplomatic way to refuse every one of the pope's requests.

6

"Did you believe anything Acquasparta just said?"

"I believe he won't travel for a fortnight," Callum said. "As to the rest, as to what he really cares about? I don't know."

"So it wasn't just me."

"It wasn't just you." Callum tapped the fingers of his left hand on the table in front of us. "I fear we can't trust him at all."

"I feel like I'm treading water and sharks are circling around my feet," I said.

"He reminded me a little of a shark," Callum said, "and I'm sure his bite is just as strong and impossible to dislodge."

Carew, who was sitting beyond Callum, nodded. "We have to be very, very careful from this moment forward."

"I thought we were being careful, but with Romeyn and Peckham in the room—" I glanced at the Archbishop of York, who was currently speaking quietly to his secretary in the doorway of the dining room. While I watched, Romeyn walked a few paces into the corridor with him.

The audience was over, along with an awkward meal. Peckham had departed with Acquasparta, who'd insisted he had to rest. The cardinal had picked at his food, barely eating or drinking anything, so I guess I had to believe him. That left Callum, Carew, and me as the only ones remaining with Romeyn. I rose to my feet and met Romeyn, who'd dismissed his secretary and returned to the doorway. It was time to speak frankly.

The Archbishop of York was near to my height and met my eyes briefly before lowering his head in a slight bow. "Sire."

"That I haven't spoken more than a few words with you before today was an oversight on my part," I said.

"It was my honor to be present at this meeting, sire."

"You took a risk on my behalf. I won't forget it."

Romeyn looked up, his features smoothing into an expression approximating detached concern. "I did only what I thought was right."

I scoffed under my breath. "You aren't that much of an idealist. Your speech was calculated down to the smallest intonation."

Romeyn blinked but had too much composure to stutter a protest. In my mind, I was recasting him in the guise of Thomas Wolsey, the adviser to Henry VIII, who would one day follow Romeyn as Archbishop of York. Wolsey had been *de facto* king at times, with extreme intelligence, organizational skills, and drive. He'd gained enormous power before falling out of favor with the king because he couldn't arrange the annulment of Henry's marriage.

"You are far too worldly and intelligent to be impressed by me," I said. "As you showed in there, you have a mind and thoughts that aren't to be dictated by others."

"If I have offended your grace in some way, I apologize." Romeyn bowed deeply.

"Stand up," I said. "That's not what I meant. You said what you thought needed to be said, and it happened to be in support of me. How can I be sorry about that? Next time, however, I'd like a little more warning of where you stand."

Romeyn straightened. "Yes, sire."

Aaron appeared out of a recess in the corridor behind Romeyn, reminding me that I needed to speak to him too. This whole thing with the pope and the papal legate had way too many moving parts. I glanced at Aaron, held up a hand to signal him to wait, and turned back to Romeyn.

"You, Peckham, and I need to have a talk in private. I'll expect you both at the castle tomorrow."

"Yes, sire." He bowed again.

Callum and Carew had joined me, and I shrugged into the black cloak Carew draped again over my shoulders, glad of it now that we were in the chilly corridor and away from the fire. While Carew, Callum, and I headed towards Aaron, Romeyn reentered the dining room.

"I am very glad to see you," I said when I reached him.

"And I you, sire," Aaron bowed his head.

"How ill is Acquasparta, really?"

"Ill enough," Aaron said. "He hasn't deceived you in that regard, even if he looked well today. I've just come from his chambers."

I studied my mother's old friend. Gray strands peppered his dark hair and his full beard was almost entirely white, but his brown eyes were just as bright and intelligent as ever. "But is he deceiving me in some other way?"

"I don't know, sire, but I feel there is more here than meets the eye," Aaron said. "I ask that you be very careful going forward."

"The audience was certainly unusual," Carew said.

Aaron and Carew were old acquaintances. Both had stood at my side since before King Edward's death. "In what way?" Aaron said.

I, too, was interested in why Carew thought so. Other than the four years I'd been King of England, I had no experience with affairs of state at the level of dealing with a papal legate. Carew hadn't had much either, but he'd at least been to court and seen the way things were done.

"He asked three things of the king, none of which he is likely to accede to easily." Carew looked at me. "And offered nothing in return."

"He thinks I'm weak," I said.

"Pope Boniface thinks you might be weak," Callum said. "I can't read Acquasparta well."

"A good emissary transmits the message without ever conveying his own thoughts," Aaron said, "but it's more than that. I think—"

Aaron didn't get a chance to finish his thought. A sudden commotion—shouts and chanting beyond the walls—had the four of us swinging around to face the front doors, which were just visible from the corridor through the anteroom that led to the main courtyard of the palace.

"Stay here, my lord." Carew strode towards the large doors.

Romeyn reappeared out of the dining room doorway and hastened past until he was at Carew's heels. Upon reaching the entryway, Callum wrenched one of the great doors open. Sound exploded into the palace. In a moment, I was at the doors too. The rain had turned to mist, and with the waning of the day a fog had risen—but I could see beyond the erect postures of my guard of thirty who were standing between me and the gates of the Archbishop's palace. The commotion lay beyond them: a crowd in the street looked determined to batter down the gate.

"What's happening?" Peckham hobbled towards us from the western wing of his palace. Acquasparta followed, though he leaned heavily on the arm of another man, who was dressed in red as he was, but much more simply. I didn't recognize the man but guessed him to be the cardinal's secretary, who hadn't been at our meeting, though I supposed he could have been hiding behind a curtain in a corner to take his notes.

"I don't know," I said.

Carew hovered in the doorway, taking in the scene, and then he and I together went down three steps to stand on the stairs, the better to get a sense of what was happening outside the gates. The chanting and shouts grew louder as a young man in his early twenties was hauled up to the gate by four men wearing the livery of the Archbishop of Canterbury. The crowd was growing by the second, and hands reached out to press them forward.

One of the men in livery shouted, "Let us in!"

Wide-eyed, the two men who manned the gatehouse moved to the gate. Justin, the captain of my guard, started forward with his hand up. "Stop!" he said, but it was too late. One of the guards had already released the lock. The four guards and their prisoner squeezed inside the courtyard, and then the two guards at the gate struggled to close it again.

With the help of Justin and two more of my men, who'd followed him, they finally managed to slide the bar home, locking out the crowd. It had grown to easily a hundred strong. And it was still growing by the second, every single member calling for the prisoner's head. The man's hands had been tied behind his back, and his face was bloody from a beating. If not for the gate between the courtyard and the crowd, this could have turned into a lynching.

The prisoner wore dirty brown breeches and a shirt of an indeterminate color. Perhaps it had once been blue, but the front was smeared with mud, soaked with rain, and torn at the left shoulder. His dark brown hair was wet from the rain and plastered to his head with a darker fluid that might have been blood. Justin hastened back towards me, his face a thundercloud, and one of the four soldiers followed. His three companions stayed nearer to the gate, holding the prisoner, who swayed on his feet but managed to remain upright. My own guard was blocking the path to the steps, but at Justin's signal, my men parted to let the Archbishop's soldier through.

He didn't look at me. Perhaps he didn't know who I was. "We found him, your eminence." He spoke to Acquasparta.

I was standing on a lower step, three down from the doorway, and turned to look up at Acquasparta, unaware that he'd taken up a position behind me. The double doorway into the palace was now fully open, with a half-dozen men, from servants to churchmen, gaping at the crowd at the gate.

Acquasparta nodded sagely. "You have done well."

Peckham edged his way into the doorway to Acquasparta's side. "What ... what have you done?" He looked from Acquasparta to the crowd, and then his hand clutched at the robes at his chest.

Even as I watched, Peckham's face paled, and he staggered slightly. Callum was standing behind him and caught him as he fell. "Aaron!" Callum called the doctor's name as three servants helped to half-carry, half-drag the Archbishop back into the recesses of the palace.

A moment later, I was in front of Acquasparta, my hands clenched, wanting to wipe the smirk from his face, but having to do it with my voice instead of my fists. "Answer the Archbishop's question!"

"We had word that a heretic had come to live in Canterbury and was gaining followers. Our only recourse was to arrest him. With the proper motivation, it may be that we can return him to the fold, guide him to the better path as Archbishop Romeyn said." Acquasparta spoke these words with a nod at Romeyn, who had come to stand on the steps too. "At the very least, he can tell us who his compatriots are and we can root out this infection before it spreads."

Acquasparta appeared to believe every word he said.

I stabbed a finger in the direction of the crowd. "Those people aren't here to question your prisoner. This is a mob. They want his head."

Behind me, the volume had risen as the people strained forward, more and more of them pressing against the gate. History told me I wasn't exaggerating. The people of Canterbury had slaughtered their Jewish neighbors in a mass riot only thirty years ago. It was easy to see how it had come about. I didn't want them to do the same to this heretic.

"Let me through! Let me through!" A palace guardsman on horseback approached the gate. The people gave way for him, but to my horror, the palace gatekeeper moved to the gate with the clear intent to open it.

As had been the case with Justin, even if he'd heard my call of "No!" over the noise of the crowd, it was too late. He'd already pulled the bar across. The gate swung open and the crowd surged past the horseman, overwhelming the guard, who stumbled backwards, his mouth wide and protesting.

"Idiot," I said to myself under my breath. "What did he think was going to happen?"

This was going to get out of control really quickly, and I didn't know if I could do anything about it. For the moment, those in the front line of the crowd seemed a bit uncertain now that they were actually inside the palace—a place none of them had probably ever been. They milled around, filling in the space between the gatehouse, the stable, and where the three guards still stood with the prisoner. Most still hung back, some of their anger dissipating now that they'd achieved their goal of entering the palace grounds. At any second, however, the volatile crowd could become violent again.

Carew stood at my right shoulder, half a step in front of me. Without weapons, all my own men could do was defend me as best they could, and they formed a tight semi-circle around the steps, buttressing and protecting the palace entrance. The commotion would eventually catch the attention of the city garrison and my other men, but it hadn't yet. They were busy with a murder and, undoubtedly, had assumed I was safe inside the Archbishop's Palace.

Acquasparta seemed either to have no idea how dangerous the situation was, or it had become exactly what he wanted, because he didn't move, just stood on the top step with a slight smile on his face.

Then Acquasparta threw fuel on the fire. "Take him to a cell!"

How anyone could hear the papal legate's words over the noise coming from the crowd I didn't know, but as soon as those in the forefront realized that the prisoner was only to be arrested, not hanged, they gave a roar and stormed forward.

A moment later, the prisoner was ripped from his guards' hands. I lost sight of him and thought he'd gone down under their feet, but then I spotted him again, another twenty paces away, wrestling with his captors. With mounting horror, I watched them drag him through the gates of the palace. Someone had already placed a rope around his neck in a noose.

I swung back to Acquasparta and hissed, "This is your fault. Do something!"

But Acquasparta's lips were white around the edges as he gaped at his handiwork. I wanted to shake him. His secretary was urging him to reenter the palace proper, for his own safety, but then Acquasparta surprised me by waving him off. He raised his hands in motion of appeasement and said, "Stop! Stop this madness!"

His words were barely audible to me, much less to the crowd, which was no longer facing the palace entrance anyway. Certainly, they had no effect. Then his secretary spoke urgently to him again in Italian, and Acquasparta retreated back into the palace, looking frailer than ever. As he left, the mist turned again to a light rain, and a gust of wind blew the fine droplets into my face.

Justin had backed up the steps to stand beside Carew to better protect me. "They're going to kill him," he said.

7

I snarled at Justin, "I know they're going to kill him!" I spun this way and that, looking for a way out of this, looking for ideas.

Carew's face was intent. "We need a plan."

"We bloody well do need a plan!" I said. "Any suggestions?"

"We can't stop it, not with only thirty of us and no weapons beyond our belt knives." Justin's red hair was plastered to his head, which was why my Welsh archers had nicknamed him *Goch*.

"I'm not sure weapons would help if it meant killing civilians," I said.

"We have to stop it. Come, sire, out of the rain while we regroup." Carew took the steps back up to the palace two at a time, passing Romeyn, who still stood in the doorway, his brow furrowed in thought.

Cursing Acquasparta and his stupidity, I gestured for my men to follow Carew. "Get everyone inside. We have maybe a minute to figure out how to stop this."

Justin gave a piercing whistle, and ten seconds later, my men had retreated inside the anteroom of the palace. Callum returned, looking grave, but I didn't ask him how Peckham was. We had no time, and the knowledge of the Archbishop's health wasn't going to save the young man out there.

"Someone said that this is Acquasparta's doing?" Callum said.

"It seems so, but he can't help," Romeyn said. "The guards arrested the heretic on his orders, but he either didn't count on the crowd or he underestimated it."

Callum nodded, accepting for now what he couldn't change. What was important was saving the young man. While that was a given to Callum, I saw hesitation in the eyes of several of my men. I didn't have time to dispel it, but perhaps I didn't have time *not* to either.

"For what purpose did God give man a mind if not to use it?" When it became clear that I was going to have a major confrontation with the Church over heresy, my mother and Callum had given me a primer on Luther, Milton, and freedom of religion. I was about to see if I could actually articulate what they'd asserted. "When did thinking become a crime in England?" As I spoke, I looked in particular at one man whose name was Thomas. His size made him a formidable fighter, but when he wasn't soldiering, he tended towards quiet and thoughtful.

Thomas answered immediately. "It could never be a crime, sire." And then he quoted from the Bible: "You then, why do you judge your brother? For we will all stand before God's judgment seat."

That was from Romans, and as soon as we were out of here, Thomas was going to get a promotion. But he was talking about the behavior of the crowd, which was reprehensible, and for which they could be condemned. The issue at hand, however, was heresy. I didn't know what this heretic believed, and I didn't care. If I was going to save him and all the others I'd welcomed into England, I needed to uproot the very idea that a man could be condemned for his beliefs.

I wasn't good at this, really, but Callum had carefully written out what to say if the occasion ever arose, so I parroted it: "Does not Exodus say, 'Who has made man's mouth? Who makes him mute, or deaf, or seeing, or blind? Is it not I, the Lord?'" I tried not to look at Romeyn. This was his jurisdiction, not mine, but he'd taken a step back from my circle of men, not interfering with my speech with them, and his face gave nothing away.

The men gathered around me to listen, and several nodded, though I saw puzzlement on others' faces. Most people in the Middle Ages didn't spend any time thinking about issues of theology. They were lectured at by priests, but services were in Latin, which few understood. It was the ritual that was important, which made the peoples' hatred of heretics all the more strange to me, since most people couldn't even tell you what the difference was between what they believed and what heretics believed and why it was important.

Acquasparta had known that, of course. Every rabble rouser since the beginning of time knew that people were easily led and once aroused would go where a charismatic man pointed.

"I say to you that each of us understands God's message according to his ability and God's grace. My England will not infringe on any man's right to come to his own understandings," I said, and then quoted Milton: "'Give me the liberty to know, to utter, and to argue freely according to conscience, above all liberties."

Except for my voice, the silence in the corridor was absolute. I had thirty faces staring at me. I didn't know that I'd ever had such an audience or such a need for eloquence. I made a fist and brandished it. "Whether you knew it or not, you have always had that right, no matter what your king or your priest said. That right is innate in all of you. And just as each one of you has the right to speak your mind in your own home or among your companions, so this man has that right. I will not take it from you. I will not allow that crowd to take it from him."

Romeyn licked his lips. "We could set fire to the stables."

I stared at him, astonished and within inches of laughing that such a suggestion had come from him. "Thank you. That might have worked if everything wasn't already soaked and the crowd had remained within the palace." I shook myself. "I have an idea: everybody strip off your livery."

Justin didn't hesitate to obey, and as he disrobed, the rest of my guard followed. In turn, I tightened my black cloak around myself, making sure I was completely covered. My breeches and boots were that of a nobleman, which couldn't be helped, but I wanted to hide that I was the king of England, up until the moment I revealed it.

"Callum and Carew are going to get me to the heretic," I said. "The rest of you must disperse through the crowd. When I reach wherever they intend to hang this man, I'm going to throw off my cloak and raise my hands above my head. That is your cue to shout, 'the king, the king' until the crowd listens. I will start to speak, and at the end of every sentence, you need to cheer me on."

"Of course, sire," Justin said, and there were nods all around.

Callum looked darkly at them. "Regardless of what he says."

I hoped Callum's words weren't necessary, but faith was a funny thing, and while everyone in my guard was an excellent fighter, not all were thinkers or leaders. Fortunately to them, I, not Acquasparta, was the highest authority after God. They would obey.

"Let's go." I headed back to the front door and down the steps. While we'd been inside, the sounds of the crowd had diminished, which had me a bit worried we'd be too late. Once outside again, however, I could hear them farther down the street.

"They're by the cathedral," Carew said.

"They're probably looking for a tree," Callum added.

We sprinted through the gate, which the guards had left open, and across the road towards the cathedral grounds. Bounding through that open gate, we entered the graveyard on the south side of the cathedral.

The crowd had grown since it had left the palace courtyard. What had started out as a hundred people had become more like two or three hundred, with people streaming towards the commotion from all directions, though all had to fit a few at a time through the gateway. Canterbury was a Benedictine monastery, and a few of the monks were just realizing that something was amiss and starting to appear too.

The ringleaders had found a tree near the east end of the graveyard past the well. One of the ringleaders had thrown one end of the rope over a branch of a great oak tree that overhung the monastery wall. The other end was looped around the young man's neck.

I hung back for a moment while my guard dispersed into the crowd ahead of me, and then I loped forward, Carew and Callum on either side of me. Taking a page from Justin's book, Carew put his fingers in his mouth and blew a whistle that was so loud it might have scorched the leaves on the tree. My ears rang, and I had to restrain myself from putting my hands over my ears.

"Sorry, sire," Carew said, with a glance at me.

"No apologies," I said.

Carew's whistle had managed what Acquasparta's feeble protestations could not. The jeers and shouts among the crowd didn't exactly stop, but a good third were now paying attention to us rather than to the imminent hanging. The hangman stopped too, which was the most important thing, and there was a second of silence in which Callum inserted, "Make way for the king!" as he began to shove his way through the crowd.

I threw off my mantle—a little earlier than I'd intended since I was still stuck in the middle of everyone—but the people needed to see that I was, in fact, the king.

My guard had slipped in among the crowd such that I couldn't distinguish more than a handful of their faces anymore. At Callum's shout, they took up the call as I'd asked. "The king!" "It's the king! "Make way for the king!"

"Kneel before the king!"

I knew that voice. It belonged to a Welshman in my guard named Rhys, whose barrel chest was more than broad enough to produce the sound, though he himself was hardly taller than five and half feet.

The shocking bark worked. Those closest to me went down on one knee, and like a wave at a football stadium, those behind bent down in response to the actions of those in front. The several executioners remained, pumped up on adrenaline, the color in their faces high and their eyes wild with hatred. The one who'd thrown the rope over the branch had caught the end and held it, though thankfully he hadn't yet hauled the prisoner into the air. It would take a bit of work to do so, but as the heretic's hands were tied behind his back, it was also possible that a single jerk on the rope could snap his neck.

The executioners gazed out over their suddenly silent crowd, shocked into stillness themselves, and then the ringleader's eyes went to mine as I made my steady way towards him. He stared at me for a second, as if not sure what he was seeing, and then his eyes widened. In a swift movement, he dropped to one knee and bent his head. Callum reached him a second before I did, took the rope from his hand, and tossed it back over the branch so that it fell in a tangle at his feet.

I turned to the crowd. Heads came up, but I didn't lift my hand to allow them to rise. I had several choices before me: I could shame them; I could chastise them; I could appeal to their better natures, if they had them; or I could deflect them. I didn't know if there was a right way to go about this. I'd never saved a man from a hanging before, but I wanted to make sure this didn't happen again, not in Canterbury. Though at some point I was going to have to address the fact that if it was happening here, towns up and down England might be facing a similar riot if the underlying tinder of prejudice was lit.

"I hear this man is a heretic." I don't know what they expected me to say, but that clearly wasn't it. A murmur of conversation filled the square, and I lifted both hands and dropped them to lower the volume. "Can any one of you tell me what that means?"

Dead silence. And then, "He defies God!" That came from the back of the crowd.

"Could be." I looked down at the heretic, who'd fallen to his knees too, the noose still around his neck, and scrapped in an instant the speech I'd been prepared to make. These people wouldn't understand it, and it wouldn't get to the heart of the matter for them—which wasn't heresy. They really didn't know what that meant. I put a hand under the prisoner's chin and brought up his face so I could see into it. "Where are you from?"

"G-g-gascony, sire," he said with a thick accent.

Some of the men in the front rows murmured—something about foreigners, I suspected. I brought my own head up, knowing now that I had my key to them. "How many of you knew this man came from France?"

Nobody moved.

"Come on. I want a show of hands." I raised my own, and a dozen or so near me followed suit, perhaps too afraid not to.

"So the rest of you thought he was an Englishman?" I exaggeratedly shook my head. "If you admit to that, you'd have to admit to murdering a fellow citizen in cold blood. Last I heard, that was against the law. I'm sure you don't want that."

Now they were confused, worried that they were damned whether or not they raised their hands, but most of them did anyway.

"That's better." I rubbed my chin as I looked at them: three hundred English folk. Ninety-nine days out of a hundred, they went about their daily business without a hitch, but like the heretic, they'd been in the wrong place at the wrong time and had been caught up in Acquasparta's schemes. At one time or another, many had probably spoken to the man they'd been about to kill. My own men remained on their knees among them. I could have had them rise and posted them at the edges of the crowd, a silent threat, but I didn't want the people afraid of anything but what they'd done.

I looked down at the heretic again and then to the men behind him. "Remove that noose."

The ringleader hobbled forward, still on his knees, hastening to obey. When I held out my hand for the rope, he gave it to me. I held it up to the crowd. "I invited this man to England because France wouldn't have him. Personally, I like thumbing my nose at France."

That actually got a bit of a laugh. They were beginning to wonder where this was going and if maybe they were going to come out of it alive.

"But when I opened our doors to people who believe differently from you and me, that made him my guest, and every one of you has just made a mockery of my invitation." I paused, and then overrode the shuffling and mumbling that followed that statement, "The truth is, I don't care what this man believes. I don't care what you believe. I intend to create an England where every man, regardless of where he was born or who his parents are, has the right to believe what he likes."

"As long as he pays his taxes." That was Rhys again.

A dozen people gasped. I felt the air leave my own chest in a *huh* at my guard's audacity, but I recovered quickly, pointing to him and grinning. "Even so. You do your job, and I will do mine. But this—" I held up the rope again. "This is not for you. Your job is to welcome foreigners, *particularly* Frenchmen who wish to give us their allegiance." I tossed the rope to the ground. As before in the anteroom at the palace when I'd spoken to my men, the silence was absolute. I gazed out at my people's bowed heads.

"Stand up." I gestured with both hands. "Up! Up!"

"King David! God save King David!"

My men came through, bellowing the call until the people around them joined in. I lifted my hands again to raise the people to their feet, even as Carew and Callum pulled the heretic away, through the gateway in the wall behind me that separated the graveyard from the monastery grounds. I had none of my men beside me, but I didn't need them. The people were on their feet, bowing as I passed them, and the threat was over.

I couldn't help thinking it wasn't what I'd said, but because I'd been the most recent person to speak to them. They'd been about to lynch a man on the word of Acquasparta. Like any crowd, they were quick to anger, slower to calm, but eager to follow whoever was willing to lead them.

For the last few minutes, that person had been me, but it had been touch-and-go there for a minute and could have just as easily ended badly. I'd been lucky.

I'd also just defied, in the most blatant and open way possible, those who wanted to see the Inquisition in England. I'd thrown down my gauntlet at Acquasparta's feet. Even if I wanted to, there was no turning back now.

8

I strode back into the great hall of Canterbury Castle, my heart still pounding from the encounter with the mob. We'd brought the heretic with us, along with the ringleaders who'd been about to hang him, for no other reason than because I couldn't simply release them all into the city again. They were cooling their heels in separate rooms in the barracks—probably adjacent to the room where Mike and Noah had been left—until we could figure out what to do with them.

In faltering English, the heretic had said his name was Martin. Once we switched to French, he became more voluble, explaining that he'd come to Canterbury from Gascony with his family, having heard that England had become a refuge for those who believed as he did. He swore he'd never shared his beliefs with anyone, and it wasn't clear how Acquasparta had learned of them. After hearing that he had a family, I'd immediately sent men to find them and bring them into the castle too. With the crowd subdued and dispersed, I hoped we could put the incident behind us.

William de Bohun, my squire, was waiting for me a few paces inside the hall. He looked to top out in height at about five foot ten, a few inches shorter than I was, but he'd filled out in the last year. Soon I would have to knight him and find myself a new squire. Before he could speak, I pointed at him. "I need my sword."

He bowed, "Yes, sire," and scuttled away to do my bidding.

I turned around to find Callum, his face calm, looking at me. His eyes flicked right and left, drawing my attention to the various onlookers in the hall. I wasn't doing a very good job of hiding my emotions, and an angry king was a fearful sight. I'd been king for only four years, and many still remembered the towering rages of King Edward. By contrast, I worked hard not to expend my temper on my underlings and never in public.

Instead of speaking—because I didn't trust myself to speak—I stalked towards the doorway that would take me to my receiving room, Callum on my heels. Once inside, I dismissed my various secretaries who were laboring over today's papers and turned on my friend. "What was that?"

"An ambush, my lord."

I waved a hand at him. "Don't call me that. David. I'm David to you right now." I paced to my throne but didn't sit, instead turning back to look at Callum. "Why did Acquasparta arrange for that man's arrest? Why the three untenable requests?"

Callum took in a breath and let it out. "He arrested that man in this city within your vicinity to test the limits of your position. He wanted to bring the matter of heresy to a head and dispatch it."

"Well, he sure did that." I was already calming down. I ran a hand through my wet hair and came to a halt before the fire, which was smoldering low in the hearth. It wasn't a cold day, but the rain, which had lessened while I was speaking with the papal legate, had picked up again during the ride back from the cathedral to the castle.

Callum added, "I do not believe he foresaw any of the events that followed, neither the mob nor the extent of your determination to prevent him from pursuing heretics in England. Fortunately for us, whatever plan he did have backfired, and now Acquasparta has nothing to show Boniface for his efforts."

"He doesn't?" I said. "Why do you say that?"

"You saved a man from a lynching," he said. "You gave a speech too, first to your men in front of Romeyn, which before today I wouldn't have recommended, and then to a crowd of commoners. But none but they heard it, and who among them could understand more than one word in three? It gives us breathing space."

I scoffed under my breath. "I would have preferred a direct challenge. I don't want breathing space."

"You do, actually," Callum said gently. "We need time to figure this out, especially after the murders."

He'd brought me back down to earth. A quiet knock at the door at the back of the room did the rest. Callum went to open it, revealing Lili standing on the threshold. She looked past him to me, and I held out an arm to her. She hurried forward and wrapped her arms around my waist, hugging me. I kissed her temple. "I'm okay."

"Carew told me what happened. First with Mike and Noah and then at the Archbishop's palace. You—" She broke off, seemingly at a loss for words.

"I did what I had to," I said.

"I know that, but you could have been hurt!" Her voice went high on the last word, and I heard tears in it.

"Nobody was going to harm me. They had no weapons—"

"Nor did you! And you didn't know that at the time." She gave a very Welsh 'ach' at the back of her throat and pounded me on the chest with the flats of both hands. "Why do I even bother? You will do what you think is right."

I took both of her hands in mine and kissed them. "I have to."

She blew out her cheeks. "I know."

"If it's any comfort, Acquasparta seemed to have been taken by surprise by the vehemence of the crowd," Callum said. "He intended to arrest the heretic in front of David, not kill him."

"Why?" Lili said, which had been my question, but before Callum could answer, Lili waved a hand. "Never mind. I know why." She looked up at me. "To test Dafydd."

I released a sigh and walked to one of the ornate chairs near the fire to sit, very tired where before I'd had too much energy to contain. "Everyone's motivations are murky. I can't figure out the purpose of the pope's demands either. Why put me in a corner, first by asking something of me he knows I can't give easily, and then by forcing me to show—in public—how far I'm willing to go to protect a heretic?"

"What demands?" Lili said.

I regaled her with the tale of Acquasparta's three issues.

Her brow furrowed. "He wants you to refuse. He wants you to deny the requests."

Callum gave a low growl. "She's right. The latter two, in particular, are outrageous. He has to know that you would never agree to them, and that you *could* never agree to them."

"That doesn't answer my question," I said. "What happens when I do refuse? Does the pope retaliate by excommunicating me? By placing all England under interdict? What would he gain by that?" While an England under interdict meant priests couldn't perform sacraments and ceremonies, the populace would still belong to the Church. Excommunication, on the other hand, would mean I was thrown out.

"The pope would gain England," Lili said, "or at the very least, control over it."

Callum nodded. "Either you capitulate, giving him authority you are currently withholding, or a fight with the Holy See could be the tipping point that forces your barons to unseat you. I wouldn't have said you were weak at home, but perhaps he knows something we don't."

"He doesn't," Lili said.

I tapped a finger on the arm of my chair. "And if the barons unseat me? What then?"

"He would seek a more malleable king," Lili said, "someone he could control more easily."

"Does he know my barons?" I said, with a laugh.

"Maybe not, but whomever he found might not be so quick to defy him. He would see what happened to you and be more conciliatory." Callum looked at Lili. "Particularly if he was young like Thomas, Edmund's son."

"Pope Boniface has to know about my family's rocky relationship with the papacy, I suppose," I said.

"How could he not?" Lili said.

At King Edward's request, the previous pope had excommunicated my father twice, in 1276 and again in 1282. My great-grandfather had been excommunicated once too for the same reason: refusing to kowtow to the English king.

"Boniface has to be wondering how much of your father's son you are," Callum said.

Lili nodded. "He would want to nip any rebellion on your part in the bud."

"My personal ancestry aside, English kings have a long history of taking a hard line against papal decrees they don't agree with," I said. "In fact, Edward persuaded the last pope to excommunicate my father in the first place by putting pressure on him through his moneylenders, who threatened to call in his loans if he didn't do as Edward asked. Boniface will know that too and think it sets a bad precedent."

"The new king wouldn't be placing his throne in jeopardy over a few heretics, either," Lili said.

"What Boniface really wants is for you to acknowledge his secular power," Callum said. "We know that. He hasn't said it out loud yet, but we don't need him to do so to know what he is thinking."

Lili looked from Callum to me. "You're talking about something that happened in Avalon's history?"

I nodded, my eyes still on Callum. "There's still something we aren't seeing. I think he does know something we don't. He feels he has an advantage over me, beyond his ability to excommunicate me, though I can't see what that might be."

"Acquasparta wasn't exactly forthcoming," Callum said.

"Did you speak to him or Peckham after you saved the heretic?" Lili said.

"No," I said. "We left as quickly as we could."

"Was that wise?" she said.

I laughed. "I don't know. I wanted to let him stew a bit, to have him unsure of what I was thinking for a change. Besides, I couldn't see talking to him after what happened."

Callum smiled. "David might have taken off his head."

"Deservedly so," Lili said.

I waved her closer, and when she obliged, I pulled her down to sit on my knee.

Callum was standing with his arms folded across his chest, staring into the fire, not looking at us. "The religious issue is important to Boniface—genuinely so—but I think it is the third item that Boniface cares most about."

"I was wondering that myself," I said. "Do you think he's made a deal with Philip?"

"From the bit Acquasparta let slip, I think he has to have," Callum said. "He has no business involving himself in Aquitaine otherwise."

Not always, but often throughout the middle ages, the kings of France had held the ear of the pope far more than the kings of England. England was too independent, with an unruly barony overly concerned about its rights, and with a thriving mercantile class that grew larger and more influential every year and didn't fit in well with the feudal system.

In classic feudalism, the stratification of society was rigid with very little movement between classes. Sitting at the top of his personal pyramid was the king, with nobles below him, followed by knights. Merchants and craftsmen took up the next level, with peasants and serfs occupying the vast bottom class. This was a generalization, of course, and Boniface felt he should be sitting pretty above the king. Not all churchmen agreed, however, and certainly very few kings did. Especially English kings.

Rather than accept such an arrangement, a little over two hundred years from now, King Henry VIII had made himself head of the Church in England, upending the social and religious order of his time and giving a huge boost to the nascent Protestant Reformation. Nobody but the few of us time travelers were even aware that such an act was possible. Certainly, it would never have occurred to this pope that I could declare myself the head of my own church. But I would rather follow in Henry's footsteps than sacrifice a single one of my beliefs on the way to giving in to Boniface.

I'd asked my mother about the exact words King Henry VIII had used the day he'd declared himself the head of a church, denying centuries of tradition. But as it turned out, Henry hadn't. He hadn't made a bold speech. He'd instituted a process, which began because he wanted to annul his marriage to one of his wives. Martin Luther had already nailed his *Ninety-Five Theses* to the church door in Germany (Saxony at the time), detailing all that was wrong with the Church. And in England there was general unrest and resentment—dating back hundreds of years—against the way the Church was run.

Over the course of the next five years, Henry worked with Parliament, getting them to pass act after act that increased his power over the Church and diminished the Church's independence from the Crown. This culminated in 1534 with the *Acts of Supremacy*, which declared Henry the "supreme head ... of the Church of England."

My Parliament wasn't nearly as long-established as Henry's, and the House of Commons was only four years old, not a couple of hundred years as in Henry's day. I'd already asked them to revoke any previous laws that prevented Jews from living freely in England, and just last month, they'd agreed that a man's religious beliefs should not subject him to sanction or punishment by the state *or* by the Church.

If the Pope had heard about that, it was no wonder he'd sent Acquasparta to urge me back into line. I was pretty sure I could convince Parliament to stand with me again if I put my mind to it. There was a reason freedom of religion was part of the first amendment to the U.S. Constitution, along with its cousins, freedom of the press and freedom of speech. I was willing to stake my entire rule on this one issue, and I'd known from the start, even from the day I'd knelt before the Archbishop of Canterbury and received my crown, that I might have to.

Then Carew entered the room, followed by Bevyn and Ieuan.

"Does the Order of the Pendragon know anything about any of this?" I said without explaining which 'this' I was referring to. Whether the murders or the papal legate's demands, I didn't care. They were all high-ranking members. They all should know.

My companions exchanged rueful looks, but it was Bevyn who committed himself to answer. "No, sire."

Though most members of the Order were fighting men, they weren't meant to be warrior monks like the Templars. For all that there was no doubt the members thought they were carrying out God's will, they were much more practical than that. Their sole mission was to protect me at all costs.

They did that not by guarding me, which they left to lesser men, but by playing politics and espionage. If Gilbert de Clare or Edmund Mortimer had been at Canterbury, they would have been in on this too. Intrigue was like bread and butter to them, which was a good thing because it didn't come naturally to me.

It did come more easily, however, to Lili and Cassie. Callum's influence had made both women members in the Order, and since then, the formerly all-male membership had grown to include several more women, the men having finally realized that women could make excellent spies. Other than those members who had direct contact with me, I didn't know the names of most of them, nor the Order's exact numbers.

When she'd first joined the Order, I'd attempted to get Lili to tell me something more about it or what they talked about at their meetings. She'd taken my face in her hands, kissed me, and refused to answer any of my questions except to say that she'd sworn an oath to keep what happened with the Order within the Order. She would never do anything that violated either my trust in her or her new responsibilities.

There'd been a wicked gleam in her eye too, which worried me a little. But my wife had as much honor as any knight I knew. I'd given up.

According to Bevyn, my ignorance in these matters was for my protection and theirs, though I secretly thought it had more to do with the fact that Bevyn liked keeping secrets, even from his king. I did know that the current concern was to keep a lid on growth, so as not to inadvertently invite a traitor into our midst. Which it seems I had done when I decided to take my trio of troublemakers off my mother's hands.

The door behind me opened, and Bronwen, Ieuan's wife, entered the room. This was becoming a party. Bronwen was a time traveler too, having chosen to come to the Middle Ages with Ieuan and me after we ended up in modern Pennsylvania seven years ago.

Lili's blue eyes flashed at the sight of her best friend, her anxiety briefly giving way to amusement, though I couldn't think what could be amusing her right now. Bronwen carried a tray with a half-dozen wooden cups and a pitcher wrapped in a cloth, which Lili rose to take from her.

"Sorry I'm late," Bronwen said. "I heard what happened and thought this might help some of you think better." She and Lili set down their burdens on the long table where I conducted cabinet meetings and signed papers, just as the last of my time traveling companions at Canterbury arrived: Peter, Darren, Cassie, and Rachel.

Rachel was Britain's chief medical officer, as I liked to call her, though only the time travelers caught the Star Trek reference. That first day in the medieval world, Rachel had accepted Anna's offer to head up her nascent medical school and to be the organizer of everything that had to do with medicine in Britain.

Rachel had spent six months setting up a college of medicine in Llangollen, training others to train others. Two weeks ago, I'd asked her to join my entourage. Medieval kings spent most of their time circumambulating their kingdoms, and I wanted her to see what was happening in the entire country.

Anna had given her a big job. Too big a job for one person, really. But if I could go from being a fourteen-year-old American kid to being the King of England, I didn't think it was too much to ask that other people take steps towards fulfilling their potential too.

Huw, who'd entered the room last, remained standing a few paces away, half-turned so he could see both me and the door. At approximately twenty, he had an earnest intentness that reminded me of myself when I was younger, though I had probably been even more innocent.

The young man had come a long way since that day when he and his father had walked across Gwynedd with me after I'd been abducted and almost killed. The traitor responsible had been among my closest guard and had been working with two others who hated me. It was a constant problem—needing to trust those close to me in order to stay sane but never knowing if any man was really my friend. I'd been wrong before, and clearly I'd been wrong again.

9

"Y ou heard what happened at the Archbishop's palace?" I said to my friends, having moved from my chair beside the fire to the table. Everyone else had found a place to sit too.

"I told them," Carew said. "Should I put out a query in regard to another meeting with Acquasparta and the Archbishops?"

"I told Romeyn I wanted to see him and Peckham here tomorrow," I said, "but you'd probably better send a message to Acquasparta too. At the very least, we should inquire about his health. He didn't look good when we left."

"Nor did Peckham," Callum said. "Aaron was seeing to him."

"Could you have a look at both of them, Rachel?" I said.

"Of course," Rachel said. "I have also looked in on the two guards Lee and the others disabled before leaving the castle. They'll both live."

I felt a slight easing in my shoulders. These were the two men Callum had tasked with keeping an eye on Lee, Mike, and

Noah. After we'd realized their charges were missing, we'd searched the castle from top to bottom, ultimately finding the two guards tied up and unconscious in one of the neglected cellars underneath a corner tower. They had no memory of how Lee had gotten the drop on them. Nor did they know where he was now.

Meanwhile, Ieuan put out a hand to Bronwen. "You don't have to be here."

"And let you boys get yourselves into all kinds of trouble without Lili and me?" Bronwen said. "I don't think so."

Ieuan gestured to the drink they'd brought. "What's this?"

Darren had pulled out a chair so Rachel could sit at the table, and now she leaned forward to smell what was in the pot. "Am I smelling coffee?"

"Sirrah, you jest!" Callum said, in a parody of medieval-speak, and sniffed too.

Bronwen grinned. "I do not jest."

"How did you achieve this?" Callum said.

"I have friends in high places," Bronwen said, with a glance at me.

"I thought coffee came from the New World?" Peter said.

"Ah, that's what they want you to think, but it doesn't." Bronwen looked very pleased with herself. "It comes from Africa."

I'd been a kid when I'd come to Wales, so I'd never developed a taste for coffee. But Bronwen's particular love for it, heavily laden with cream and sugar, was well known. Crusaders had brought sugar back from the Holy Land a hundred years ago, and since London had become one of the foremost trading capitals of Europe, it was now possible to get it in quantity, especially if you were the King of England. Cream, of course, was easy.

I took a cup from Bronwen, allowing the aroma to wash over me. It smelled like morning. My mother had drunk coffee too, once upon a time.

"I didn't know if you all liked coffee," Bronwen said, "but Cassie assured me you did."

"I might be British born and raised," Rachel said, "but nobody makes it through medical school or residency on tea alone. This is sugar?" She picked up one of the cups filled with brown crystals.

"Sugar and cream, just like the doctor ordered," Bronwen said, watching Rachel scoop both into her cup. "You are a girl after my own heart."

"May I?" Rachel held up her cup to me.

I still hadn't taken a drink of mine, and nobody—even close friends such as this—could drink before the king. I nodded.

She took a sip and then closed her eyes. "Heaven. Thank you, Bronwen, from the bottom of my heart."

"It hasn't been that long for you," Bronwen said. "I haven't had coffee since 1285."

That was seven years ago. It had been only ten months since the bus had taken Rachel and forty other people through the barrier that separated this world from Avalon. If I still felt like an alien from another planet half the time, it wasn't any wonder that so many passengers were having a hard time of it. Rachel had grown up in Wales and spoke Welsh, but that was about as far as she or any of the others got towards familiarity with the medieval world.

Bevyn cleared his throat. He admired Bronwen, so he'd briefly shown amusement at the interruption, but now he returned to his usual intensity. "Men are continuing to hunt for Lee, but the longer we go without finding him, the less likely we'll be able to bring him back."

Lili put a hand on my shoulder. "Lee is stranded in the Middle Ages with few friends and almost no possessions. He has murdered his companions and could cause more trouble—he's certainly giving Dafydd a headache—but other than sowing discontent and harming those guards, I honestly can't see how Lee could be that much of a threat to Dafydd's rule."

"We know what he planned in Wales," Callum said. "I won't underestimate him."

Bronwen looked from Callum to me. "Good riddance, I say—" She stopped, her expression faltering at the look on my face that I didn't master as quickly as I should have. Clearly she hadn't liked Lee either. She gave a slight cough. "Sorry."

"We have been many steps behind them from the start," I said, "because once Lee left Avalon on the bus, we have had no access to information about him other than what he told us. In fact, it seems now that, back in Caerphilly, Lee may have deliberately provoked and encouraged Noah and Mike in their rudeness and misbehavior in order to keep our attention on them, leaving him free to plot and plan with impunity."

"The best-case scenario is that he fled too soon, before whatever he was plotting was complete. While he could terrorize a town," Callum said, "that pales in comparison to what he could do if he has made contact with David's enemies, as he did in Wales with King Llywelyn's foes."

I studied my friend. This wasn't an exclusive family gathering, and yet he had used my given name. He must have been really upset to have done so. It was never my intent to turn friends into inferiors, but we all knew the reality of everyone else's relative position to mine. Fortunately, we were among friends and his use of my name went unnoticed—or at least unremarked.

"I can tell you that Lee isn't from London originally," Rachel said, "even though that's what he told everyone. I can hear traces of an accent in his voice, but I can't place it. I'm not even sure he's from England."

"I can hear it too," Darren said. "It bothered me at first, but he'd hardly be the first man to teach himself a new accent as a way to improve his lot in life."

And Darren should know. The son of an African father and a white mother, Darren had started out at nineteen as a bobby on the streets of London. He'd gone to university at night and risen through the ranks—not without some resentment on the part of those who weren't rising as fast, with accusations of reverse racism. Darren had ignored the naysayers by focusing rigidly on his goal to get off the street and make detective, which he'd done at the relatively young age of twenty-eight. A year later, he'd applied to MI-5 and been accepted. Callum had snapped him up for Cardiff as soon as Darren's file had crossed his desk.

"In this case, however, it seems Lee might have done it to hide his identity," I said.

"The fact is we know very little about any of the bus passengers, not having access to records that would tell us more. I apologize for not bringing all of you into the loop sooner." Callum gestured to Huw, who up until now had been standing off to one side, completely silent. He took his duties to the Order so seriously it was almost a fault. I, for one, would like to see him unbend enough to joke with his fellows. And the last time I'd asked if he had a girl somewhere, he said he hadn't time for such frivolity. "Tell them."

"Once King David made the decision to take the three men out of Caerphilly and include them in his court, the Order decided to find out more about what they'd been doing since they arrived." Huw held himself straight and spoke formally. "Such was my task."

"I should have been the one to ask," I said.

"You thought all they'd been doing was drinking," Lili said.

I sighed. "That's all I wanted them to be doing, and I didn't inquire further because I didn't want to deal with them. You may laugh at me, especially after what we've all been through together, but just the thought of forty new needy people was overwhelming to me."

"Nobody's laughing," Bronwen said flatly.

"It was never your job to deal with them. It was Callum's and mine," Cassie said. "It's our fault more than anyone else's."

"I didn't see it either," Bronwen said, "and I've spent more time at Caerphilly this year than any of you."

I felt my irritation rising. This was the same conversation I'd had this morning with Callum and Carew. "Will one of you let me admit I was wrong, just this once?"

"We'll let you admit it when it's your fault," Bronwen said. "As always, you take too much on yourself." She could have concluded with *so there*, but I was glad she didn't. Instead, she gave me a flinty smile, and I subsided. Bronwen never had trouble speaking her mind, and seven years in the Middle Ages had only made her see more clearly what was important. Her graduate program's loss was my gain.

"Up until their arrival at the king's court, Mike and Noah may have been only what they appeared to be," Huw said as if the interruption hadn't happened. "And that was what led us astray. They drank, they whored around, and they had no occupation other than their own pleasure. Once they arrived in London, however, it appears that Lee took them into his confidence."

I held up my hand to interrupt. "You all may have noted the moderation in Mike's and Noah's behavior since their transfer from Caerphilly to my court."

There were a few nods around the table.

"I took it as a good sign," Bronwen said. "I thought your plan might be working."

"Apparently not," I said.

"Who in Wales in particular did he bribe?" Bronwen said. Ieuan's lands were in eastern Powys, and Bronwen would know all the players there.

"Several barons we thought loyal to King Llywelyn," Bevyn said. "We have spoken with the king and have set a watch on them. If Lee is still in contact with them or has plans that will undermine the king, we will know of it before it happens."

Most of these lords lived in the former March—the southern and eastern portions of Wales—which for two centuries had been fought over by Welsh and Norman barons, and where, in many places, the people had grown accustomed to English rule. Consequently, it was here that my father's rule was least accepted.

"Why would Lee do any of this?" Peter said. "Why murder his only friends? What's his motivation?"

"We don't know," Callum said. "It probably has something to do with freeing Ireland from Norman control, but frankly, we don't know anything about him or what he's doing beyond what the few people who were willing to talk told us. It isn't much."

"I saw fear in their eyes when I spoke with some of them," Huw said, uncharacteristically offering information for which he hadn't been asked. "I haven't seen fear like that in grown men in a long time. Maybe not since I was a boy."

Bronwen took another sip of her coffee, sighed, and set it down. "He didn't just arrive in the Middle Ages and decide to become a traitor. He's done something like this before."

"You aren't wrong, Bronwen," I said. "Callum, Cassie, and I were talking about what happened last year in Cardiff and wondering if Lee had played a role in the bombings."

Carew's brow furrowed as he looked at me. "My lord, given the effort Lee expended plotting treason against your father in Wales, I'm surprised he consented to come to England in the first place."

I tsked under my breath. "I wondered that today too. He may have seen it as an opportunity, and I didn't really give any of them a choice. I spoke to them personally, at my mother's request. Mike sneered, Noah looked blank—"

"—as he always did," Lili said, "not to speak ill of the dead."

"—as he did," I agreed. "Lee gave me an appraising look before nodding his consent. At the time, I was simply relieved that I wasn't going to have to drag them away from Caerphilly in chains. My mother couldn't have endured any of them for another day."

"When did you start to think that we'd misjudged Lee, sire?" Darren said.

"That's a very generous, 'we', Darren," I said, "and sadly, I didn't. Not more than a little, and certainly not enough to do more than wonder. It was the Order, at Callum's urging, that decided to take another look at everything we thought we knew about them."

Since coming to the Middle Ages, I'd encountered more than a few men of dubious morality. Mike had fallen into one of the lower levels of bruiser/brawler/drunk. If he'd had a wife, he might have hit her. Over time if Mike had remained in the modern world, his personal trajectory might have resulted in an expanded waistline and diminished prospects, both of which would have soured him on everything and everyone until he fell into a bottle and never came out.

Noah, on the other hand, had struck me from the start as cut from a different cloth. Small and wiry where Mike was big and blustery, he'd done nothing since he'd arrived in the Middle Ages. Quite literally. I hadn't ever heard him speak more than a few words except those to me when I spoke to him directly. He seemed to know better than to openly defy either me or my father, and he seemed to fit somewhere in the middle between Lee and Mike. He had been a follower, but a loyal one, and appeared to do as he was told.

I really wished I'd paid more attention to what had been happening at Caerphilly, and I blamed myself for being blind and innocent—more innocent than Huw. My friends might be frustrated at the way I took the responsibility for their actions onto myself, but I was the King of England. Whether or not any of them liked it, the blame and responsibility for those in my charge always trickled up to me.

"For my part," Callum said, "vague curiosity coalesced into actual concern when Lee started associating with the king. I set men to watch all three and make note of their doings, and I asked the Order of the Pendragon to trace their activities in Caerphilly." Callum gestured to Huw. "This is the result."

"Once it became clear that Lee had been plotting treason," Bevyn said, "Huw and I rode for London as quickly as we could."

"But I wasn't there," I said.

"Thus the further delay." Bevyn's expression was one of frustration, which I shared. He'd been ten steps behind Lee from the start. While I had missed the starter's gun entirely, he'd almost caught up, but almost hadn't been good enough.

"Obviously, we should have arrested them first and asked questions later." Callum glowered in the direction of the door, as if he could time travel back to a point three months ago when he'd made the decision to watch them.

"So what's Lee's plan, and what are we going to do about it?" Bronwen said.

"We won't know that until we catch him," Callum said.

Cassie lifted her hand to gain everyone's attention. "Has it occurred to anyone else that there now may be two people who want to unseat David: Lee and the pope? Is that too much of a coincidence?"

Callum spread his hands wide. "How could Lee and Acquasparta possibly be working together?"

Cassie lifted one shoulder. "I'm just asking the question."

"It's a disconcerting thought," I said.

"If Lee does have you in his sights," Bronwen said, "who's to say the next King of England wouldn't be as strong as you and far more ruthless."

Ieuan snorted under his breath. "Gilbert de Clare springs to mind, even if he has no royal blood."

"To sum up," Bronwen said, cutting through the chatter, "we know of no connection between the current Irish resistance to Norman rule and Lee. We have no clue as to why Lee murdered Mike and Noah, and little insight as to why he took their murders as the opportune time to splash his slogan above their bodies. Is that about right?"

I laughed. I couldn't help it. "Pretty much."

"Then maybe, for now, we need to put aside the why and focus on what happens next," Bronwen said.

I sobered instantly. "I was going to suggest that we have too many simultaneous problems, and we need to take a multi-pronged approach."

Bevyn's brow furrowed. "What was that?"

I'd used an Americanism he didn't know. Searching for how better to explain what I meant, I waggled my hand at Callum, who obligingly stepped in.

"We need to come at our current troubles from many directions," he said. "We can't choose only one path, because we don't know which one will turn out to be the best."

"Right," I said. "We may have very little time until Lee reveals himself again, or we may have weeks. Acquasparta, on the other hand, is more of a known quantity. I urge the Order put aside the issue of Lee for now."

"I agree with the king," Callum said. "His pursuit requires fairly straightforward police work."

Darren bobbed his head. "Peter and I are on it."

I nodded, confident in their abilities. The color of Darren's skin was no more a barrier to getting the job done here than it had been in Avalon. On one hand, he stood out in medieval England and attracted attention wherever he went. On the other hand, people came right up to him who otherwise might have avoided the authority he represented, and he'd found that those who felt out of place or beleaguered recognized themselves in him and were more likely to open up and speak the truth.

"What do you require from the Order, then?" Bevyn said.

"I need to know everything about Boniface there is to know: his weaknesses, his debts, to whom he owes obligations, and what he may have said privately about me," I said. "I am asking both you and our trading partners for this information."

Bevyn shot a quick glance at the others before nodding. "We will see to it, as quickly as we may. I know that our Jewish friends already have an extensive portfolio on him. The Order has not paid him as much attention up until now as perhaps we should have."

That initial group of Jewish merchants who'd come to Wales after my mother's return from Avalon had grown to a network of spies, moneylenders, and merchants that stretched from Aberystwyth to Constantinople. The Pope usually didn't choose to borrow money from Jews, but that didn't mean they wouldn't know everything there was to know about him as a matter of self-preservation.

"How did you leave it with Cardinal Acquasparta, my lord?" Ieuan said.

I grimaced. "We set a tentative date of two weeks from now for some kind of response from me regarding the Pope's 'concerns', as Acquasparta called them."

Bevyn grunted. "Two weeks."

"A lot can happen in two weeks," Cassie said.

"A lot has happened in one day," Bronwen said.

"What's the other avenue you thought to pursue, Dafydd?" Lili said.

"A more familiar one," I said. "Do we know where Gilbert de Clare is at present?"

"My maid says he's in Kent," Lili said, speaking of Branwen, who was not so much an inveterate gossip as an able listener. Lili had invited her into the Order of the Pendragon, but she'd sniffed her disdain and commented that she would prefer to join whatever order was designed to protect Lili, a sentiment for which I could only honor her. "He may not know you are here, however."

"I need him," I said.

"Why in particular?" Carew said.

"I may have to start a war—or at least pretend to."

As one, my companions gaped at me, but I laughed. They'd reacted as I'd hoped. My constant preoccupation with politics meant I had to take my amusement where I could. "Boniface is concerned about my claim to Aquitaine, right? He fears that if I pursue it, we will have a war with Philip of France, who also claims it."

"So you want to go ahead and start that war now?" Cassie said.

"I want him to believe that I plan to," I said. "Look—the cardinal brought out three items that he wants from me: he wants to prosecute heretics in England; he wants the money Pope Nicholas gave me from his *taxatio*; and he wants me to back off from my claim to Aquitaine. Doesn't it strike you as an odd list? On the surface, the first item should be the most important to him. Refusing it is certainly the most important to me, and today Acquasparta gave every impression that heretics are to be rounded up whenever they are found."

"But you don't think that's really it?" Cassie said.

I made a *maybe* motion with my head. "He cares about it. Callum and Carew assure me that he cares about it, but we're talking about a handful of people in the whole of England."

"There are more in Wales," Lili said. "It may be that the pope is pursuing you first as a way to set a precedent for negotiations with your father, who he deems the stronger."

"You are usually right about these things," I said, "but the numbers are still small—certainly fewer than a hundred people."

"So far," Cassie said.

"Okay, true," I said.

"The principle is the important thing," Carew said. "You openly defied the Church when you welcomed heretics into England. He can't have that. It sets a bad precedent for the rest of Europe."

"I know that," I said, annoyed that they were undermining my well-conceived thesis with their logic. "But I don't see why he would link that issue with these other requests, ones much more material in nature if heresy is really his chief concern. Specifically, he has no business meddling in Aquitaine, which a) has nothing whatsoever to do with the pope, b) indicates an alliance with Philip, all of which, c) seems deliberately designed to raise my hackles. It feels like he *wants* me to defy him."

"Which is why we were thinking that Aquitaine might be what Boniface cares most about," Callum said. "If that's the case, by pretending we care most about it too, we might induce him to bend on the issue of heresy."

"That is remarkably devious of you, my lord," Cassie said. "I'm impressed."

She never used my title except in public, so I smirked and bowed. "Thank you."

"So, I gather that by calling in Clare and marshalling his forces as well as yours, you want to give the impression of going to war," Ieuan said. "Will Clare support such a move?"

"Of course he will," Carew said. "His new wife brings him lands in Aquitaine. He wouldn't want to see the duchy fall to the King of France."

I might rail against having to spend so much of my energies on politics, but Gilbert de Clare *lived* them. As a young man, he'd fought with Simon de Montfort to unseat King Henry III. He'd allied with my father at that time to divide Britain among the three of them, and then switched sides at a crucial moment, all but giving the country to Henry and bringing about Montfort's death. He'd also led a massacre of Jews right here in Canterbury nearly thirty years ago, as part of Montfort's plan to wipe out the indebtedness of the nobility in one go. As with many aspects of the persecution of Jews, their treatment had less to do with religion than with money and power.

After the Barons' War, Clare had gone on Crusade with Edward, who was not yet king, to atone for his sins. I hadn't asked if he counted the massacre as one of them, but he had never objected to my open door policy towards Jews. Clare was nothing if not pragmatic. He cared little, if anything, for high-minded ideals. His wealth and lands had grown under my watch, and I had no doubt that he would embrace the idea of going to war—or pretending to—if it gave him the opportunity to add to his lands in France.

"What will Pope Boniface say when he discovers you are marshalling men to cross the Channel?" Cassie said.

"We won't know for a while, will we?" I said.

WARDEN OF TIME

"That would be great, but what if your plan doesn't work?" Cassie said. "What's the worst thing that could happen? Besides war, I mean, which is bad enough."

"If David doesn't bow to the pope on these issues, Boniface could put England under interdict and excommunicate him," Callum said.

Understanding had grown in Ieuan's eyes too, but it was replaced almost immediately by puzzlement. "What if Boniface calls your bluff? Would you really take England to war against France?"

"If I have to," I said. "I will not give way on what matters most. I will not."

10

I lay in bed, staring up at the canopy, my brain churning with worst-case scenarios.

Lili rolled over and put a hand on my shoulder. "You could at least close your eyes and pretend to be trying to sleep."

"I'm deciding whether or not to get up." I flung a forearm over my eyes, forcing them closed. They itched with tiredness, but my brain wouldn't let me rest. It had been a wild day.

"If you don't sleep, you won't be good for anything tomorrow." Lili laid her head on my chest, and I put my arm around her.

"That's why I hadn't gotten up yet." I turned my head to look towards the window. I'd left the shutters open to better hear the rain on the window, hoping the steady drumming would help me empty my brain. Lili's breathing slid into sleep, and after a moment, I eased away from her, leaving her head pillowed in the crook of her arm.

I was a lucky man, no doubt about it. I didn't actually intend to throw my kingship away, which was one reason I'd focused my attention today on rescuing the heretic rather than repeating my speech about freedom of religion to the townspeople. I would fight for my throne as long as there was something to fight for, because I didn't feel like my work was finished yet, but knowing that I had Lili to come home to made the possibility of any other loss easier to bear.

I'd sent a rider to Clare at Tonbridge, but his castle was in western Kent, forty miles away. It would be a day or two before I would hear back from him. I tried not to wish for a cell phone more than once a day. Since the busload of people had arrived, we'd acquired some technical ability we hadn't had before, and a telegraph line was in our future. But not yet, and even if we did have it, odds were it wouldn't have run from Canterbury to Tonbridge.

Meanwhile, I'd spent the day in conference with my advisers and cabinet, preparing for the possibility of war. The logistics were ridiculous. Just feeding the thousands of men I'd have to bring across the channel took an army of cooks. Weapons, ships, siege engines—not to mention strategy—all had to be worked out. The pope was not going to be pleased. And even if the preparations were a complicated bluff, it had to look real. It had to be more than talk and pretense, and that meant some serious activity on our part.

If Acquasparta had spies at Canterbury Castle, I wanted them to be reporting to him that I was going to war. I wanted him to be lying awake staring up at the ceiling too.

I pulled on my breeches and boots, since stone floors are really cold on the feet, tucked in my shirt, and threw the warm black cloak I'd worn to the Archbishop's palace around my shoulders.

Before leaving the room, I poked my nose through the doorway to where Arthur slept in an adjacent room. My three-year-old son lay tucked up in his big bed, as befitted the future King of England. His nanny slept on a trundle bed beside him. Most nights, he ended up in our room anyway, wiggling under the covers between Lili and me. It was early enough that he hadn't yet woken. I was thinking it must be somewhere around two in the morning. I'd lain awake a long while, but we still had some hours before dawn.

"Sire." The guard on duty outside my door bowed as I passed him.

"As you were," I said.

Another guard stood at the top of the stairs at the end of the corridor. At the sight of me coming towards him, he disappeared, only to return almost immediately. I knew what he was doing: the word would be spreading throughout the keep that the king was awake and on the move. It wasn't fair that everyone else had to be awake when I was, which was why I hadn't left my room earlier.

The monarchy had all sorts of hereditary and appointed offices, many of which were really cabinet members—the Lord High Treasurer, for instance, or the Lord High Chancellor. Clare,

Bohun, Mortimer, Callum, and Carew all had their places. They didn't serve in the royal household, however—though if the king was awake at two in the morning, certain companions might show up. As King of England, I had remarkably little authority over my own household, and whenever I tried to change these kinds of details, I only ended up hurting the feelings of the people whose job it was to be awake. I felt guilty about waking the castle, but not enough to return to bed.

At least I'd managed to dress myself without Jeeves, my manservant, but even as I thought that, Jeeves hustled down the hall towards me, straightening his soft hat. "Sire." He bowed deeply. "What do you require?"

"I require you to go back to sleep," I said. "How am I to trust your assessment of my attire if I know you're operating on half a night's sleep?"

"My lord—"

"Go, Jeeves. I'm fine. Just off to do a little paperwork."

"Yes, sire." Jeeves bowed and backed away. I hoped he would actually sleep, but more likely he'd lie down fully dressed to await events.

The square keep of Canterbury Castle stood six stories high, with towers on the corners adding the last level to the battlement. The exterior was all stone, but the interior was constructed in wood, which made the whole structure far more comfortable than it would have been had the castle been built all in stone. The corridors and stairs were built inside the eleven-foot-thick walls, allowing passage from room to room. The toilets (sometimes called *garderobes*) were in the walls too, accessible usually by an offset hallway in an attempt keep the smell contained and discourage it from wafting into the corridors.

Great wooden beams supported each ceiling and floor above. The bottom floor contained the kitchen and storage areas. Next up was the great hall, which took up almost the whole of the level, but also included my receiving room/office for smaller gatherings, in which I met my advisers throughout the day. Above that were the apartments of lords such as Callum and Ieuan. Then came a whole floor devoted to my needs, though Ieuan and Bronwen, with their small daughter, Catrin, had a room there too. And above that were more apartments and quarters.

The stone stairways were in circular towers on opposite corners of each floor. They spiraled down to the right, so if an invader was moving up towards me, he'd have to fight me left-handed. Fortunately, that wasn't a problem today, and I met no opposition as I went down the steps to my office. When I reached the next level down, however, I glanced into the corridor to see three men of the garrison in heated conversation halfway along it. It was dark in the stairwell, so they didn't notice me right away, but when the conversation continued, and after a moment included the words, 'wake Lord Ieuan,' I revealed myself and came forward. "Is there a problem?"

The eyes of the guard closest to me bugged out. "S-s-sire!" All three men stiffened to attention, bowed, and stiffened again as if unable to decide which form of obeisance was most appropriate when caught unawares at two in the morning in a corridor with the King of England.

These men belonged to Canterbury's garrison, and I didn't recognize any of them. Still, I canted my head, waiting for an answer. After a few seconds' pause, one of the other guards, a young man of perhaps twenty, spoke up. "I noticed an unusual light coming from the toilet just now. We were wondering if we should wake someone to inspect it."

"What's your name?"

"George, sire."

"Unusual how?" I said, though I hadn't ever seen a medieval toilet with any light coming from it at all unless someone had left a candle burning in a sconce. I thought back to the Spiderman nightlight that had been plugged in above the sink in my bathroom back in Oregon. Even after I'd repainted my bedroom and bath orange at the age of thirteen to reflect the loyalties of my new teenage self, I'd left the nightlight in the socket.

"Well—" The soldier glanced at each of his companions, neither of whom gave him any help. "There's a ... a ... glow coming up the shaft."

"Show me," I said.

George turned smartly on his heel and paced away down the corridor towards the far end. He took me first to the guard room that marked the corner of the keep, and then through it to the toilet.

Medieval latrines varied in quality and cleanliness. My sister, Anna, had a thing about them, and designing a better toilet had been a quest of hers. The best simple latrines consisted of a small room with one or two wooden toilet seats, which wouldn't have been out of place in any American home, placed over a chute of varying sizes that emptied outside the curtain wall.

The most hygienic and best-smelling ones dropped the waste into a moat or a channel filled with water, which then had a mechanism to move the waste away from the castle. The monastery associated with Canterbury's cathedral, like other monasteries I'd visited in Wales and England, had an elaborate underground water system with channels and pipes that moved fresh water into the complex and waste water out of it. The monks had built these systems without access to modern concepts of cleanliness or disease. It wasn't rocket science—just forward thinking and a basic knowledge of hydraulics.

The toilets in this castle, however, were less advanced because the keep wasn't built into the curtain wall. While the guarderobe looked the same as anywhere—a narrow cubby hole built into the wall of the keep—the toilet shafts consisted of a chute leading to a cesspit below.

"My apologies, sire, but you have to look right inside," George said, wincing at having to ask.

I peered past the seat to where he was pointing and then, holding in a breath, looked closer. A faint white glow lit the interior of the chute about eighteen inches below the level of the toilet seat. A flashlight would have been better, but I swung around to one of the other soldiers who'd come with us and snapped my fingers at him. "Get me a candle."

He ran to the nearest sconce on the wall, which held three candles behind a clay shield to block drafts, took out one candle, and brought it to me. Leaning with it into the toilet chute, trying to breathe only through my nose and hoping the flame wouldn't ignite the methane gases that had built up in the chute from the waste below, I tried to figure out where the light was coming from. Now that I'd brought the candle closer, the glow had diminished in comparison, but it was still there, emanating from a block of clay that had been smushed into the crevices between the stones that made up the toilet shaft.

The light would have been brighter if a layer of the clay hadn't been inexpertly smeared over it. By the same token, if the clay had been laid on a bit thicker, hiding the light inside the brick, and the toilet had been less engulfed in darkness, nobody would have seen it at all.

Which would have been a disaster beyond imagining.

My heart beating out of my ears, I straightened up, bringing the light with me, and looked at the soldier who'd brought me the candle. "Wake Lord Callum and send him here. Right now."

"Yes, sire!"

Before the soldier took a step, however, I caught his arm. "And when you've done that, wake Lord Bevyn, Lord Carew, and everyone else on the floors above us."

The man nodded and ran off.

I pointed at George. "Lord Ieuan's chamber is opposite mine. He will rouse the men of the garrison. Wake him, and then go to my wife and son. It will be your job to get them out of the castle. Tell her 'Cilmeri', and she'll come with you."

Without cell phones, I'd worried that in times of danger I would almost always have to send a messenger to Lili instead of going myself. 'Cilmeri' was the emergency code word Lili and I had chosen.

"Get everyone up: William de Bohun, Arthur's nanny, Jeeves—all of whom should be sleeping in rooms adjacent to my chamber. Take all of them out of the castle by the wicket gate to St. Mildred's Church. You know it?"

It was a little church a stone's throw from the castle. It was the first place that came to mind that was a safe distance away but was also where I could find them easily. The Archbishop's palace was too far away, and I didn't want to send them there anyway.

George nodded vigorously, though his brow furrowed. "Cilmeri?"

"She'll know when you say it that your message came from me." Cilmeri was the place where my father would have died in an ambush had Anna and I not arrived in my aunt's minivan to save him. "Everyone must be as quiet as possible. I don't want anyone outside the castle to know that the alarm has been raised until it's impossible to hide. Get them out!"

Wide-eyed but obedient, George disappeared. I looked at the last soldier, an older man with white in his beard and calm gray eyes. My urgency was clear, but he gazed at me steadily, awaiting orders.

"We need the whole castle cleared, down to the last man, woman, and child," I said. "Go first to Sir Thomas in his quarters above the gatehouse. He will wake everyone else. Send the women and children to St. Mildred's chapel, same as George. Quietly."

"What about the men?"

"Once they've cleared everyone out, they need to get out too. Don't wait for me or further orders. Do you understand?"

"I do."

I didn't think we could avoid a panic, but since I was the only one who knew what the glow in the toilet might be about, I hoped to contain everyone's fear as long as I could. I didn't want whoever had put the bomb in the toilet to panic and set it off prematurely. Particularly when I was standing on top of it. Whether or not that was a danger depended on whether the bomb had a timer or could be detonated remotely.

The soldier left, replaced within a few seconds by Callum. "What is it?"

Never in my life had I been more relieved to see anyone than I was to see him in that moment. Callum was the soldier, not me, and I was out of my depth in this.

I directed Callum's attention to the light shining up from the shaft below the toilet seat. Wordlessly, Callum took the candle from me and, as I had, leaned close so he could look into the chute to see what was causing the glow. "It's PE-4, what you call C-4." He kept the tone of his voice completely even. When I'd given the orders to the guards, I'd had to grit my teeth to stop them from chattering so badly I couldn't speak. Still bent over, Callum turned his head to look up at me. "I can dismantle this right now, but are there more explosives somewhere else? In other toilets perhaps?"

"I don't know," I said. "I don't think we have the time to go toilet to toilet, not if whoever planted this here discovers that we've found it. It could be set off remotely, right?"

"I think it's a timer with a digital clock," Callum said. "This one looks like it came right out of a terrorist's manual. You can find out how to make one in two minutes on the internet."

"Last I checked, we have no internet," I said.

"We do not. Nor C-4." He glanced at me. "Given the amount of C-4 here, telling you to stand back is perhaps a waste of air, but I'd like you to stand back."

I obeyed, moving outside the guarderobe itself into the little corridor that led to the main gallery running through the walls of the keep.

"It's the timer that caused the glow." Callum's voice echoed out of the little room. "You can buy ones that don't light up, but it seems whoever did this didn't think about that until he put the bomb together. C-4 is quite stable and explodes only when combined with a detonator. It's the detonator that is set off by an electrical charge, which then sets off the C-4."

"My God," I said. It was such a simple arrangement to cause the incredible destruction we were facing if we couldn't stop it. I peered around the corner again, so I could see him. "Can you make this one safe for now?"

"When it isn't connected, the detonator is more dangerous than the C-4," Callum said. "But that isn't to say—"

He broke off as feet pounded toward us, coming along the corridor. So much for quiet. The older soldier had returned. I stepped out of the doorway into the passage and grabbed his arm. "My family—"

"George woke them. They're out, and the top floors are cleared." He looked around the corner to see Callum on his knees, his arm reaching into the toilet chute. "His lordship's wife went with them. What do you want me to do now?"

Before I could answer, Ieuan arrived, skidding to a halt behind the soldier. "I have done as you ordered. Bevyn is awake and has the evacuation well in hand. Many of your guard are reluctant to leave before you, but they are following orders anyway, particularly once told that you'd sent Lili and Arthur to St. Mildred's. Why are we doing this?"

"Explosives," I said. C-4 would mean nothing to him, but he'd seen the effect of gunpowder. Only Callum and I knew that C-4 would result in a much greater explosion than any gunpowder producible in the Middle Ages.

Then Justin appeared at Ieuan's right shoulder, having brought a half-dozen of my men with him. Any more and I'd have a small army. They ranged down the corridor behind him, ready for whatever threat came at them, though the one we were facing couldn't be stopped by any of them. Another man I didn't recognize, slender and stooped, who couldn't have been more than a few inches over five feet, stood a pace behind Justin, wringing his hands.

"The soldier you sent to me spoke of a glow in the toilet," Justin said. "I don't know what this is about, but your urgency infected him to the point that I sent a few men to find out if other toilets in the keep have a glow inside them too. And I found Tom, here, thinking that I would bring him to you to see if he could help. He is one of the men who cleans the latrines."

This was why I kept Justin around. His initiative had always impressed me. "When was the last time you cleaned this latrine, Tom?" I said.

"Yesterday morning, sire." Tom's voice shook. "Just after midnight, it was."

I put a hand on his shoulder, trying to calm him. "How many latrines are there in the keep?"

"Er—"

I gazed at him, waiting for an answer.

"He can't count, sire," Justin said. "I believe there are ten, two on each level but the first."

"I just wants to do my job, my lord," Tom said.

"Are you saying you like cleaning the latrines?"

Tom ducked his head. "Nobody bothers me. I just do my work, sire, and don't have to talk."

I'd never considered the possible benefits of being a latrine cleaner before, but I could see how a certain personality might prefer it to many other jobs. "But the smell—"

"Oh, you get used to it, sire. I find I can't smell anything anymore. Or taste anything neither." Then Tom looked past me, his eyes widening.

I turned to see Callum, still on one knee in the guarderobe. He'd carefully removed the detonator and laid out the pieces of the bomb on the stone floor: the block of C-4, a slim silver detonator with wires running to a nine-volt battery, and a kitchen timer, purchasable at any store back in Avalon.

While we watched, he detached the timer from the battery and detonator, and then he stared down to where it lay in the palm of his hand. The faint white glow that had lit the toilet chute now shone into his face. His look of concern had me taking a few steps toward him. "Callum?"

He looked up, hesitated for a second, and then handed the timer to me.

It read 14:53. As I watched, the readout went to 14:52, and then 14:51.

"We can't assume this bomb is the only one. We have to move," I said. "Now."

11

We moved. We only had to go down another flight of steps, cross the great hall, and exit by the main stairs to get out of the keep, but Justin took us down another flight to the kitchen. "I feel like you're a target, my lord," he said to me by way of explanation. "I don't know who's waiting for us out there. By now, we've evacuated a hundred people from the castle. More. If the danger is as great as you say, and the men who did this are watching, they'll know the alarm has been raised."

"There was no help for that after a certain point," I said.

"We don't have to think too hard about who set the explosives," Callum said as we ran across the deserted kitchen and exited through the back door, which had been left open.

"No, we don't," I said. "How many hours in advance could that timer have been set?"

"Up to twenty-four hours, I'd guess," he said. "I'd have to look at the timer once it stops counting down, but it's a clock too and appears to have the capacity for keeping military time."

A flight of steps led up to the bailey, and we took them. Carew was waiting for me at the top. He was another who hadn't been willing to leave the castle without me.

The rain had stopped, which was too bad. Pouring rain could have gone a long way to damping things down after an explosion, and it would have made the people more likely to move faster in order to get under cover.

I halted on the top step, taking in my surroundings with a swift glance. The evacuation of the keep may have occurred with dispatch, but the bailey was in chaos. Every horse had been released from the stable and now many milled about, undirected, as the men who'd released them went back for other animals or people. Too many people had too many possessions they didn't want to leave behind. Canterbury Castle obviously hadn't done a fire drill in far too long.

I spied Bevyn and Huw near the town gate. Bevyn's mouth was open, shouting at the people to get them moving, though I couldn't hear his words and few seemed to be heeding them. Huw had his arm around a woman with a baby in her arms. More soldiers were trying to herd the people in question—craftspeople, servants, and hangers-on to my court—all in varying stages of undress, towards either gate. One man went so far as to throw a woman, who'd been screaming incoherently at him, over his shoulder and run with her to the exit.

"Only a few understand the danger," Ieuan said.

"They can't," Callum said. "None have seen what C-4 can do. The gases expand at eight thousand meters per second."

"Fire?" Ieuan said.

"It isn't like black powder. It doesn't set things on fire, but fire is part of the explosion." Callum looked at me, a helpless expression on his face at trying to explain the unexplainable. He took in a breath. "Short answer, it won't set the keep on fire." Ieuan looked relieved, but Callum's face was white and drawn. "David, it won't matter. We can't outrun this explosion. It isn't like in the movies. Half a kilogram of C-4 can destroy a lorry."

I hadn't actually wanted to hear that. In Avalon, I'd seen the remains of royal castles destroyed by explosives during the time of Oliver Cromwell. He'd blown big holes in them and undermined towers, for the express purpose of making them indefensible. At that time, people hadn't been living in them, but Canterbury keep was home to many. Even if the walls didn't entirely come down—which they might since C-4 had many times the power of seventeenth century gunpowder—it would destroy everything inside. Including people, if any had been left behind.

"We need to get the people moving," I said.

"Sir Justin!" A young soldier burst from the entrance to the keep and ran towards us. He pulled up panting. "We counted at least three more lights!"

"Did you touch them?" Justin said to the soldier.

He shook his head. "We did as you ordered, sir."

Justin nodded and looked at me. "I told them to look for them and then to run."

"As they should have," I said. If we'd known sooner, between Callum, Peter, and Darren, maybe we could have disarmed them all, but now we didn't have time.

Three more soldiers spilled out of the main entrance to the keep. One of them raised his hand, signaling to us. "That's everyone!"

Ieuan held my upper arm in a strong grip. "Dafydd, we need to get you to safety."

Justin nodded vigorously.

What kind of time do we have, Callum?" I said.

He checked the timer. "Not quite eleven minutes."

It had taken only four minutes to get this far. I looked back up to the keep. Despite the soldiers' assurances, I wasn't convinced that nobody had remained inside, but we were past the point where anyone could go back to check. Even three bricks of C-4, properly placed, could reduce an entire floor to smithereens.

It shouldn't destroy the castle.

Maybe.

It depended on their location and if they were tied to some kind of accelerant. In Avalon, gasoline could multiply an explosion many times. We didn't have that here, but I didn't know if putting the bombs in the latrine chutes, with their stew of gases, would have a similar effect.

Cassie ran up, leading a horse.

"You were supposed to have gone with Lili," I said.

She looked at me blankly for a second, because I didn't often tell her what to do, and then said, "I've been helping. The people aren't leaving. They don't understand why they should. I don't understand why they should."

Callum took the horse's bridle from her. "C-4, Cassie. There are at least three more bombs beyond the one I defused."

Her face paled. She was from the modern world, and while she hadn't been a soldier there, she was lately of MI-5. She knew C-4's destructive power. She'd seen it with her own eyes in Cardiff last year when it had brought down the courthouse and city hall. I hadn't been there, but everyone had told me what it had been like. I hoped the castle didn't contain as much explosive as had been used then, though it would take far less to reduce Canterbury Castle to rubble.

"Are Bronwen and Catrin here too?" Ieuan was looking at Cassie, fear for his wife and daughter in his eyes.

"They went with Lili and Arthur," Cassie said, and then looked past Ieuan to me. "William went with them to keep them safe. Others too."

I took in a breath, turning my attention to the people before me. Both gates were wide open. One led straight into the town along Castle Street, the other to farmers' fields. These people needed to go through them. I glanced at Callum. Another two minutes gone. My heart was pounding hard, but not so much it deafened me—or stopped me from thinking.

I threw myself onto the horse Cassie had brought. "The people will go if I order them to. Find horses for yourselves because we'll need them later, and then get out of here. I want this bailey cleared with two minutes to spare. These people aren't sheep, but they'll move together if we get them going." I slapped the reins on the horse's side. "Ya!"

I didn't wait to see what the others did, but directed the horse to the left. A young man was dragging a crate across the bailey. He saw me coming and looked up wide-eyed. I slowed as I approached him, leaned down, and said, "Run."

I didn't need a crown on my head for everyone at Canterbury Castle to know me by sight. His mouth dropped open. And then he ran.

Like a sheepdog herding his flock, I sent the horse through the center of the bailey, riding in a curving arc to herd the people towards Bevyn and Huw at the town gate. Then I turned back and rode the other way, urging everyone who remained towards the back gate. A little girl crouched crying on the ground while her older brother tried to drag her with him. I reached down my hand. "Pick her up. She can ride with me, and then you need to follow us out of here."

The boy grasped his sister around the waist and lifted her. I got my arm around her waist and tugged her across my lap. She was heavier than she looked. Then I raised one hand into the air, wishing I had my sword too. I pointed at the keep and shouted. "My friends! The keep is coming down. We must leave here now!"

Callum, who'd found a horse to ride, cupped his hands around his mouth. "Four minutes, sire!"

"Go!" I bellowed the word, and finally the fifty people who'd remained in the bailey surged towards the two gates.

Ieuan appeared out of the crowd, running between two horses. Cassie had mounted my horse, Cadfan, and three more horses followed on leading reins behind her. With her long black hair flowing down her back and her cloak wrapped around her tightly, she could have been a native princess in the wild west, rounding up wild horses. Justin and each of my soldiers had mounted too, and then Carew swung onto one of the horses Cassie had corralled.

Fortunately, the remaining untethered horses weren't wild and wanted to follow. Although the people were panicked because we'd woken them in the middle of the night to evacuate the castle—and because they'd heard a fear in my voice that hadn't ever been there before—the keep was still intact. The threat was still theoretical.

I pulled in beside Callum. We had only fifty feet to go to reach the gate. "What's the time?"

"Two minutes, thirty-eight seconds," he said.

I glanced up at the keep. "I want this to be a hoax. I would give anything for it to be a hoax."

"That C-4 in the toilet chute was real. So is this timer," Callum said. "I count us lucky that the bombs are on a timer and not activated remotely. If they had been, we would have been dead the moment he realized we knew about the bombs and were evacuating the castle."

"I tried to keep it quiet for that reason," I said.

"It doesn't matter now," Callum said. "We'll see in two minutes if this was real or all for nothing."

"Not nothing, regardless," I said. "Canterbury Castle was unprepared to evacuate in an orderly fashion. Can you imagine what this would have been like if we were in London? On a typical day, Westminster Palace houses three times this many people."

"Something else to put on your to-do list," Callum said.

And then we were through the gate and across the drawbridge that protected it. Most of the people veered to the left towards the town gate that lay to the north along the town wall, but I turned my horse's head to race along the road that followed the castle moat and the curtain wall. Only as we passed by the keep did I realize the danger—that I'd inadvertently brought us closer to the keep than we'd been at the gate. My heart caught in my throat, praying I hadn't misjudged the time.

But then we were past the corner of the wall and racing for the little chapel, which lay the length of a football field away, where I'd sent Lili and Arthur. Now that it came to it, I had a bad feeling the chapel wasn't quite far enough from the castle for real safety, but there was nothing I could do about it now. At least a hundred people milled about under the trees, with more moving in and out of the church. The men of my guard—men-at-arms and archers alike—had formed a perimeter, standing shoulder to shoulder to protect the people in the little chapel and its grounds.

Several men moved aside to let our company through, of course, and I pulled up to shouts of, "The king!"

Lili flew from the chapel entrance, Arthur in her arms. She'd been waiting for me. I passed the girl I'd rescued to someone else, dismounted, and then caught Lili and Arthur in an embrace. Even as I did so, I turned my head to look back the way we'd come. The keep loomed up on the other side of the field, a dark bulk against the sky. Clouds covered the sky from horizon to horizon, indicating more rain in our future, so the castle was lit only by the torches that had been left burning on the wall-walk.

My companions had reined in with me, along with several dozen others who'd decided to come this way instead of entering the town with the rest of the refugees. As Ieuan had promised, my *teulu* had obeyed him and evacuated quickly. I traveled with fifty knights and men-at-arms, just as my personal guard, plus two hundred Welsh archers. Nearly two-thirds of these stood nearby, and I hoped the rest were on duty as they should have been on the wall-walk of the town. If any men had slept through the alarm and remained in the barracks, it might be too late for them, and I spared a thought for the latrines in the smaller buildings in the bailey, realizing only at this late moment that the C-4 could have been placed there as well.

William de Bohun loped towards me, and it was with real relief that I saw my sword in his hand. As the King of England, I had many swords, but I wore by preference the one my father had made for me after my crowning. Callum had kept it safe for me for the two years he'd spent in the modern world and returned it last year.

"Thank you for staying with my family," I said to William.

He swallowed. "I feared for you—"

"You did your duty," I said.

"Did we get everyone out?" Lili said.

"We think so." My arms were still wrapped around her and Arthur, though he was wiggling to get down. I wasn't prepared to put him down, however, and whispered in his ear, the words coming as quickly as my heart was beating, "Stay still. This is important."

Arthur clung to my neck as he hitched himself higher in my arms. Not for the first time I marveled at his child's awareness of his surroundings. He had no idea what was going on, but the adults were tense, and he had made my life easier by choosing not to disobey.

"Callum," I said.

"Twenty seconds," he said.

Bevyn and Huw came puffing up, and Bevyn answered my raised eyebrows with a nod of his head. He, too, thought we'd succeeded in rescuing everyone we could.

I counted silently. Others did the same. Then, before our staring eyes, a wave of dust engulfed the castle and obscured our view at the same moment as a percussive *BOOM* rang out across the fields. I instinctively ducked, clutching Arthur and Lili to me and shielding them with my body. I hadn't been in Cardiff during the bombing that had sent the bus to the Middle Ages with my mom and sister in it, but I had to think it must have been like this. The noise of the explosion was far louder than I'd expected it to be.

As the noise faded, I raised my head and strained my eyes towards the castle. Smoke puffed out all around the keep. If we'd been any closer, the dust would have been choking. While no rain fell, the wind was blowing strongly from the southwest, as it usually did, serving to send the smoke and dust over the town of Canterbury which lay to the northeast of the castle.

Gradually, the debris in the air cleared. Part of one tower still showed above the wall, but most of the keep was just ... gone. The curtain wall on our side had also been demolished, turned in an instant from solid stone to dust.

Nobody screamed. Perhaps everyone was too shocked. Men and women stood with their hands to their mouths, staring in the direction of the castle.

Callum cleared his throat and spoke into the silence. "It is my guess that the explosives were placed in the latrines on the middle floors. The explosion blew out the walls, causing the stones of the top two floors to simply drop onto the basement since there was no longer anything to hold them up."

Nobody had an answer to that or any reason to question Callum's evaluation. I was as shocked as everyone else, never mind that I was from Avalon. The destruction was mind-boggling, no less to me for having some idea in advance of what it might look like.

Then Arthur wiggled in my arms. "You're squeezing me, Daddy!"

I lowered Arthur to the ground, and he plopped in the grass at my feet to dig with a stick he found.

"Nobody could have survived that, my lord." Ieuan's voice came low in my ear.

"No," I said.

"He meant to kill us all," Lili said.

Her daughter, Catrin, on her hip, Bronwen stood with Ieuan, and he held her as I held Lili—tightly. I didn't want to let my wife go. I didn't want time to start up again because the world was looking like a much scarier place than it had a half-hour ago—and it had been frightening enough. Whatever I chose to do next, I couldn't do it with Lili. I needed to lead, now, from the front as always. It would be her job to protect Arthur and our unborn child.

So I took in a breath and said what needed to be said: "We have to move. We have to get the women and children out of Canterbury, preferably to a fortress with a sizable garrison. It wasn't just me who was meant to die, but my family too—all of our families. My son."

I was having trouble speaking coherently, but the rage building inside me had me trembling more than the earlier fear. We all knew who *he* was, and we'd so far avoided saying his name out loud. That time had passed.

Lee.

He'd meant to kill us all. Destroying Canterbury Castle had been a personal attack. I'd spent three months with the man. He'd eaten my food and accepted the hospitality I offered him—and then he'd tried to kill me, my family, and hundreds of other people. I'd known he was intelligent, but it was terrifying to have his mind directed towards something so villainous I could barely get my head around the magnitude of the crime.

I didn't know why Lee had done it. I didn't know what he hoped to gain from my death and the loss of Canterbury Castle. I didn't know where he'd gotten the C-4 either, but I pictured Lee's duffel bag, which had always gone everywhere with him. It hadn't been in his room when we'd searched it. He had it with him, along with God knows how many more bricks of explosive.

We had to find him, and we had to find him fast.

12

"The question we are all asking ourselves, and I guess I can be the first to say it, is *how* Lee knew we were on to him such that he planted those bombs and set the timer before he left." Callum looked at Darren and Peter, who had just joined our little group.

Rachel was moving among the evacuees, speaking to one after the other to gauge if anyone was injured. Justin was evaluating the condition of the men. We were safe at the chapel for now. I wanted to wait for the dust to settle before returning to the castle, as well as ensure that no more bombs had been set to go off on a delayed timer. We had a few minutes to think before we made our next move.

"I have no answers." Darren said. While Huw and Bevyn had been in charge of the town gate, Peter and Darren had been the last ones through the back gate, taking upon themselves the job of ensuring everyone got out.

"That may be the question you're asking, Callum, but I want to know what Lee hoped to gain from David's death," Cassie said. "All I can see is chaos."

"He wanted chaos. He had to have," I said. "What I don't understand is why he didn't kill me himself, or arrange for it to happen in a way that could be more controlled. Poison, for instance."

"Because he wanted all of us dead. Arthur too." Lili had given Arthur to his nanny to hold and returned to wrap her arms around my waist.

I lifted my arm so she could duck under it. "You don't need to be here."

"You don't have to protect me, Dafydd." Then she looked at Callum. "Before we go any further, is there any doubt that it was he who did this?"

"I have no doubt, and nobody else should either," Callum said. "The explosives came from Avalon. That is a fact. Lee murdered Noah and Mike. That is also a fact. I don't see another explanation unless a different bus passenger is unaccounted for and has a vendetta we don't know about."

Lili bit her lip. "I don't mean to confuse the issue, but is there any chance that someone else from Avalon could have come here without you knowing? Someone who doesn't believe you should be king?"

Callum and I exchanged a swift look. "I—" I shook my head. "You mean someone like Cassie or Marty? Or are you wondering if someone else could have my family's ability to travel here from Avalon?"

"Either. Both," she said.

"I can't speculate," I said. "I have to believe not—until I have some indication otherwise. Furthermore, what are the chances that such a person would have brought C-4 to the Middle Ages?"

"Zero," Cassie said.

"I would have to agree," Callum said.

Cassie put her arm around Lili's shoulder and squeezed. "We're going to stop him, Lili. Nobody is going to get to David or Arthur." Then she looked at Callum. "Have we decided, then, that Lee was part of this ELF group?"

"Elf?" Lili said.

"ELF is the acronym for the Economic Liberation Front, which claimed responsibility for the bombing at Cheltenham back in Avalon," Callum said.

"What were the group's aims?" I said.

"That wasn't yet clear by the time we left," Callum said. "Fostering chaos, certainly, but we had no manifesto from them. There was the usual talk about corruption at the highest levels of government. It was all in a file that crossed my desk a year ago. We flagged it and passed it on. Believe me, after the bombing of GCHQ, if I'd ever made it back to my office, I would have looked at it more closely."

"As I recall, their aims were along the lines of 'economic equality for all'," Cassie said.

Peter leaned into the conversation. "Thinking about what Lili asked, I have a crazy idea: what if Lee somehow knew you were going to be on that bus?"

"That's not possible." Darren shook his head at his friend. "We didn't even know we were going to be on that bus until twenty minutes before we boarded it."

"Lee wanted to make a statement. Had I not woken, had George the soldier been less nosy, we would all be dead." I shook my head. "It was like using a trebuchet to kill an ant."

Bevyn cleared his throat. "You are no ant, sire."

"That may be, but I would be surprised if Lee doesn't see me that way. I am nothing to him," I said.

Callum stood with his hand on the hilt of his sword, which he'd had the foresight to put on before he left his room, urgent summons or no urgent summons. "People become terrorists for different reasons. If Lee's actions arise from a desire for disorder and anarchy—in other words, to disrupt the social order—then it's easy to see why working against David and the monarchy would be a given for him. If he wants something else—power for himself, for example—then killing David should lead to him getting it. Given that he's an outsider, though, I find it hard to see how."

"Because he's working for someone else," Lili said.

"That's another option," Callum said. "He could be a hired gun."

"Not with pounds and pounds of C-4 in his bag," Cassie said. "He brought that with him. I think we have to conclude that he was at least partly responsible for the bombing in Cardiff."

"And up until now, I have assumed that the Cardiff bombs and the ones that went off earlier at GCHQ in Cheltenham were connected," Callum said. "I'm wondering now if that assumption was mistaken."

"I'll leave you to it." Lili said abruptly, turning on her heel. She headed to where Bronwen knelt on the ground nearby, hovering over Catrin and Arthur.

My own stomach roiled as I watched her go, and I forced myself to damp down the anger that I wasn't sure would ever go away, even if we caught Lee and hanged him from the nearest tower that was still standing.

I turned back to the others. "That leads to my next thought: yesterday, because of the fist he painted on the wall, we learned that Lee's focus is on Ireland," I said. "At the time, we didn't discuss the IRA because we saw him as a murderer rather than a terrorist. I think we need to reexamine that assumption." Back in Avalon, the Irish Republican Army, the military arm of the Irish resistance to English rule, had operated for most of the twentieth century but had disbanded during the peace accords in the late 1990s.

Cassie tugged on her braid, which she tended to do when she was thinking. "It's been twenty years since the IRA was active."

"We all know how long these hatreds last," I said.

Ieuan's brow furrowed. "I fail to see the connection between Lee blowing up Canterbury Castle and the unrest in Ireland."

"Ireland is under the Norman thumb—my thumb," I said. "We all know it. Lee would bomb Canterbury for the same reason that the IRA used to bomb London—and why they may have bombed Cardiff last year: to draw attention to its cause."

"Except we're only guessing at his motives," Cassie said. "Lee hasn't sent out a manifesto, and if you died, the future king would be far less likely than you to change course."

"The crazy thing is that I am trying to change course," I said, "but it would do no good for me to revoke my barons' rights in Ireland. They'd rebel against me."

Cassie made a noise of disgust in the back of her throat. "Lee hasn't even been to Ireland!"

"Not while he's been in this world," I said, "but it wouldn't stop him from working with emissaries from Ireland, given the opportunity."

Callum nodded. "There's no reason Lee's goals would have changed just because he found himself in the Middle Ages. In fact, as King David and I discussed yesterday, he could have been filled with a greater urgency because this is when the subjugation of Ireland started. He might think he has the chance here to stop it before it really sets in."

"It's already been a hundred years," Ieuan said. "The barons aren't going to give up on estates that their families have held for several generations."

"We know that," I said. "That's not to say Lee does."

He cleared his throat. "And I might as well point out the precedent. It isn't all that different from what you and your family have accomplished."

I raised one shoulder. "I can't argue with that. I wouldn't have argued with Lee if he'd ever talked to me about it."

"Getting back to Callum's original question," Darren said, "someone must have warned Lee that he was under investigation."

"Maybe so," Ieuan said, "but until we find out who, we can't know if it was out of innocence or intent."

"It could simply be that Bevyn's arrival forced Lee to move up his plans slightly," Cassie said. "Lee could have intended to depart within hours of when he actually did. What if he set the timers early yesterday morning, after the latrine cleaners finished their work, and they were always supposed to go off tonight?"

"The cleaners do work only at night," Ieuan said.

"Lee and the others were allowed to roam unchecked throughout Canterbury and wherever else they've been these last three months," I said. "How long would it have taken for Lee to worm himself into the confidence of a few of the guards here at Canterbury?"

"We've been here just three days, and I did have men watching him." Callum grimaced. "Though it seems now that Lee was running circles around them all along."

"Lee made few mistakes. You meant to have him under surveillance only when he left the castle, right?" I said, and at Callum's nod, I added, "If he'd been seen going in and out of the latrines would your men have said anything to you about it?"

"Perhaps not. We'll never know now, since they can't remember anything after the evening meal two days ago." Callum looked towards the destroyed castle. "I wish I could take them at their word."

"If they knew something, Lee would have killed them and hidden the bodies, not dosed them with poppy juice," Bevyn said. "They'd be buried somewhere underneath that rubble."

Callum looked down at the ground. I reached out a hand to grip his shoulder, frustrated as Callum and far more at fault than he. "We're going to shake this off. Everybody is alive, and because Lee set off the bombs by timer rather than by remote control, he might not know that we've only lost a castle. We can stand here and blame each other, or we can work towards making this right."

"David—" Bronwen joined the circle, having left Catrin with her nanny. "Does Lee speak Middle English?"

"I asked him once if he wanted help with it," I said. "He laughed and said it would be a waste of my time because he was sure he'd never get it right."

"Which means he's completely fluent," Bronwen said. "We brought him here, and he's been way ahead of us from the start."

Callum raised his hands. "We're going in circles. I think it would be better if we table this discussion for now. We need to look at what is right in front of us. We can talk about the why of it later. All we have right now is speculation and no answers."

I turned to Ieuan. "We need to know who among my men interacted with Lee and the others most often. Did they have friends among my *teulu*? I have no intention of accusing anyone but Lee of treason just yet, but I would bet my crown that money changed hands. Somebody is going to know something about something, and with the sight of the explosion fresh in everyone's minds, we might get answers now that we won't get later."

"Yes, my lord." Ieuan jerked his head to Bevyn and Huw, and the three of them moved away into the crowd.

"Cassie, Lili, and I will talk to the women," Bronwen said. "I agree that somebody is going to know something." Bronwen and Cassie moved off.

"That's a start." I rubbed my forehead, trying to ease the headache that had taken up residence above my right eyebrow. Carew so far hadn't added to the conversation. He often didn't when those of us from Avalon got going, whether because he found our conversations hard to follow, or because he never spoke unless he had something to contribute.

Now, however, seeing me rub my forehead, he went to one of the horses and returned with a water skin. "Drink."

I did as he ordered, closing my eyes as I felt the cool water slide down my dry throat. Everybody was going to need food and water soon. I had hundreds of people whose needs had to be met, and a destroyed castle that could no longer meet them. "We have two things before us, then: finding Lee, and getting our people someplace safe."

"We should retire to the Archbishop's palace for what's left of tonight," Carew said.

"Some of us can stay there," I said. "Before the riot, I would have agreed to shelter with the Archbishop in a heartbeat, but it's no longer my first choice, not with Acquasparta there. Additionally, Peckham's palace can't take in as many people as we have here."

Then my eyes narrowed. "Did anyone think to release our heretic?"

"He left the castle after the evening meal," Darren said.

"What about his family?" I said.

"The men you sent to find them and bring them to the castle were unsuccessful. They went to the lodgings the heretic indicated, but there was nobody there, and the landlord claimed to have no idea who we were asking about."

"That's ... odd." I ran a hand through my hair. "Well, nothing to be done about him for now. We have bigger fish to fry."

13

Callum was looking at me carefully. "I know that look, sire. I've never liked it."

I met his gaze, interested that Callum was back to referring to me by my title. "We could stay here for the rest of the night, but I don't think that's a good idea. It's time to go."

"Tell us your plan," Callum said. "I can see you have one."

I put my hand on Carew's shoulder. "I want the women and children out of Canterbury, and I need a place where they can be safe. Where can they go?"

"Chilham Castle," Carew said immediately. "Five or six miles."

"Who holds it?"

"Alexander Balliol, cousin to the King of Scotland," Carew said.

I swallowed down a laugh. If anyone owed me one, it was John Balliol. "That sounds promising. How many men do you need?"

"What? No, my lord. I won't leave you—"

"Thirty should be enough," Callum said, answering for Carew. "Any more and it will slow you down too much. You should be able to reach it before dawn."

I was still looking at Carew, who glowered at Callum before turning back to me. "Sire—"

"I am placing my wife and son in your care," I said, "and my unborn child."

That shut him up.

"That's only half a plan," Callum said. "Tell me the part I won't like."

"First of all, if I leave Canterbury now, it will look as if I've abandoned this city and these people."

Callum gave a reluctant nod. "It will look like that."

"But that doesn't mean I can't keep Lili and Arthur safe," I said.

Carew's jaw firmed, finally acquiescing. "You are correct, as usual, sire. I will care for the queen and prince."

"Second, we were expected to die, right? Obviously, we did not. And that means we have a very narrow window where our enemy doesn't know what we're going to do. There are a hundred horses in the stables just over that rise." I pointed with my chin to the west. With so many men at Canterbury, there were too many horses to lodge inside the castle. "With the horses we have here, we have enough to mount a strong force to protect both Lili's company and mine."

"What are you thinking of doing?" Callum said.

"*We,*" I said.

"We, then."

"We are going to find Lee," I said.

"How? The king can't search door-to-door through Canterbury."

"Of course not—"

"Sire." Cassie appeared at my left shoulder, holding the elbow of a sobbing woman, who held her arm across her waist as if her stomach pained her. "Beatrice, here, has something to tell you."

Beatrice wore a nightgown and cloak, though she had boots on her feet, and her dark hair had come loose from its night braid. She looked as if she was in her late twenties, though she could have been younger. As Cassie stopped, the woman looked up, saw me, blanched, and then put her head into her hands to sob some more.

"Who is she?" I said.

"She was brought into the castle from the town to help with the extra work caused by your arrival," Cassie said. "I overheard her talking to her friends just now. I think it's important that you listen."

Beatrice continued to cry, though the overt sobs had lessened as she realized that everyone's eyes were on her.

"Tell him." Cassie prodded Beatrice's arm.

"Do you know something about the explosion and who did it?" I said.

Beatrice took a trembling breath. "I know about Lee."

"Tell me," I said.

Beatrice licked her lips. "He-he asked me to keep watch early yesterday morning for him—for him and the other men he was with, Mike and Noah."

"Keep watch where?" I said.

"In the keep. Outside the toilets."

"When was this exactly?" I said.

"Shortly before dawn," she said. "I remember because it was dark when we started. I was still tired and hadn't wanted to rise."

"Why would he want you to watch outside the toilets?" I said, not because I didn't know, but because she needed to speak for herself. I didn't want to put words in her mouth, even if it would make this go faster.

"I-I don't know," she said, and then at my skeptical look, she put out an imploring hand. "He didn't say. At first I thought he might be ill, but then he went from toilet to toilet. He couldn't have been sick in all of them."

"When he was done, what did you do?" I said.

Now Beatrice looked shamefaced. "I looked inside. But I didn't see anything! Not anything that would have caused that!" She flung out a hand in the direction of the ruined castle.

"Why did you do as he asked?" I said.

"He was in favor with-with—"

"With me," I said.

Beatrice ducked her head in a nod. "I thought—I thought he might—he said—"

"What did he promise you?" I said.

"I could become a permanent maid," she said. "Leave the inn where I usually work."

I caught the scoff Cassie immediately swallowed down. To distract Beatrice from Cassie's disbelief, I said, "Did he give you money too?"

"No. No money, but he bought me this." She held up her wrist to show the slender silver bracelet adorning it. She'd traded my life and hers for a trinket. It was easy to blame her, but of course, the blame really lay with me.

"Do you have any idea where Lee might have gone?" I said.

The tears came again. "I don't know! I swear it!" She glanced again at the ruined castle.

"He wasn't your friend." Callum stepped in. "He meant for you to die with all of us."

"I know." She pressed her sleeve into her eyes to dry her tears. "He met men—I don't know who—in the Old Bull Inn where I work most days."

Callum nodded as if he knew the place she was talking about. "When was this?"

"Two days ago," she said.

"Again, you actually saw him meet these men yourself?" Callum said.

Beatrice's shoulders sagged in resignation and exhaustion. "I was giving my cousin, who owns the place, a hand in between my duties at the castle. I couldn't tell you what they said, though. They were foreigners."

"How do you know that?"

"They spoke English funny," she said, "and when they talked to Lee they spoke in French."

Twenty-four hours ago I would hardly have thought twice about Frenchmen in Canterbury. Lee could meet with whom he liked. But yesterday I hadn't known that the pope was worried about me going to war against King Philip, or that he supported Philip's claim to the Duchy of Aquitaine. That Lee was meeting with Frenchmen seemed too much of a coincidence to dismiss.

"Is there anything else you can tell us about Lee that might help us find him? Anything at all?" I said.

Halfway through shaking her head, Beatrice stopped. "Well, he was having some trouble with his foot."

"His foot?" Cassie said.

"His big toe where it met the nail was full of pus." She made a face. "I told him he had to have the nail pulled out or he might die. He didn't want to do it."

"When was this?" I said.

"Last night. I mean—the night before this one." Beatrice was looking at me sideways.

"You were with him all night?" I said. "This is the night before the morning he asked you to watch the corridor while he was in the toilets?"

She nodded.

I tipped my head to Cassie. "Anything else?"

"She shouldn't leave Canterbury in case we need her again," Cassie said.

I looked at Beatrice, who was staring at the ground. "I expect we can find you at the inn."

"Yes, sire." She curtseyed, and Cassie escorted her away.

Ieuan sneered. "Frenchmen."

I ran a hand through my hair. This was a piece I really hadn't wanted to fit into the puzzle.

"I can't see how that helps us find Lee," Darren said, but at the general silence that followed, he looked from one of us to the other. "What?"

I felt a chill at the back of my neck as Callum said, "Actually, it could."

"The enemy of my enemy is my friend?" I said.

"Scotland allied with France against England at various times throughout history," Callum said.

"Llywelyn Fawr, my great-grandfather, reached out in that direction too." I said. "It might seem natural for interests in Ireland to look to France for help in ridding Ireland of the Norman menace."

Darren was still looking puzzled. "If Ireland unites with France to overthrow you, that still doesn't rid Ireland of the Norman barons."

"But as we discussed before, it creates chaos," I said. "Upon my death, those same Norman barons would be looking to their estates in England, leaving their holdings in Ireland exposed."

"Or so Lee might think," Callum said.

I looked over my companions, calculating who I could spare from my side and what tasks I needed them to do. I started with Bevyn and Huw, who'd been moving among the refugees. I waved them over to me and gave them a rundown of the discussion so far. "I need every bit of information the Order can muster from its contacts."

"Yes, my lord." Bevyn said immediately, but then he hesitated, seeming about to say something else.

"What is it?" I said.

Bevyn moved in close. "The Order failed you, sire. We should have known what Lee was up to even before Huw brought his news from Wales. And now with this French link—if Lee was meeting with your enemies, we should have known about it."

"You will have to address that within the Order," I said. "Now is not the time for recriminations."

Bevyn cleared his throat. "What I meant was that you might be better off using others for this task. I don't want to fail you again."

I scowled at him. "You tried to resign from my service once, as I recall. It didn't go well."

Bevyn's eyes strayed to what remained of the castle, but he didn't speak. I caught his arm. "You could not have predicted what happened. It is far beyond your experience."

"As I was saying, sire," he said. "You need someone else for this."

"Who do you suggest?" I said. "You and your Order are what I have to work with, so I am expecting you to find out the information I need to stop Lee before he does something equally terrible. He spoke with Frenchmen. Start there. I want to know who they are, how long they were in Canterbury, and the name of their master."

Bevyn swallowed. "Yes, sire."

"Don't doubt now. I have others for that." Turning away before Bevyn could say anything else, I left the circle under the trees and strode towards Lili, who was talking quietly with Carew. "So you know already?" I said to my wife.

Lili nodded, though she looked hard at me for a second before putting her arms around my neck and looking up at me. "Don't you dare do anything foolish." And then before I could assure her that I wouldn't, she shook a finger in my face. "You swore you wouldn't last time, but you did anyway and you almost died."

"I will do my best to stay out of harm's way," I said. "I always do."

Lili took in a breath. "But you are the King of England. There's only so much you can do to protect yourself. I know."

I kissed her. "I love you."

"Lee wants you dead," she said. "You have never faced anyone like him before, not even Valence."

"More than Lee, it may be his employer who wants me dead," I said.

Lili raised her eyebrows. "His employer?"

"The King of France."

"Ah. So that's it." She shrugged. "Well, better to know than to not know."

We walked together to where Bronwen sat with Catrin and Arthur. While Catrin slept in Bronwen's lap, Arthur was awake again, and he left the shelter of her arm at my approach.

I knelt in front of him and took his shoulders in my hands. "You have been very brave."

"Someone blew up our castle."

I'd spoken to him in American English, and he'd responded in the same language.

"Someone did," I said. "Because of it, Daddy has to go to work now, and you can't come with me."

"Are you going to find the man who did it?"

"I am." I looked into his eyes. "It will be your job to protect your mother and your little sister or brother until I get back."

He nodded. The idea that a three-year-old could protect his mother was absurd, but it was something a father asked of his son, and Arthur would see the responsibility as his right. He would be king himself one day, and tonight he'd grown a little bit more in that role.

"Good boy." I kissed his forehead, and he wrapped his arms around my neck.

I stood up, still hugging him. He was so big now that his feet almost reached my knees. "It's going to be okay. We lost a castle, but we're all safe."

"I was scared," he said.

"I know. I was too. It's okay to be scared. What's important is to do the brave thing anyway," I said. "That's what I do."

He nodded into the hollow of my neck. Lili approached and hugged us both, and I transferred Arthur to her arms. "You need to go." I kissed her and then kissed Arthur one more time.

Carew had been waiting in the shadows under a nearby tree for me to finish saying my goodbyes. I tipped my head to him, and he bent his head in a slight bow. Then he helped Lili mount one of the horses that had been brought from the castle and handed Arthur up to her. Ieuan assisted Bronwen and Catrin onto another horse. The stables, where the rest of the company could find mounts, were just over the rise. It would take no more than a few minutes to reach it.

As for me, it was time for a speech.

I leapt onto the stone stile that allowed parishioners to enter the graveyard without going through the gate. My sword banged against my thigh. Somewhere along the way, William had girded me, but I had no memory of it. I raised a hand above my head.

Ieuan barked, "Quiet!"

Stragglers had been coming into the churchyard since the castle had fallen, people who'd panicked as they'd run from the gatehouse but who were now seeking friends and companions. Members of Parliament who'd come to Canterbury to consult about a tax bill mingled with ladies-in-waiting, servants, a few minor lords, and various friends and relations of the above. More than a hundred faces looked up at me, and I was reminded strongly of the speech I'd made yesterday in the churchyard of the cathedral. It felt like a lifetime ago.

"Someone tried to hurt us," I said. "He failed."

A few people shifted their feet, their expressions showing puzzlement. They were thinking: *how did he fail? Isn't Canterbury Castle destroyed?* So I got straight to the point.

"That castle behind us is the same pile of stones it was an hour ago." I shrugged and gave a half smile. "It's just been rearranged slightly."

That got a laugh from those closest to where I was standing, which was what I was looking for.

"Castles can be rebuilt. Lives are irreplaceable. Thanks to a soldier named George whom I hadn't met until today, you are standing before me. You may have lost your possessions. You may be scared and apprehensive about the future. But you are otherwise unharmed."

In the back of the crowd, a few soldiers were jostling, and I recognized George being buffeted around the head and shoulders by his fellows. I gestured with one hand. "Come up here, George!"

George was half-dragged, half-shoved towards the front of the crowd, his face flushed very red. When he reached me, I clapped him on the shoulder. "How about a round of applause for George?"

The crowd cheered; George bowed and finally managed a big grin before I sent him back to his friends.

"We have some cleaning up to do." I pointed to the castellan, Thomas Fairfax, to whom I hadn't yet spoken. "Sir Thomas will see to the salvage."

Thomas raised a hand and nodded, bowing towards me as he accepted the assignment.

"We will rise from the ashes," I said. "We will not be defeated."

General cheers now.

"For now, we have no home to return to. Those of you who are able-bodied, who can help Sir Thomas, will of course be asked to do so. For their safety, Queen Lili and Prince Arthur, along with many of our staff and guard, will not stay here. If any of you do not feel you can return to Canterbury just yet, you are welcome to go with them." I pointed to where Carew waited with Lili, Bronwen, and the children. A small crowd of people were already gathered around them, along with Carew's hand-picked guard of thirty men, about one-third archers and the rest men-at-arms.

"Where are they going, sire?" asked a woman near me.

"With Lord Carew," I said. "For their safety and yours, I will not tell you their destination."

That got a murmur of both consternation and approval.

"We have been attacked. I can name the man responsible. I do not know why he destroyed my castle, nor for whom he destroyed it."

"Them Frenchies!" someone said from the rear of the crowd.

I raised a hand in acknowledgement of the accusation, interested that it was to the French that the man's mind had gone. And he didn't even know what I knew.

"I cannot say, and I won't speculate. It does us no good to name enemies without proof. The one I can name is the man responsible for the destruction. He goes by the name of Lee. Many of you might have seen him or known him, for he has lived at my court since May." A babble of incomprehensible responses rose up, and I made a shushing motion to dispel it. "If you know something about his activities, please speak to someone who can get that word to me."

I jumped off the stile to find William de Bohun planted in front of me. "I'm staying with you."

"You're not," I said. "I need you with Lili and Arthur."

"They have many men to guard them. I can help you. I speak perfect French, and I am the son of Humphrey de Bohun." William, with his bright blond hair, narrow chin, and patrician nose, looked far more noble than I did. By comparison, my features were those of a typical American mutt.

I studied him without answering.

"I am also your squire. I would stand by you even were you to enter the gates of hell."

"I hope it won't come to that." I stepped to one side to go around him, but he put a hand to my chest to stop me. Touching the king was a brave move for a medieval man.

He knew it too, but he was too far gone to care. His fierce look could have melted iron. "Take me with you. Please, sire."

I shook him off and strode past him. I was two paces beyond his position before I said, loud enough to make sure he heard, "Did you hear me say no?"

I smiled as I heard him hustling behind me to catch up.

14

The King of England could never go anywhere without a personal guard of fifty or more, and I always had a company of archers as well. The company existed to protect me, and I had to accept that. What I didn't have to accept was for my whole court to stay at my side. The majority had to be sent back to London, so as to leave me with a workable number of personal companions in this time of crisis: Ieuan, Callum and Cassie, William, Rachel, Peter, and Darren—with Justin, as always, as captain of my guard.

"Where to first?" Justin said once Ieuan and I had seen Lili and Bronwen on their way and encouraged some of the nobles to put their heads together to arrange for their return to London.

"Back to the castle," I said. "I need to see it up close."

Justin didn't argue with me. I figured he was happy I hadn't ordered him to stay with Lili, as I could have. Leading Cadfan and with Sir Thomas pacing along at my side, I skirted the damaged curtain wall and headed towards the back gate. This was the same gate through which we'd left the castle before the explosion. It was the closest entrance into the castle bailey and didn't require us to go through the town of Canterbury itself, which was protected by stone walls and had many gates of its own.

It was still full dark—perhaps darker even then before. We'd stayed at the chapel for an hour, but if it had been two in the morning when the castle blew up, we could have hours until dawn. The wind blew on the back of my neck, bringing with it the smell of imminent rain. I checked the sky. The cloud cover was absolute.

Before I crossed the drawbridge, I was met by the captain of my archers, a man named Afan. Unusual for a northern Welshman, he was an expert shot and the best I'd ever encountered. The expression of relief on his face at seeing me coming towards him would have been comical if the situation were less serious.

"My prince." He bowed.

One of the affectations of my Welsh guard was that their allegiance to me derived from the fact that I was a prince of Wales and the heir to the Welsh throne, not because I was the King of England, a station about which they adamantly cared nothing. And they were right not to care. England and Wales were allies, but England had no authority over Wales. When—hopefully in the far distant future—my father died, and I ruled both countries, they would continue as separate nations. Such an arrangement had precedent: when William the Bastard conquered England, he ruled England as its king and Normandy as its Duke.

This double authority had also created the situation in Aquitaine to which the pope so objected. I could rule England as its king, like William had, but rule the Duchy of Aquitaine as its Duke, in fief to the King of France.

Afan fell in beside me as I passed underneath the gatehouse, and we all came to a halt within a few paces of the entrance to the bailey. I stopped and stared, and then at a nudge in my back from Cassie, moved aside so the people behind me could press forward. The keep presented a shocking sight. What had once been a magnificent square tower was now little more than rubble. In addition, several of the smaller wooden buildings adjacent to the keep were on fire, flames shooting through their thatched roofs.

"I thought C-4 didn't start fires," Cassie said.

"The dust and rubble suppressed the fires that were burning in the keep before the explosion, but the shock wave probably knocked over an oil lamp in one of those huts," Callum said.

Only the barracks, located on the opposite side of the bailey from the keep, were still intact. We needed to keep them that way.

"Was it foresight, my lord, that you didn't bring the Treasury with you?" Ieuan spoke in an undertone about three inches from my ear.

I tried to laugh, but the sound came out forced. Ieuan, for all that he was trying to make a joke, actually had a point. I too was glad that it was no longer possible for the king to bring his gold with him wherever he went like in the old days. It had been necessary to do so because of the nomadic nature of the court. Not to boast, but my wealth wouldn't fit in a few treasure chests and was back at Westminster under lock and key.

Justin stayed glued to my left shoulder. "I don't feel comfortable with you so exposed, my lord. Someone tried to kill you. There could be more explosives, archers, or even an army of assassins within hailing distance of us right now. The castle is entirely indefensible."

"That's why I sent Lili and Arthur away," I said, "and I'm not exactly wearing my crown, am I? Nobody but we few need to know where the King of England is right now."

Rachel was holding onto Darren's arm as they moved past me into the bailey. "My God," she said.

"What were the injuries?" I said to her.

She raised one shoulder, and then turned towards me to answer more fully. "A twisted ankle from misstepping in the dark. One old fellow was feeling pains that might indicate an underlying heart condition. That's about the extent of it."

"We were very lucky," Darren said.

"We need to keep making our own luck," I said. "Let's get some buckets, shall we?"

To their credit, nobody raised an eyebrow that the King of England was going to help put out the fire at the castle. They knew as well as I that we would need every helping hand before the sun rose.

The moat around the castle was fed by a small stream that ran between St. Mildred's Church and the castle. Before we'd even reached the castle, Sir Thomas had sent someone to open the sluice gate wider, and the line of people passing buckets of water from hand to hand had already formed. It felt like a ridiculously pathetic effort, given the destroyed keep, but this was how fires were put out in the Middle Ages: one bucket at a time.

We joined the line of exhausted, strung-out people, many of whom had fled to the town initially but had since returned. Cassie tossed her braid over her shoulder and swung a bucket to me, which I caught and passed on to Ieuan. We'd found a spot in the middle of the line, within the confines of the bailey but still fifty yards from the keep. Bucket after bucket followed until my hands reddened from the wet, rough wooden handles. Another minute and blisters would start to form.

"Could Lee have gotten cold feet at the last minute, which is why he made it so the lights weren't completely covered?" Cassie handed me another bucket. "Could he have meant to give us a fighting chance?"

Callum grunted as he handed a bucket on to her, having taken it from Rachel, who had taken it from Darren on her other side. "You have a kind heart."

Her brow furrowed. "I'm serious."

"I don't see us as anything less than very, very lucky," I said.

"Are you suggesting George was a plant?" Callum said. "That Lee left him in the castle to warn us?"

"Even then, it was only because I couldn't sleep that I ran into George in the first place, and he showed me the light in the toilet," I said. "Lee meant to kill us all."

"All right," Cassie said. "Just checking."

I turned to look at her, surprised at her easy acquiescence, but Rachel said, "I get it. She's playing the tenth man, though there are only nine of us here."

"What's that?" I said.

"If everyone agrees about something, it's the duty of the tenth person to disagree as a matter of course," Rachel said. "Isn't that right, Cassie?"

Cassie nodded. "We've condemned the man, all of us. I'm trying to get inside his head."

"I don't know that you want to spend any time inside Lee's head," I said, "but the idea of the tenth man sounds useful, and I'll keep it in mind. I am well aware that it's very easy for everyone to agree with me all the time."

"David," Cassie said under her breath. "You do realize Callum talked to the Order about Lee for the same reason. He'd expressed his worries—"

"And I dismissed them," I said. "Believe me, I know, and I'm grateful, even if it's after the fact."

"Lee was very charming when he wanted to be." Cassie looked at her left hand, hissing at the new blister on her palm before passing another bucket to me with her right hand.

Seeing Justin approach, I made a slashing motion with my hand to stop the conversation and stepped out of line. I turned the gesture into a welcoming one to him, while saying to my friends, "We'll consider this later."

"My lord." Justin hadn't been helping with the fire because he'd been inspecting what defenses remained, talking to the guards at the gates, and patrolling among the survivors. He didn't believe the threat was over. The moment we arrived, he'd climbed onto the walls—those that were still standing that is—to supervise the men and women watching from them.

"Are we being attacked?" I said.

"Not at the moment, sire."

I put a hand on his shoulder, knowing it was unfair to mock him. "I'm sorry. I'm tired."

"You need sleep, sire," he said.

"We all do."

"Sire." Sir Thomas had followed closely behind Justin, and he bowed before me.

"You have your work cut out for you," I said. "Are you up to the task?"

"It depends upon what you want done, sire." Thomas indicated the destruction behind me. "As soon as the fire is put out, I can start the salvage work. If you want the castle rebuilt, that will take considerable time and money."

"Salvage what you can for now. No doubt the interior is a total loss. We'll confer later about where we go from here, though—" I rubbed the end of my nose in thought, "—I think we need to rebuild this castle."

"I can't disagree, my lord," Thomas said.

Justin had stepped briefly into my place in the bucket line while I spoke with Thomas, but now he pointed with his chin towards the town gate. "Archbishop Peckham has arrived, my lord."

I looked where he'd indicated. Sure enough, a small party had entered the bailey. One of Peckham's servants helped the Archbishop out of his carriage, and then he stood in the dirt of the bailey, one hand to his mouth and a second clutching the hand of the man who'd helped him. Archbishop Romeyn alighted beside him. Both men appeared to have dressed hastily, as we all had, though Peckham was wrapped in a thick cloak and wore a woven hat pulled down close over his ears to keep out the cold.

"I'd better see to them," I said.

Acquasparta had not come, a fact for which he could be forgiven, given the hour and his illness. Peckham shouldn't have been here either, which I said to him when I reached him.

"I had to come. Some said you—" He broke off, unable to finish his sentence.

"I am not dead, as you can see."

Peckham transferred his clutching hand to my arm. "I am so glad, my dear boy." He took a breath, as if hesitating to speak, and then said, "You don't think this has anything to do with ... with ..."

"The incident yesterday?" I said. "I can't say as yet. Do you have some reason to think the two events might be linked?"

Peckham's eyes were fixed on the ruined keep. "How did this happen?" He took a few steps past me to where Sir Thomas stood. The castellan bowed and took the Archbishop's other arm to assist him.

I looked beyond him to Romeyn, whose face was very grave. I'd never seen a churchman in breeches and shirt, but that's what Romeyn wore, his brown cloak frayed at the edges and his boots scuffed and unpolished from much use.

"I am glad to see you before me, sire."

"It was a near thing," I said.

"Is it safe for you to be here?"

"Is anywhere safe after this?" I said.

Romeyn looked at me carefully, his eyes narrowing. "I'm guessing you wouldn't be here if you thought there was real danger. Do you know who did this, sire?"

"I know who brought the castle down," I said. "I am still in the dark as to why or with whom he might be working. Perhaps you have a thought?"

Romeyn blanched. "I'm sure I couldn't say."

I just looked at him.

"Sire—Acquasparta could have nothing to do with this," Romeyn said, replying to the conclusion I'd drawn but hadn't articulated. "He couldn't."

"He incited a riot to catch a heretic," I said. "Why would the destruction of a castle be beyond him?"

"I know what he did, but surely—" Romeyn stopped, pressing his lips together tightly. Then he bowed. "If the events are linked, if Acquasparta has had any hand in the destruction before us, I would urge you to find out."

I canted my head. "I intend to."

Peckham was back. His hand shook as he put it on my forearm but his voice no longer wavered. "What could have caused this destruction?"

"The castle was brought down by an explosive force more powerful than black powder," I said bluntly.

Peckham let go of my arm at my vehemence. Then he gave me a rueful smile, showing that he was gaining control of his shock. "If there is anything I can do for you, my dear boy, anything, please let me know."

"Actually, if you had a spare bed," I said, "for me and my companions, I would be grateful."

Dawn was nearly upon us, but being twenty-three didn't mean I could get by on no sleep at all, not if I was going to be capable of decision-making anytime soon. And I needed to be.

"Of course! Of course! It would be my honor." Peckham's eyes strayed to the keep again.

"My people and I will arrive shortly."

He nodded and moved towards his carriage, but then he turned back. "Will your party include the queen and Prince Arthur?" He gazed around the bailey. "I don't see them."

"They are well. I have sent them elsewhere for their own safety."

"Good. Good."

I gestured to where Cassie and Rachel were still passing buckets in the line. "Two women will be among us."

"I will make the necessary arrangements." Peckham reentered the carriage.

Romeyn waited until Peckham was seated before entering himself.

I put a hand on the window frame. "Be careful. There is much here that we don't yet understand."

Romeyn bowed his head. "Sire."

Ieuan came up beside me to watch the archbishops leave.

"I neglected to ask you earlier if Bronwen objected to leaving with Lili," I said.

"You've had a lot on your mind," Ieuan said. "And of course she didn't. Bronwen was shaken up like we all are, but she's sensible." He leaned in. "I know they don't like it, and they think it's sexist of you, but you were right to send them away, if only for the sake of the children."

I blinked. "I can't believe you know that word."

He raised his eyebrows. "In my household? How could I not know it?"

Callum approached. "Have you seen enough, sire?"

I lifted a hand and then dropped it in a helpless gesture. In truth, there wasn't much of anything I could do here. It had been important to come back. The people needed to see me, to know that I hadn't died and that I cared enough about them not to leave them to their own devices. Perhaps nobody would have blamed me for leaving for Chilham with Lili since we weren't going to rebuild this castle tonight. But I wouldn't have it said, especially after yesterday's riot, that I'd turned tail and run. If I had enemies in England who were working secretly with Lee, I wouldn't give them that ammunition to use against me.

15

We left the castle. The fire was almost out, and the people were dispersing throughout Canterbury. Morning would bring enough work to keep everyone occupied for many days and weeks to come. I left a small guard—the bulk of the normal castle garrison—to watch over what remained. With the barracks still intact, along with the gatehouse where Sir Thomas's quarters were, they had a place to lay their heads if they took it in shifts. The bodies of Mike and Noah still lay in their room in the barracks. Sir Thomas said he'd speak to the priest at St. Mildred's about a burial.

The rest of us rode along the same street that led to the Archbishop's Palace on which I'd traveled yesterday. The circumstances were so dramatically different, it was hard to believe the town itself remained unchanged, barring the dust from the castle that had settled on everything.

As we passed under the gatehouse at the town gate, onlookers made way for us. Despite the early hour, townspeople were lining up to cross the drawbridge going the other way, to get a look at the fallen castle and to help put out the flames. As I passed, people pressed in around my horse, patting my leg and the horse's withers, expressing their relief that I lived. After the incident with the heretic, I hadn't been entirely sure what my standing might be with them, but there was nothing like a crisis to bring people together in support of their leader. Wars had always been good for that. And, apparently, so were exploded castles.

Justin edged up on my right while Ieuan buttressed me on the left, both uncomfortable with the people getting so close. If I hadn't been so tired, I might have protested, but I also knew that the threat against me was real. My companions were only trying to keep me alive. Still, with more enthusiasm than I'd shown yesterday, I raised a hand to people hanging out of upper story windows.

"Perfect." Cassie spoke from behind me, and I turned to look at her, my expression questioning. She pointed towards the sky. "It's starting to rain."

I let out a laugh, more in relief than genuine humor. It *was* perfect. We needed the rain. Still, I was grateful it didn't start in earnest until we were within a few yards of the Archbishop's palace. This time, the gate was already open when we reached it, and we rode straight under the gatehouse and across the cobbles to the front door. I slid off Cadfan, and took a moment to rest my forehead against his withers.

"This way, David." Callum nudged my elbow.

"Coming." But I didn't move. In the time it had taken to dismount, the events of the day had overwhelmed me. My heart was pounding out of my ears, and my breath was suddenly coming so fast it wasn't doing my lungs any good. I shut my eyes, trying to get a grip on myself. I was clenching my fists so tightly my fingernails were cutting into the palms of my hands.

Callum's hand gripped my shoulder, and he gently guided me away, though I didn't know where he was taking me because I kept my gaze fixed on my boots. I was grateful for the rain yet again, because with my hood up and the darkness in the courtyard, my inability to function hadn't caught the general attention of my men.

We ended up near a corner of the porch by the door, just out of the weather and the torchlight. Folding his arms across his chest, Callum leaned his shoulder against the wall, shielding me from the gaze of anyone whose eyes might stray in my direction. "You can talk to me," he said after a minute had passed and I still hadn't looked up. "This is me, remember? The man who washes his hands ten times a day."

"Still?"

His calm words had cut through the static in my head, and I managed to meet his eyes. My heart twisted at the pity and understanding I saw in them.

"Still," he said.

I shivered and sweated at the same time. My hands, once I managed to unfist them, shook. "We could have died, Callum."

My friend took in a breath and let it out in a long, slow sigh. As he did so, I could feel the tension ease out of him. After a second, I realized he'd done it on purpose, because my body had involuntarily mimicked his, and oxygen was finally flowing to my brain.

"I know," he said.

My mouth felt dry, and I licked my lips. "How can I do this to my family? It is one thing for Lee to come after me, but ... if something were to happen to them, it would be all my fault."

"Again, it would not be," Callum said. "It is, however, the price you pay for being king."

"I don't want it."

"I know," Callum said.

"I can't walk away, though." I put my free hand to my forehead, rubbing hard with my thumb and forefinger. I didn't feel like I was going to pass out anymore, but I found myself growing angry. "What is that about? I'm willing to risk the lives of my family and everyone I love so I can—" I stopped again, frustrated with myself, and this world, and Lee, and everything else. I glared at Callum, who looked back at me calmly, absorbing my anger without returning it.

"You do it so you can change the world," Callum said. "You do it to make your peoples' lives better."

I fell back to earth with a thud. My anger had continued what Callum had started, normalizing my breathing and allowing me to regain control over my limbs. The panic attack faded. Its absence left me more tired than before, and I turned to put my back to the wall.

Callum dropped his arm from my shoulder, the worry in his eyes vying with relief that I'd stopped quivering. He'd talked openly about his PTSD from his time in Afghanistan. It was pretty clear I had it too.

And possibly, after tonight, so did everyone here.

Cassie approached, concern on her face. She held her shoulders tightly and had the same green-around-the-gills look that I'd been feeling. "Are you okay, David?"

"Not really," I said.

I spoke the truth, but the words came out normally.

"We should get inside," Callum said.

I nodded. I'd never panicked like that before, not even after my first battle at fourteen. I didn't see it as a sign of weakness—Callum would be really angry at me if I did—but if it had happened once, it could happen again. Right now I was among friends, but who was to say that the next time I would be.

I hoped that at least Peckham, if not Romeyn, had gone back to bed so I wouldn't have to speak to anyone before I slept.

Peckham had, but both Romeyn and Aaron were waiting for me at the door. "Sire," Aaron said as I reached him. He bowed so low his long beard almost touched his knees. Romeyn had exchanged his workman's clothes for the traditional robe of an archbishop, though without the crown or chain of office. He had deep circles under his eyes, as I was sure I did too.

"Rise, Aaron," I said. "I'm too tired for that. You should have stayed in bed."

Aaron looked offended. He could no more sleep when I was in danger than Justin could. "I'm glad to see you alive, sire. I would hate to have to explain to your mother why you weren't."

"You and me both," I said, without irony. My mother had made her position clear: if she lost me because I'd taken less care of myself than I should have, she would never forgive me. I knew it was her love for me speaking. There was no greater pain than the loss of a child. Anna had lost her second son to illness, and I was coming to realize that it was a loss from which she would never recover.

"I wish you hadn't come here, sire," Aaron said.

A little perturbed, I took a few more steps into the anteroom at the front of the palace. Romeyn and Aaron came with me. "How can you say that, Aaron?"

His hands behind his back, Romeyn stood beside Aaron. "Hear him out, your grace." Perhaps I shouldn't have been surprised by an alliance between these two very intelligent men.

My men had followed me under the gatehouse into the courtyard, and Peckham's steward was speaking with Justin about arranging for food and shelter for my men for what remained of the night. Cadfan had already been taken away to the stables.

"I've been eavesdropping, as you requested, sire," Aaron said as if my request and his acceding to it were the most natural thing in the world to speak about out loud in the presence of the Archbishop of York. "I was dozing beside the cardinal when his secretary woke him to tell him of the destruction of the castle. Acquasparta said something I think you need to know about."

I observed him, waiting.

Aaron took in a breath. "The cardinal didn't express shock or surprise, as if he'd been expecting the news. Then he said, 'I looked, and behold, a white horse, and he who sat on it had a bow; and a crown was given to him, and he went out conquering and to conquer.'"

My eyes narrowed. "That's from Revelations."

"I know that, sire," Aaron said.

"Putting aside how you know that, what does this have to do with my coming here?" I said. "I don't even ride a white horse."

"True, but King Philip does," Romeyn said. "He is known for it."

Aaron put out a hand to me. "I know it sounds absurd on the surface, but I can't think why else Acquasparta would have quoted that particular passage. It worries me."

I bent my head, feeling exhaustion wash over me. Philip as a stand-in for Christ himself had my stomach churning. My brain was working clearly, however, and I took in an easy breath.

"I have to sleep for a few hours. We all do." I turned to Callum, who'd entered the anteroom with Cassie while I'd been speaking with Romeyn and Aaron. "What do you think?"

"I think we perhaps should have gone to Chilham with Carew," Callum said.

"We still can." Cassie slipped her hand into Callum's.

"What is the hour?" I said.

"Five in the morning, give or take," Cassie said.

I shook my head. "I just need three hours of sleep. We can be in Chilham by noon, depending on what the dawn brings us."

Romeyn and Aaron exchanged an inscrutable look, one at which both of them seemed very accomplished, and Romeyn said, "This way, sire, if you will."

Romeyn ignored the steward, who'd been hovering on the far side of the anteroom, and who'd wanted to take me elsewhere. Instead, Romeyn led me to his own room on the first floor of the palace. I loosened my sword belt, removing it in order to lean my sword against the wall, and fell face first onto the bed fully clothed. I heard the door close behind me, and then I slept.

16

I'd learned over the last four years to put away troubles in a locked box in my mind so as to clear it for sleep. I was so exhausted, I didn't have to do that this time, but my dreams were troubled: a presence with Darth Vader's voice recited a laundry list of incomprehensible tasks that faced me, while fire and smoke poured out of a hole in the ground in front of me. I woke with a start to a sunlit room and the squeak of a door opening behind me.

In a flash, I spun off the bed, my belt knife in my hand. William stood before me, his mouth open in surprise. I stopped when I saw him and straightened, slipping my knife into its sheath. "Sorry."

William bowed. "I apologize, sire, but you asked to be woken in three hours. It has been four."

Now that I was upright, the room came into focus. I'd slept in a four-poster bed with gold curtains that I hadn't bothered to undo and sleep behind. Someone had thrown a blanket across my back—I credited Cassie for the thought—and I hadn't moved from the position I'd first lain down in. I was standing on a wooden floor, worn in places but otherwise spotless. Steam rose from a basin of water on a table near the window. I hadn't heard the maid come in to bring it.

"I don't fault you. Obviously, I needed the sleep. Did you manage any?"

He shrugged. "A little."

I took that to mean 'no'.

"I slept a few hours in the castle before it blew up."

"What did I miss?" I said.

"Nothing of note, sire. Lord Ieuan sent a rider to the constable at Dover Castle to tell him what happened here at Canterbury and that we fear French involvement, though we have no proof of it. It is too soon to have heard back."

"I'm glad someone was thinking last night," I said.

"The men of Dover are always ready for an attack from across the Channel, so that will be nothing new to them," he said, "but they will warn the other ports to be on the alert."

Located on the east coast of Kent, less than twenty miles from Canterbury, Dover town and castle was one of the longest-established communities in England, dating to Anglo-Saxon times. Ports like Dover had protected England from foreign invasion since before there was an England. I also saw them as our first line of defense against diseases coming from the Continent and had worked extensively with the ports' representatives to document all boats coming in and out of England. At times I'd felt almost like a supplicant. The men of the ports had a strong independent streak and were not to be dictated to, even by the king. Perhaps especially not by the king.

But although medieval people struggled with the concept of invisible pathogens, once the portsmen understood that my aim wasn't to tax them to death, they'd risen to the challenge. Most of the new policies and procedures that regulated shipping had been proposed by them. The Black Death might still be sixty years away, but it wasn't the only incipient pandemic out there, and the only way it was getting to England was by sea.

Thus I was glad Ieuan had the foresight to send word to the constable at Dover, one Stephen de Pencester. He operated under the oversight of Edmund Mortimer, whom I'd named Lord Warden of the Cinque Ports, one of the most powerful positions in England. Mortimer represented these port towns in my cabinet. Although he'd had little connection to eastern England up until now, I'd essentially bribed him with this responsibility to keep his eyes off opportunities for expansion of his personal estates into Ireland. It was one of the things about being King of England I hated most—doing something I wouldn't normally have approved of in order to accomplish what I saw as a greater good.

"What about Lee?" I said.

"No, my lord. No sign."

I nodded, having expected nothing better. In retrospect, Lee seemed too much of a professional to have stuck around to watch the destruction of Canterbury Castle. He wasn't a criminal or a serial arsonist, at least as far as I knew. He was a terrorist, with specific goals and aims. Getting caught watching the results of his handiwork would have been sloppy of him.

Though he'd met with Frenchmen, I wasn't sure what kind of connection there could be between Lee and King Philip, or Lee and Acquasparta, but I could easily see a link between Acquasparta and Philip, since it was Acquasparta himself who had informed me of the pope's support of Philip's claim to Aquitaine. The pope or Acquasparta wouldn't even have needed to speak to Philip directly, and all three could be working through underlings. Plausible deniability wasn't a modern invention. Any one of them might want to be able to stand before me, or another questioner, without having to lie outright.

Cassie appeared in the doorway, tipping her head to William to indicate that he was dismissed. She had a fresh shirt and tunic bundled in her arms, and she handed them to me. I splashed water on my face from the basin of warm water, and as I dried my skin, I eyed her warily. She wanted to talk. I wasn't sure I was going to be happy with what she wanted to talk about.

"Does Callum know you're here?" I said.

She laughed. "Are you afraid of what I'm going to say?" We were speaking American English, which allowed her to leave off 'my lord' or 'sire'.

"Where is he?" I said.

"He went off with Darren and Peter, 'pursuing a lead'." She shook her head. "I had my eyes closed at the time so I didn't ask for more."

"I need to talk to him."

She ignored that. "I don't agree that you should be a part of the team that goes after Lee. He isn't worth your direct attention."

"How can you say that? Lee tried to kill me." I stripped off my shirt, dropped it beside the basin, and pulled the new one over my head, tucking it into my breeches and then tying the strings that kept the neck closed. Next I put on the dark green tunic, which was slightly shorter than those I normally wore, falling to just above my knees. It fit me across the shoulders, and I suspected that Cassie had quested among my men for a spare that would fit. She helped me buckle my sword belt around my waist to keep everything in place.

Cassie shook out my cloak, now clean and dry, and swung it around my shoulders. "Exactly. It's personal with you. I don't think it is with him."

"I don't think you're right in that," I said. "Looking back, he played me perfectly. He wasn't a sycophant—he knew I wouldn't respond well to flattery—he was acerbic and witty, with just the right amount of irreverence to draw me in."

Cassie didn't respond right away, and I added, "You saw right through him, didn't you?"

She scoffed. "Hardly. It was Lili who was paying the most attention. She didn't say anything because she was afraid her worry came from jealousy, because he was from Avalon and she wasn't. She feared that because of it, she couldn't understand what you needed—and that you needed something more than she could give you."

I groaned. It was clear I had some patching up to do with my wife, and I wished she were right in front of me so I could make a start. "She wasn't jealous. She was smart. Unlike me."

"Like I said, I don't think you should take this personally," Cassie said. "Lee is one man, and while he did a lot of damage, you have bigger fish to fry. This thing with the pope, for starters."

"This thing with the pope, as you say, may be tied to this thing with Lee." I shook my head. "I need to do something other than running back to London to hide. If I do that, it feels like I've ceded the whole country to him."

Cassie wrinkled her nose at me.

"What?"

"You do realize that some of us—I'm not talking about me—have experience investigating terrorism, right?" she said. "That was Callum's *job* back in Avalon."

I made a gurgling sound in the back of my throat. It wasn't like I'd forgotten. We'd talked about it while standing under the trees near the chapel. I started to wonder if my decision to stay in Canterbury had been the right one, even if it had felt right in the heat of the moment. I'd probably just get in Callum's way.

"I haven't thanked you and Callum yet, by the way."

"For what?"

"For siccing the Order of the Pendragon on Lee," I said.

Cassie shook her head ruefully. "It was too little too late."

"Without you, I might have lost more than a castle," I said.

"The people will take it as a sign that God is still with you."

I didn't voice the disparaging comment that formed on my tongue. It was an honor to be the King of England, and the people deserved something more than cynicism for having placed their trust in me.

"Sire!" William de Bohun was back. He swung around the frame of the door, holding onto it with one hand to stop himself from hurtling too far into the room. "News has come from Dover!"

I caught William by the arms. "Slow down."

"The queen sends word from Dover that two French spies were caught trying to leave the beach under cover of darkness!" The boy could hardly breathe in his excitement.

I couldn't make sense of what he was saying, seeing as how I'd gotten stuck on "the queen sends word" and "Dover". Before I could ask for more information, Ieuan appeared behind William in the doorway. "The boy speaks the truth. Word has just come from Dover Castle that two Frenchmen were apprehended as they tried to sail from Dover without passing inspection first."

"William said *the queen*," I said. "What does he mean by that?"

Ieuan grunted. "For some reason, Lili didn't go to Chilham. She went to Dover."

"Where two French spies were caught trying to flee England." I put both hands up to the sides of my head and squeezed. Four hours of sleep clearly hadn't been enough. "Your sister—"

"She's your wife, my friend," Ieuan said. "I had some idea when you married her that you'd rein her in, but it was never more than a faint hope."

The two of us looked at each other, shaking our heads and smiling. Dover Castle was possibly the largest and most well-defended castle in England. I could hardly complain about her safety now, even if getting there might have been riskier than going to Chilham.

"David, you and Ieuan should head to Dover," Cassie said. "Leave Lee to the rest of us."

"I hate to part with any of you, but events seem to be conspiring to make me accept that you're right." My thinking from the start had been that it would be best if modern people were at the forefront of the pursuit. My departure would leave only modern people in the party, since I would take Justin, Ieuan, and William with me.

"They will be more than up to the task," Ieuan said.

"I hate to think what kind of damage Lee can do with a sack full of C-4," I said, "but I concede that this can't be about my personal issues with Lee. I need to speak to these Frenchmen." I looked at Ieuan. "Any word from Clare?"

"No, my lord," Ieuan said, "though with the dawn, word of the destruction of Canterbury Castle will be spreading far and wide."

"Lee will know, if he doesn't already, that he failed to kill me," I said.

Ieuan chewed on his lower lip. "Will he try again?"

"Unless Canterbury has some intrinsic value I don't know about, and its destruction, not my death, was the point, he may well believe he has to," I said.

"Don't mention that to Callum unless he brings it up himself," Cassie said. "He won't want to let you out of his sight."

"He will have to accept that neither of us can be in two places at once, just like I have to." I turned to William. "Where's your father?"

"Hereford, I think," he said.

"Too far. I need his men now, not in two weeks," I said.

"Why do you need his men?" William said.

"To defend the coast, of course," I said.

"Who do you think is planning to invade?" Ieuan said. "Philip?"

"How can I not think it?" I said. "Too many threads are coming together before our eyes. They point to a conspiracy that somehow involves Acquasparta, Philip, and Lee, though how each of them fits into it I don't know. I can't imagine how they all got together. I never would have wanted to see Canterbury in a pile of rubble. I certainly don't want to fight a war with the King of France, even if I threatened Acquasparta with it yesterday. But Lee met with Frenchmen, and we've captured two French spies. Pope

Boniface supports Philip's claim to Aquitaine over mine. If Philip has plans for me, we need to be prepared."

"I will send a rider to Dover to inform Lili and Sir Stephen that you will be arriving later today." Ieuan bowed and departed, taking William with him.

"You can't defend the coast with two hundred archers and fifty men-at-arms," Cassie said.

"Since when have you been such a defeatist?" I said. "Anyway—" I waved a hand. "—I walked away from a destroyed castle with no casualties. You were right to say that my people will believe God is still with me. They will come when I call. As it turns out, Lee might have done me a favor by destroying my castle. It will rally the people around me."

The definition of a great king in the Middle Ages was one who won battles. Back in Avalon, King Edward was almost universally lauded for his strength, though he'd won the accolade at the expense of Wales, Scotland, Ireland, and France. The English—and the historians who wrote about Edward—didn't consider the cost in their evaluation.

Similarly, Richard the Lionheart had spent all of six months in England during his ten-year reign but was remembered as a good king. Nobody seemed to care, then or since, that ransoming him when he was captured by an Austrian duke on his way home from the Crusades had bankrupted the country.

I wasn't much concerned about my legacy, but I did want the power to do what I thought England needed while I was king.

And for that to happen, keeping the overall goodwill of the people was essential.

Acquasparta himself appeared in the corridor as I left Romeyn's room, and I halted when I reached him, fighting down the feeling of animosity that rose within me at the sight of him. "Your color is better than yesterday, your eminence," I said.

He had a handkerchief clutched in his right hand, and he dabbed the sweat from his forehead with it. "The fever has broken again."

"You shouldn't be upright at all," I said. "You'll bring on another relapse."

"I needed to speak to you before you left," he said, and at the beginnings of another protest on my part, he raised one shoulder in a classic Italian shrug. "I assure you, King David, that I never intended for the arrest of that heretic to result in a riot. Canterbury is known for its holiness and peaceful acceptance of pilgrims."

I just managed not to laugh. "Thirty years ago, the people of Canterbury slaughtered the Jews in this town. Surely you were aware of that?"

"The Jews killed Christ. What happened to them in Canterbury is another matter entirely," he said.

I contemplated him a moment, suppressing my disgust— and disconcerted that he'd actually brought up the issue of blood libel, which Pope Innocent had called baseless as recently as 1247. I was also shocked by Acquasparta's complete disregard for the actual reason the populace had been incited to riot then—and why they had rioted yesterday. Again, it wasn't because the Jews killed Christ or because heretics believed something different from what the Church taught.

The people had followed where a powerful and charismatic man had led.

Thirty years ago, that man had been Gilbert de Clare at Simon de Montfort's request. Yesterday, it was on behalf of Acquasparta and the Church. "We will have to agree to differ on the cause of that atrocity. Popes have asked that kings such as I protect the Jewish communities in the lands we rule, but it is heretics, not Jews, who brought you to England."

"Indeed. I am grateful to you for defusing the situation, but that does not detract from the underlying issue at hand. The Church must be allowed to prosecute those who deviate from the true Faith." He paused briefly, and when I didn't reply, he added, "It is my duty to warn you that this might not be the only such incident if you continue on the path you have chosen."

Genuinely appalled at where this was going, I moved closer to him and lowered my voice. "You will not arrange for the arrest of any more men in my country, whether or not you believe them to be heretics. You will not incite my people to riot."

"The arrest was at the command of His Holiness, the Vicar of Christ," Acquasparta said defiantly, though it didn't come off as he might have hoped, since he was swaying on his feet from his illness. "I do not answer to you."

"As long as you are in England, you do."

Acquasparta gazed at me, his shoulders stiff. I longed to shake him, or to see him shaken, but he was unbending. "I have heard your words and will convey them to the pontiff. I cannot promise what his response will be."

"I have no desire to dispute with the pope, but you can tell him that I do not fear his wrath. Regardless of the action he takes, I can promise him that my answer will remain the same." It was a hard line to take, openly and at this stage of the game, but I had almost been blown up a few hours ago, and I wasn't feeling conciliatory. I also didn't like the fact that Acquasparta was treating me like a boy who could be bullied into conformity. If he thought I would bend, he had sorely misjudged my resolve.

We were also speaking before several witnesses. Cassie was standing silently at my side, though Acquasparta so far hadn't even deigned to look at her. She was hard to miss, too, with her deep black hair and high cheekbones—not to mention masculine breeches. Romeyn hovered a few paces away, listening closely beside Acquasparta's secretary. I didn't mind who heard me, but down the road, Acquasparta might regret having threatened me before so many witnesses.

"Pope Boniface does not see these events as you do," Acquasparta said.

"That is not my problem," I said, "though I am happy to explain my position to you—and to him—as many times as I need to."

"I do not think it would help," Acquasparta said. "I fear the supreme pontiff might need to take extreme measures in the coming months if an agreement cannot be reached." He didn't seem to realize how much better off he'd be if he chose to quit while he was ahead—or at least before he pushed me into saying something even more radical than I already had.

Too late.

"You speak of placing England under interdict," I said, "and perhaps even excommunication?"

Acquasparta's gaze was steady on mine. "As you say."

In the past, such censor—or the threat of it—had almost always brought rulers into line eventually. It just wasn't going to work this time. Not on me. Acquasparta could threaten all he wanted. I was even willing to accept that Acquasparta, the pope, and all these other Churchmen were sincere. They thought it was their God-given responsibility to keep the populace thinking straight. But that I disagreed was going to be to their loss, not mine.

"He should do what he feels he must," I said. "The responsibility for what follows will be his."

"Do you actually ... threaten His Holiness?" Acquasparta said, puzzlement in his voice.

That was rich, considering that he'd just threatened me. "It wasn't a threat," I said. "Again, I simply state the facts as I see them."

Acquasparta bowed. "I will convey your response."

I turned away, though not before I saw something change in Acquasparta's eyes—a flash of annoyance, perhaps, or calculation.

I nodded to Romeyn, who was looking at me with consternation. We didn't speak—I wasn't sure I could without shouting—and Cassie and I paced towards the exit doors side by side.

"I really have stuck my neck out now, haven't I?" I said.

"Yes," she said. "You have."

17

The memory of my earlier panic haunted me. It had left a bitter residue on my tongue. The cold light of morning didn't alleviate any of my troubles either. I still had two dead time travelers, a terrorist on the run, and was no closer to resolving my conflict with the pope. I did have Romeyn as an unexpected ally, and I considered sending him to Italy on the first boat. It had occurred to me by now that not only did I need better spies in Rome, I had sorely underestimated my need for a permanent ambassador there.

Actually, if I were to send Romeyn, he wouldn't be going to Rome, but to a place called Orvieto. A few centuries ago, the popes had started moving around Italy like medieval kings, and a bunch of them in the last century had preferred Orvieto to Rome as their home base. Since, like kings, they brought their stuff with them when they moved, it wasn't as big a deal now as it would be in modern Avalon to move the papal seat.

Callum had gone to speak to the owner of the inn, which the maid Beatrice had mentioned last night. When I asked if he'd learned anything new, he shrugged. "It's a start. This is the way investigations work: you ask questions and follow your nose until you either run into a wall or learn something that leads you to more questions."

Once I brought Callum and the others up to speed on our latest news from Dover, I said, "What we have to ask ourselves now is where Lee went from here, and what role the French have played in his plans."

"Frenchmen in Canterbury and French spies at Dover have me envisioning white sails on the horizon," Callum said.

"That was my first thought, too. It isn't something I want to see in my lifetime," I said.

England had been invaded from Europe many times. The Romans had done it. The Saxons/English themselves were the product of a long invasion process over the course of several hundred years, which had pushed the Britons into Wales and turned them Welsh. In 1066, William the Bastard had successfully landed at Pevensy before marching up the coast to Hastings, where he defeated the Saxon king, Harold, to open the path to taking the throne of England himself.

Since then, French troops had landed on England's shores in two wars: during the civil war between Empress Maud and King Stephen a hundred and fifty years ago, and in the time of King John when many barons had been discontented with John's rule and essentially invited the French king in.

However, without a support network in England to prepare the way for the invasion, crossing the English Channel to disembark safely on one of its many beaches was a daunting task. It might be only twenty-one miles across the Channel (to Dover), but the Channel was a fickle body of water. Storms could blow up without warning. Ships were small and an invader needed dozens, if not hundreds, to carry the requisite number of troops and horses, making the organizational aspect of the conquest daunting. Finding a hospitable beach was a huge task in and of itself, since no port would welcome them. Plus, no matter who was making the attempt, they would surely be woefully outnumbered by the soldiers who faced them.

King Philip had shown himself to be a daring ruler, however, and if he was already working with the pope to weaken my position in Aquitaine, he might believe himself so strong he was willing to attempt it. I had been working to grow my navy since my crowning, but Philip had a head start. Since 1284, the French crown had been building a naval base at Rouen, modeled after the Spanish shipyard at Seville. He was building Genoese-style galleys and clinker-built barges, not dissimilar from the English barges for which the Thames was famous. My spies had informed me ages ago that Philip's endeavor was on a similar scale to my own galley-building program.

Unlike the historical England of this time, I was in the process of building a standing navy. It functioned more like a border patrol most of the time, with a dose of search and rescue thrown in for good measure. The men of the navy worked with the Cinque Ports—not to limit their power, but to augment their forces. Most of the patrolling occurred along the stretch of coast that fronted the European continent. Dover, as the closest geographical point to France, was at the center of the patrol. This concession had appeased the men of the Cinque Ports and reaffirmed their importance and power.

"I couldn't attest to the seaworthiness of Philip's ships or their ability to cross the English Channel in a storm, but if Philip wanted to invade, it might well be that he had the wherewithal to do it.

"I'm torn between wanting to pursue Lee wherever he's gone and believing I should be coming with you to Dover," Callum said, "because that's where you're going next, isn't it?"

"I have to," I said. "You, however, can do more good here. I have other men who can help me deal with the Church and the French. As your wife pointed out to me ten minutes ago, you were trained for this kind of thing."

"Darren and Peter even more than I."

I waved my hand dismissively. "You are the Earl of Shrewsbury and from Avalon. Your presence will give weight to their authority, and you have access to how Lee thinks. Find him. Ieuan and Justin are more than capable of keeping me safe on the road to Dover."

Callum nodded his consent. "By the way, I checked in with Sir Thomas. Mike and Noah will be put in the ground by noon. Shall Cassie and I attend the burial as your representatives? I can't imagine there'll be a large crowd."

I sighed. "Yes, go. It should be me, but—"

"You should go to Dover," Callum said. "Their deaths are not your fault."

"Have you figured out yet why Lee killed them?" I said.

Peter had been standing a few feet away, talking to Cassie, while Callum and I had been speaking. Now he cleared his throat and came closer. "My guess, my lord, is that they'd become a liability. They knew too much about Lee and his plans."

"That seems likely," Callum said. "They helped Lee set the charges in the early hours of yesterday morning, left the castle with him, and then before they'd gone far at all, he killed them rather than risk exposure through them. Wherever he was going, he didn't want them to come."

"He no longer believed he needed their help." Peter started to turn away, but then he stopped and looked back.

"What is it?" I said. "If you know anything that might help us here, don't keep quiet."

"Well—thinking about Lee's connection with Ireland. Please correct me if I'm wrong, but last night did you say that you want the Normans to leave Ireland but haven't yet found a way to make it happen?"

"Yes, of course," I said. "Didn't you know that?"

Peter licked his lips. "No. You've played those cards close to your chest, my lord. It occurs to me that Lee and I have talked about some things that I should have shared with you sooner."

We'd moved to one side of the courtyard, away from the stamping of horses' hooves as my men prepared to ride yet again. The smell of fresh bread wafted to me from the palace kitchen, and my stomach growled. I hadn't eaten yet, and I would have given a small fortune to surprise the cook with the pleasure of serving the King of England. Perhaps it was callous of me to be thinking of my stomach at a time like this. Regardless, I felt events pressing me forward, so I simply gestured that Peter should continue.

"Lee's uncle died when he was five," he said. "He was killed in the Greysteel massacre. I'd never heard of it before Lee told me about it."

"I know of it," Callum said. "That would have been around 1993, at the start of the peace process."

"I don't know anything about it," I said.

Peter sighed. "Members of the Ulster Defense Force opened fire during a Halloween party at an Irish Catholic pub."

"Oh," I said.

Atrocities had been committed by both sides during the centuries of strife between Catholics and Protestants, Irish and Anglo-Irish, for the rule of Ireland—to neither side's credit.

"He never talked about any of this to you?" Peter said.

"No," I said. "I'm coming to realize that he never talked about anything of importance to me."

A clattering of hooves on the cobbles drew our attention to the gate, through which Darren appeared. He reined in and dismounted, and then made a beeline for us.

"You've found something," Callum said.

Darren's eyes were bright. "We found where he was staying. He was there as late as this morning, though he left with the dawn. We're canvassing the area now for anyone else who noticed where he might have been headed."

The lines around Callum's eyes smoothed for the first time since I'd shown him the bomb in the latrine. "That's our first bit of luck. It means we aren't as far behind him as I feared."

18

Thankfully, the journey to Dover was the most uneventful thing that had happened to me in the last two days. It didn't even rain during the ride. We came over a slight rise to the north of the castle by early afternoon, and suddenly there it was, just across a few fields from us. I'd sent scouts ahead of me, of course, and they hadn't reported anything amiss when they'd returned, but I didn't want to walk into another trap either. We took a moment to regroup before riding the last third of a mile to the gatehouse.

I was suspicious enough of everyone that I even feared the message from Dover hadn't come from Lili at all but had been a means to lure me into an ambush. "What do you think?" I didn't need to pass Ieuan the binoculars through which I'd been examining the castle. Bronwen had given him his own pair last Christmas, made by artisans in London who'd combined technology from Avalon with knowledge learned from Muslim scientists in the Holy Land.

I had never been to Dover, which now that I was here, I realized was an oversight on my part. The castle was huge, even by

London standards, and overlooked the English Channel from the top of the white limestone cliffs for which Dover was famous. It had a great square keep, designed by the same man who'd designed Canterbury, along with inner and outer curtain walls, towers, and gates. It had an actual counter-defense tunnel, too, built years ago during the first Barons' War at the time of King John, when *he'd* had to defend against a French invasion.

"It looks okay," Ieuan said. "The flags fly normally, and I see men along the wall-walk. They appear to be in a state of alert."

"As they should be," I said. "Hopefully the castellan has had enough time to prepare for our arrival."

"Lili will have him eating out of her palm by now," Ieuan said.

With that hope, we left the relative safety of the woods and showed ourselves to the men on the battlements. Carew and Sir Stephen, the Dover constable, met us as we entered the castle grounds. I greeted them quickly and immediately asked to see Lili. Leaving Ieuan and Justin to sort out the men and horses, I went to the hall, where she was waiting for me. I hugged her tightly, heedless of who was watching, and moved to a smaller receiving room off of it so she and I could speak in private.

In crossing under the gatehouse, for all that I was the King of England, I had felt like we were breaching the walls of an enemy fortress—and that was essentially what Lili said to me when she explained why she'd come to Dover instead of riding to Chilham. "We fought the English for years, you know."

"I fought the English for years too," I said. "How does that explain your presence here?"

"You sent me to Chilham, I know, but once we arrived at the stable to collect the horses for the men who would accompany me, I started thinking more carefully about what Lee had done and why. I remembered the Frenchmen he'd met with, whom we didn't know anything about. Ieuan had sent men to do a house-to-house search of Canterbury yesterday, but with the castle destroyed, I thought there was a good chance the Frenchmen had gone already rather than stay to watch Lee's handiwork."

"With the castle fallen, the Frenchmen would have been worried about accusations and blame directed at them," I said.

"That's what I thought too. And then I put myself in the place of any of us before you became the King of England. Your father almost died ten years ago. At that time, we would have rejoiced to have had the means to destroy Canterbury Castle."

"I wouldn't have liked killing civilians," I said, "but you're right. C-4 would have felt like a godsend."

"We've become the very people we despised," Lili said.

I shook my head, wanting to deny what she was saying but knowing that I couldn't. Lili put out a hand to me. "For the people of Wales and Scotland, nothing could be further from the truth, but to the King of France, or to the native Irish in lands conquered by your barons, you are still the enemy."

"I can see that," I said. "How does this get you to Dover again?"

She smiled. "I simply started thinking like a Welshman, and what we would have done ten years ago. We wouldn't have stayed to view our handiwork. You and your men would have fled back to Wales. These men, however, are from France. It occurred to me that they—"

"—would try to go home to France. Of course," I said, glad I had Lili to do my thinking for me because I'd been really slow on the uptake.

"I explained my thinking to Carew," she said. "He didn't want to go against your wishes, and we spent precious minutes debating the right course of action. But then he decided that I could be right—and if I was, it was worth the extra ten miles of riding to find out."

"I'm glad he listened to you," I said.

She waved a hand dismissively. "It is you, however, who really made their capture possible."

I scoffed because it couldn't possibly be true. "How kind of you to say. Why?"

"You've locked up our ports so tightly that no ship comes in or out without inspection. It's easier to get *out* of England because your primary concern is disease, not smuggling, but your patrol ships stop boats and check for papers. Dover patrol had already caught the French spies, who'd put to sea from the beach rather than the harbor, before we arrived. Carew was all set to mobilize a small army to scout for them, but then it wasn't necessary because the patrol boat returned to port with the Frenchmen in custody. Then it was merely a matter of sending word to you."

"Wow." I shook my head at Lili. "You well deserve your membership in the Order of the Pendragon."

She smirked. "So Carew said."

I laughed, remembering what Callum had taught me about managing any organization, whether medieval or modern: find the best people—people you trust, pay them well, and then leave them alone to do their job. It just so happened that one of the most trustworthy and intelligent people I knew was my own wife.

Lili laughed with me, but then she sobered. "The constable here, Sir Stephen, has also had a message from Henry de Lacy."

As the Earl of Lincoln, Lacy had been a confidant of King Edward before his death. At Gilbert de Clare's urging, in another blatant act of bribery, I'd named him commander of my tiny Royal Navy. It wasn't that he needed greater standing in court, since he was already one of the wealthiest and most powerful men in Britain. Standing meant nothing, however, without the king's trust. I didn't want him working behind my back because he thought he didn't have it.

And as it turned out, he'd been a good choice, having a personality that was both demanding and precise. He also wasn't averse to using new technologies when he saw with his own eyes that they worked. Military men, whatever their lineage, could appreciate a cannon when they saw one fired.

"He fears the King of France is planning to cross the channel with an invasion army," she said.

I pressed my lips together. It wasn't as if Callum and I hadn't discussed such an invasion earlier this morning. But to hear someone else from outside my circle arrive at the same conclusion when he didn't have access to the same information I had was disconcerting to say the least. "Why does he think that?"

"His patrol has seen movement along the Seine and in the shipyard at Rouen in France," she said. "He feels certain that Philip is gathering a fleet, and he believes it prudent to assume that Philip plans to sail towards us and not elsewhere."

"We must prepare."

"Sir Stephen has already sent word to the Portsman of Dover to marshal his ships and men," Lili said. "He hadn't done it initially, since the first message from Ieuan only talked about the destruction of Canterbury Castle. But the capture of two French spies, Lacy's news, and what I could tell him about Lee convinced him. If in the end it proves to be a false alarm, so be it."

"At worst, it will be a good training exercise," I said.

"At best, you mean," Lili said. "Otherwise it will be war."

19

I tipped my head in acknowledgement of Lili's point. "How come the Order didn't know this already?"

"I don't know," she said, "but messenger pigeons can fall afoul of predators or bad weather, and we don't have as many contacts at the French court as we would like."

"I wasn't assuming treachery," I said, "but I don't like it that Lacy's reach is further than mine, and this is the second time the Order has been caught on the hop. Lacy sent a rider, you say?"

"That's only the beginning," she said. "Lacy is concerned enough that he is coming himself, bringing whatever ships he can gather quickly, though he says it will take at least three days to arrive here. That's really what persuaded Sir Stephen to call in the Portsmen—he didn't want the Cinque Ports shown up by the navy."

One of the hardest things to adjust to about the Middle Ages was incredibly mundane: things took a long time to happen. Travel was treacherous, weather unpredictable, and communication difficult if not impossible. Nobody knew what anyone else was doing or had done until they managed to connect.

Three days for my navy to muster wasn't that long to wait, until three days turned into six, or a fortnight. A horse, when pressed, could travel fifty miles a day. It was only twenty miles across the English Channel, but if the weather wasn't good, no amount of sailing was going to allow Philip to cross it today, tomorrow, or next week. I was suddenly grateful for the rainy summer we'd been experiencing, and for the gray clouds I'd seen to the southwest when I'd been looking at Dover through my binoculars.

"Does he have any indication of where they intend to land?" I said. This was one battle I wanted over before it started. I hadn't had to kill anyone recently and would prefer not to have to. But it was unlikely that I was going to get what I wanted.

"Lacy is working on it," she said. "I think he hopes to meet them in the Channel, and thus win the day before they reach our shores."

"Can these French spies you captured for me help us with this?" I said. "Have they answered any questions yet?"

As when my father and I had prepared for the last battle we'd fought—the one that had ended with the arrival of the modern bus—uncertainty of travel made planning frustrating. It meant that wherever the French landed, we'd be at a disadvantage. They would be landing in a foreign country, but we wouldn't know exactly where Philip meant to land until he did. Unless, perhaps, we could get these French spies to talk.

Dover was a sophisticated port (for the time), but an invasion army needed a big, sandy beach to land on, preferably not under the watching eyes of the garrison of a massive castle. William the Bastard had landed at Pevensy, thirty-five miles to the southwest of Dover, and Julius Caesar had landed seven miles north, probably at Walmer. When a general decided to make the attempt to conquer England, it was generally best if nobody knew about the invasion in advance, and even better if the actual landing happened far from anyone paying attention. That way, there'd be enough time to unload the luggage, get the horses and men together and in good order, and set off marching for London.

"Carew has them locked in the dungeon," Lili said. "Didn't you see him when you came in?"

"Very briefly," I said. "I came straight to you."

"When you're tired, you do tend to get very focused—"

Lili broke off at the sound of multiple heavy boots coming towards us. A moment later, a knock came at the door, and at my welcome, it opened to admit Carew and another man.

"My lord." Carew gestured to the man who'd accompanied him. "I'm sure you remember Geoffrey de Geneville."

"Sire." White haired and slender—and a little stiff from his ride—Geoffrey bent at the waist in a bow, first to me and then to Lili. "My queen, you are as radiant as ever."

Lili nodded graciously at this bit of courtliness, and I made a motion to raise him up.

Geoffrey came forward while Lili headed towards a side door. She didn't have to leave, but men like Geoffrey, who weren't part of my inner circle, weren't on the same page about what women were good for. She generally kept herself out of my meetings with men like him.

"Carew, please stay," I said when he showed signs of leaving too.

Carew gave me a short bow and took up a position by the door.

King Edward had trusted Geoffrey de Geneville, heaping accolades and honors upon him. He was of an older generation, born around the same time as my father. He had once held extensive lands in the March, but he'd bestowed them upon his son, Peter, ten years ago. Peter had subsequently lost half of them to my father back in 1285, and then had died in June of this year, leaving Geoffrey with only a granddaughter to inherit all his wealth. My mother had informed me that this granddaughter would one day marry Roger Mortimer, the son of my adviser, Edmund.

That is, she would marry him if things worked out here the way they had in Avalon, which I was really hoping they wouldn't— not because I objected to the marriage or to Geoffrey, in fact. It was Roger Mortimer I was worried about. Although no future was a given, in Avalon he grew up to be the rebellious baron who'd had an affair with the Queen of England and for a time usurped the throne of King Edward II.

I hadn't seen Geoffrey since his son died, and though I'd sent a message of condolence, I gave him a nod and said, "I'm sorry for your loss."

I hadn't wanted to make him feel bad or remind him of it, and it seemed those weren't the first words he expected to come out of my mouth, because he froze for a second. Then he blinked twice and bowed again. "Thank you, sire."

I nodded. I didn't have to be as sensitive as Lili to realize that he didn't want to talk about it. "What brings you to Dover, Geneville?" Last I'd heard, he was doing his grieving at his seat in Trim, Ireland. I found it somewhat ironic to have one of the Norman barons to whom Lee so objected standing before me, live and in color. "And how did you know I was here? We didn't raise the flag."

My personal banner always flew from the castle in which I was staying, but Ieuan had suggested we forgo that tradition today. Lee had destroyed one castle. Hopefully, he was very far from here, but I didn't want anyone to know where I was, not until I heard back from Callum, we'd sorted out more clearly the sequence of events that had led to Canterbury's destruction, and we'd determined who had been involved in Lee's conspiracy.

Geoffrey finally looked me in the eye. "I came to Dover with every intention of sailing to my brother in Champagne. I'm sure you know that he is the steward of Champagne for King Philip of France. It is a journey I make once a year if I can. However, we heard on the dock that the harbor patrol had captured two Frenchmen they were calling spies."

"They did." It would be common knowledge by now throughout the town and port.

"One of my men is cousin to a portsman here, and when I inquired of him as to their location, he informed me of the trouble that has arisen between you and Philip, and that these men are now in the castle dungeon. I was wondering if I could offer you assistance with … ah … your inquiries in any way."

I gave a short laugh. Family connections among all classes of society were intertwined. *Cousin* covered a broad spectrum of relationships, and it wasn't only the Welsh who could recite their ancestry to the seventh generation. I rubbed my chin, feeling the scruff of my unshaven beard, which I hadn't had a chance to remove. The gesture bought me time while I decided how to respond. It was true that Geoffrey's long association with King Edward didn't endear him to me. Edward had trusted him, which meant that I wasn't convinced I could, but if I spurned barons because of that, I would find myself with few allies within my own court.

I caught Carew's eye, and he nodded his head infinitesimally. He was suggesting that I proceed, albeit with caution. "What kind of assistance did you have in mind?" I said.

"Have the men spoken yet?" Geoffrey said.

"No," Carew said.

Geoffrey turned slightly to acknowledge Carew, who came forward. "May I ask what they are being held for?" Geoffrey said.

"Colluding with a traitor on behalf of the King of France," I said.

Geoffrey's eyes widened. "Is that so?"

Carew said bluntly, "You can't be unaware of what happened in Canterbury yesterday."

"I did hear that the papal legate was to meet with King David," Geoffrey said. "That meeting did not go well?"

I almost laughed again. Geoffrey was giving nothing away and looked genuinely curious. I spun around and headed for my ornate chair, set on a low dais near the back of the room, in a similar arrangement to my demolished receiving room at Canterbury. I found it oddly comforting to think that King Edward had once sat here. I had despised the man in life, but his strength and arrogance—and his ability to face down far more formidable threats than Geoffrey—were something I could draw upon.

Carew answered for me, having followed me with Geoffrey to a spot five paces from my seat. "Cardinal Acquasparta arranged for the arrest of an accused heretic, who was brought to the Archbishop's Palace while he and the Archbishops of York and Canterbury were meeting with King David. Matters quickly grew tense, and it was only the king's quick action that prevented a full-scale riot."

Geoffrey's eyes narrowed, but he didn't respond immediately, either with outrage, surprise, or even interest. It was as I would have expected from a man of his age who'd spent his life around the English court. He had to resent being shunted aside in favor of younger (and, to his mind, lesser) men, but he had never shown it. He'd been in Ireland during the events of 1288 that had led to my crowning. Since Ireland lacked good cell phone reception in the Middle Ages, he'd missed out on them entirely. Once he'd returned, he'd bowed his neck and given me homage for his lands, as was his duty.

"I see," he said, after a few more seconds of deliberation. "There is precedent for matters of the Church remaining within the Church."

"I will not allow the prosecution of heretics—or the massacre of Jews, for that matter—in my England." My tone was flat and without inflection.

Geoffrey recognized it, as he should have, as the voice of a king, and one that no man was to argue with, even if he thought I was an uncouth Welsh upstart who had no right to the crown I wore. He nodded and said, "Unrest creates difficulties for us all. Best to avoid arousing the passions of the populace."

Carew cleared his throat, stepping into the fray again. "It is good you agree."

"May I ask what this has to do with King Philip?" Geoffrey said.

"Before the incident with the heretic, Cardinal Acquasparta put to me three requests from Pope Boniface: he asked me to allow the Church to prosecute heretics; he requested that I return the proceeds from the *taxatio*—"

That actually got a raised eyebrow from Geoffrey.

"— and His Holiness also asked that I withdraw my claim to Aquitaine," I said.

Geoffrey pressed his lips together for a second in a brief sign of displeasure, and then said, "You are understandably loath to do so. Is it your thought that the Frenchmen you have incarcerated were here to influence the papal legate in some way?"

For a moment, I struggled to reply. Geoffrey was being neither standoffish nor unhelpful as I might have expected. He appeared genuinely interested in advising me, like a grandfather expressing interest in a respected grandchild. "It has crossed my mind. If you are willing to assist me as you said, that would be something I'd like them to tell me. At the moment, however, I'm more concerned about the destruction of Canterbury Castle last night."

I was watching him carefully as I spoke, and at last Geoffrey allowed a real reaction to show on his face and let out a *whuf* of surprise. "Pardon me, sire, if I misunderstand. Did you say Canterbury Castle is destroyed?"

"The keep is little more than rubble," I said. "We escaped with no lives lost thanks to an observant soldier and God's grace. You had not heard this on the dock too?"

"No." Geoffrey's face flushed for a moment, in embarrassment or perhaps anger at being caught unawares. I was impressed that the portsmen he'd spoken to had been so close-mouthed. "Do you think these Frenchmen might have had something to do with this tragedy as well as the pope's query about Aquitaine?"

"We know the traitor responsible," Carew said, "and it has been reported that he met with Frenchmen beforehand."

"And since you have Frenchmen in custody, and you suspect them of being King Philip's men, you are wondering if it was they who met with the traitor. Perhaps you also wonder if this traitor serves Philip directly?" Geoffrey said.

"Yes," I said, and the last letter came out as a hiss. "The traitor's name is Lee."

Geoffrey's brow furrowed. "Not the Lee whom I met at court a few months ago?"

"The same," I said shortly.

"He is from Avalon," Geoffrey said.

"I am aware of my own culpability in this matter," I said. "I will deal with him according to his crimes when we find him. The key is to find him."

Geoffrey said, "Sacré Dieu," in an undertone.

"My sentiments exactly," I said.

So far, our conversation had been more than cordial—and was resulting in a far longer interaction than I'd ever had with Geoffrey. We were still feeling each other out, but I was coming to realize the more we talked that I should have sought him out sooner instead of being worried about his loyalties. Having been stabbed in the back only yesterday, I needed to be careful where I placed my trust, but trusting Geoffrey and respecting the advice he gave me weren't the same thing.

He was also an important and powerful member of the older generation of barons. They'd given Edward their loyalty as a matter of course. Maybe I needed to stop feeling afraid of what they thought of me.

After a careful glance in my direction, Carew said, "The king believes Lee was ejected from Avalon because of his transgressions. Unfortunately, that means he is now able to wreak havoc here. We must find him and stop him before he does any further damage."

Carew was making this up completely, but Geoffrey's brow furrowed. "If he had the power to destroy Canterbury, he cannot be allowed to roam freely to act again."

"We agree," I said.

"It has also come to the king's attention that Lee's motivations derive from a hatred of the Norman presence in Ireland," Carew said. "It may be that he will attempt to journey there."

"Would it be in keeping with King Philip's character to ally himself with an Irish lord or two in an attempt to undermine my rule—and yours?" I said.

Geoffrey licked his lips. "Sadly, yes." The pretenses that had formed a barrier between us continued to drop lower. Geoffrey didn't know that I, like Lee, regretted the Norman presence in Ireland, even if I was the country's ruler. "And I can see why he might view such an alliance as useful."

"Which brings us to our current predicament," Carew said.

Geoffrey bowed for an unprecedented third time. "My lord, if you will allow it, I would speak to your prisoners now."

20

For all that Dover Castle was massive, with endless towers, two curtain walls, and a deep moat that was part of its outer defenses, it didn't have a classic dungeon the way my modern self might have expected (or wanted). Movie-making aside, there were no caverns, heavy oak doors, or instruments of torture lining the walls. Dover did have basements in the keep and under every guard tower along the wall, however, and Sir Stephen, Dover's constable, had put them to good use. He kept his rooms in the upper level of the massive double-towered gatehouse, and it was beneath the ground floor guardroom that the two Frenchmen were being kept, to keep a better eye—and ear—on them.

Like many men who'd achieved middle age, Sir Stephen had developed a paunch and a slower step, and I'd heard he had something of a severe and inflexible outlook. There'd been some discontent among the representatives from Dover's port at his heavy-handedness in his dealings with them. I'd wondered at Mortimer's reappointment of him, since Stephen had been the constable under Edward too, but so far he hadn't said or done anything that had upheld my initial concerns.

After a brief conference as to the specifics of the Frenchmen's capture and the circumstances surrounding it, just to bring Geoffrey and me up to speed, Sir Stephen led us down the spiral stone steps. The single holding cell at the bottom did, in fact, conform to my expectations. Floor-to-ceiling iron bars formed a wall between the prisoners and us. As we entered the small guardroom in front of the cell, the two Frenchmen, who'd been arguing with each other in low voices, broke off and looked in our direction.

At the sight of what were obviously men of standing, one of the Frenchmen came to the door and put his hands around two bars. He had black hair, dark eyes, and olive skin, making him look more Greek than French. However, he spoke in French to Geoffrey and his words were urgent. "We have done nothing! Have mercy!"

With a smothered laugh, I realized the man thought Geoffrey was the highest ranking nobleman here. I couldn't blame him for thinking it. My shirt was sweat-stained from the ride from Canterbury to Dover, and while my borrowed tunic was in respectable shape, I still wore the breeches—much the worse for wear—that I'd put on at Canterbury Castle in the middle of the night. My boots were well and truly scuffed (Jeeves was going to have a heart attack when he saw them), and because it wasn't raining, I'd shucked off the cloak I'd worn from the Archbishop's palace.

I looked nothing like a king should, particularly as a Frenchman understood it. King Edward had been a warrior and the very definition of a man of action, and my style was similar to his. I tried to minimize the little traditions and rituals that had become ingrained in my court. King Philip's court, on the other hand, was known for its ornate ceremonies and formalities, and Philip sweated only in private.

What I wasn't wearing was my armor—and my Kevlar vest, *damn it!*—with the usual long surcoat emblazoned with my crest over the top. My wardrobe was buried under several tons of rubble back at Canterbury. I'd see what kind of condition the armor was in if and when the site was cleared and it was recovered. I had faith in Sir Thomas that he would get to work right away, but he had only hands, rather than heavy machinery, to help him.

Geoffrey must have realized the Frenchman's mistake too, and in the same split second, decided to play his part. "Clear the room."

Carew bent his head, his eyes flicking quickly to me. I tapped one finger down by my thigh to indicate that he should play along too. The two soldiers, who'd been guarding the spies and might not actually know who I was, bowed themselves out the door. Geoffrey and I hadn't discussed how we would play this, but I was very much content for him to take the lead. If his plan was to make the Frenchmen think I was nothing but a servant, he'd hit upon an idea that might get them to talk.

I found a chair next to the table, sat in it, and kept my eyes on the stone floor. I tried to make myself small and inconsequential, which is hard to do when one is six foot two. Fortunately, Geoffrey kept the Frenchmen's attention on him by saying, also in French, "I am Geoffrey de Geneville, Baron of Trim. Tell me your names."

I looked up in time to see the faces of both Frenchmen fill with eager hope, indicating they recognized the name. If they were connected to the French court, they should have known who Geoffrey's brother was.

The first Frenchman, who continued to lead, said, "We are brothers, Jacques and Piers de Reims. We are here on commission from our father, seeking English wool for weaving into fine garments."

Geoffrey studied them for a moment, one eyebrow raised, probably noting, as I had, that they looked nothing alike. Piers, Jacques' supposed brother, had sandy brown hair, blue eyes, and pale skin. Piers was shorter than Jacques, too, by several inches.

"You were stopped on board a boat that did not depart from the harbor," Geoffrey said. "You had no certificate to show you'd paid the mooring fee or had your ship inspected."

"An oversight. Please let us pay the fine, and we'll never break the rules again." Jacques affected a sheepish look, which I found ironic given his purported business. Besides, no reputable trader would risk losing his cargo for lack of a few pence to pay the port master.

"Your ship contained no samples. You had no papers on your person indicating your business," Geoffrey said.

"We found no wool that pleased us, and we lost our papers overboard during our arrest," Jacques said.

He had an answer for everything, but Geoffrey was having none of it. He made a chopping motion with his hand. "You and I both know that you are not merchants. I can help you, but you have to be honest with me about your true business in England."

I returned my eyes to the ground and stilled my leg, which had been bouncing up and down under the table—a habit I often couldn't help when I was sitting. Above all, I didn't want to draw attention to myself. Jacques hadn't asked who I was, and by now I hoped that he'd forgotten I was even in the room. He would never talk if he knew I was the king, other than perhaps to beg for his life.

Jacques glanced at Piers, who, after initial interest, had spent the conversation sitting on the floor. Now Piers got to his feet and came forward to stand beside Jacques. It occurred to me that his disinterest had been feigned, and that it was really he who was the leader, rather than his brother.

Piers said, "I have been to your brother's court. He speaks well of you. You have been a friend to France."

"I have. My brother and I are very close. I was at King Philip's court last year, and we discussed matters of—" Geoffrey's paused, and I gave him credit for not glancing towards me, "—mutual concern."

"Then you know what a difficult few years this has been since the loss of—" Piers stopped, and this time he did look at me.

I'd been watching him out of the corner of my eye as he spoke, pretending to study my fingernails. I didn't move, hoping Piers was assuming now that I was one of Geoffrey's English lackeys and didn't speak French well. Or at the very least was uninterested in their conversation.

When I didn't look up or give any indication that I was listening, he added, "—the loss of King Edward. He and Philip's father might have had their differences, but he was the rightful heir to Aquitaine. Now—"

"Now it is a mare's nest of claimants, none of whom have clear title, especially King David," Geoffrey finished for him.

"And yet, he is obviously the most powerful adversary Philip faces," Jacques said.

Jacques and Piers let Geoffrey think about that for a minute. So far, they hadn't entirely given the game away, though they were close. Geoffrey was proving to be a masterful questioner, and I was glad he was on my side today. I was pretty sure I knew what matters of mutual concern he'd discussed with King Philip last year, even after he'd bowed to me and sworn fealty. He'd been speaking the truth about that. In a way, I would have been disappointed to learn that Geoffrey wasn't playing both sides against the middle.

"King Philip must be very disturbed indeed by King David's claim to Aquitaine if he sent you," Geoffrey said. "It was bold of him to enlist the papal envoy to assist him."

"You know about that?" Jacques said before Piers' hand shot out and grabbed his wrist.

Geoffrey picked at his lower lip with the nail of his pinky finger. "I have my spies too. What isn't as clear to me is the pope's hand in all this."

Jacques and Piers exchanged a glance, but neither replied.

"I can't help you if you won't talk to me," Geoffrey said. "If I'm to stick my neck out for you and lie to the king, I need to know everything you know. I hate surprises—and I would hate to discover after the fact that you were keeping something from me that would have made the difference between success and failure."

Piers hesitated for another few seconds, but then finally he said, "We don't know."

"If our companion hadn't been captured by King David's men, we would have been able to tell you more," Jacques said.

I managed to control my startled reaction. Geoffrey, for his part, canted his head and said, "He was imprisoned by King David?"

Piers snorted in disgust. "It had been determined that it was too dangerous to speak with the papal legate directly, so Acquasparta arranged to arrest Guillaume as a heretic. They would have had plenty of time to talk, and nobody would have thought anything of the attention the legate paid him. But the plan went awry, and Guillaume ended up in King David's custody instead."

My God. The heretic was a plant. I could still see the fear in the man's face and the blood on his head. At the time both had appeared completely genuine. Certainly the crowd had been. What a debacle.

"You abandoned him?" Geoffrey said, allowing disdain at this dishonorable behavior to enter his voice.

"The mission is the most important thing," Piers said. "We were due in France and time was of the essence."

Jacques looked eagerly into Geoffrey's face. "Can you free us?"

"I need to know first about your contact within King David's court," Geoffrey said. "A man named Lee, I believe?"

Piers made a guttural sound at the back of his throat. "If you already know it all, why are you asking me? Nothing I say should come as a surprise to you. Is the news from Canterbury true? The king is dead?"

"The castle is destroyed," Geoffrey said, as if he hadn't heard about it only a half-hour before. "I can't say about the king."

"Ah," Piers said.

"How did you know what happened in Canterbury if you left yesterday? No word of anything that happened there last night had come to me before I spoke to the castellan here," Geoffrey said. "Did you hear about it from Lee?"

"No." Jacques ran a hand through his black hair. "But he swore it would be done, and we overheard talk among our jailers in the last hour that the castle had, indeed, fallen."

Piers nodded, more to himself than to Geoffrey. "King David must still be alive. That is why Sir Stephen gave no sign of discomfit, and the flag still flies above the gatehouse."

"Perhaps," Geoffrey said.

Jacques pushed away from the bars, clearly frustrated. "Lee failed."

"You can't be sure of that," Geoffrey said. "He did bring down Canterbury Castle."

Piers tapped a finger to his lips. "But the king wasn't in it. King Philip should hear of this as soon as possible. Lee reached too far beyond his abilities."

"He has betrayed us!" Jacques' color was high and his mouth in a grimace. Somehow a switch had been flipped inside him, and he was in a rage. He clutched the bars of his cell, twisting his hands as if he could wrench them apart. "You must get us out now! Whether or not the king is dead, Canterbury Castle is no more. Sir Stephen might believe we had a hand in it and keep us here."

"You did have a hand in it," Geoffrey said.

Piers waved a hand dismissively, unaffected by Jacques' rage. "Lee came to us. We listened. That is all."

"You gave him money," Geoffrey said, not as a question.

"Of course," Piers said, "and encouragement. But we had no part in what he chose to do with it. We didn't help."

Geoffrey smirked. "Everyone needs to be able to stand before their lord and deny all responsibility, do they not?"

Piers canted his head. "Our instructions were quite specific."

"And what were they?"

Now that Geoffrey was their friend, Jacques was a font of information. "To find the traitor in King David's court we'd heard about and aid him if we could."

"I see," Geoffrey said. "Is it in Philip's mind that if King David were to die, the throne would be vacant but for a three-year-old boy? England needs a strong king, and Philip has as much claim to the English throne as King David does to Aquitaine."

"Exactly," Jacques said.

I thought about taking offense but decided not to. It wasn't as if Philip was wrong; he had *more* right to the throne of England than I had to Aquitaine.

"We did little, in truth," Piers said, with a glance at his more voluble companion.

"If King David were dead, what would be King Philip's next move? Invasion?" Geoffrey said.

"Yes," Jacques said.

Piers gripped his companion's arm and glowered at him. Jacques seemed to think that getting on Geoffrey's good side meant telling him everything in the most confident way possible, whereas Piers wanted to be more circumspect. A smile twitched around Geoffrey's mouth, but he didn't look at me. My eyes bored into his back, and perhaps he could feel them because he rolled his shoulders while the two Frenchmen warred at each other without speaking.

Finally, Piers turned back to Geoffrey. He fisted his hand and beat it into the bar of his cell. "King Philip has two thousand men who will sail on his word."

"When?" Geoffrey said.

"We released the pigeon before we sailed." Piers' upper lip lifted to form a disgruntled sneer. "He's coming now, and nobody can stop him."

"But David isn't dead."

"We told him that we didn't know the outcome for certain. There are factions in Philip's court who support an invasion without regard to the success of Lee's plan. They are loath to rely upon the actions of one Englishman, and believe Philip is strong enough to overcome any opposition."

That, to me, sounded like people were telling Philip what he wanted to hear rather than the truth. But of course, I was biased.

"Where will he land?"

Piers shrugged. "We don't know."

"What about Ireland?" Geoffrey said. "What's King Philip's interest there?"

Piers' brow furrowed. "I don't know. It was Guillaume who spoke with Lee in that regard."

"Guillaume was your leader?" Geoffrey said.

Piers nodded.

The trickle of unease I'd been feeling at the back of my neck turned into a torrent as I recalled that the heretic had departed the castle after the evening meal yesterday. If Lee hadn't left Canterbury until the next morning, the two could have met up again. They could be working together still.

And even if they weren't, Guillaume hadn't come to Dover and connected with his fellow spies, which meant that he, too, was roaming freely around my country. Geoffrey didn't know that, however—and nor did Jacques or Pier—or the conversation might have been headed in a different direction.

Geoffrey said, "I want to speak to Lee. Where is he?"

"I do not know that either," Piers said. "We offered him a place on our ship, but he declined. He said he would make his own way to the French court once his business in England was complete."

I didn't like the sound of that.

"Surely Lee couldn't believe any place in England would be safe for him after what he did," Geoffrey said.

"He told us he'd made his own plans," Piers said. "Besides, with the king dead, who was there to realize what he'd done?"

Piers had a point there. Lee would have murdered me, my immediate family, and half my advisers in one blow. It was only because of Bevyn's arrival that we had known that Lee was dangerous. I felt a curl of satisfaction in my belly. We'd been lucky, but we'd been good too, and sometimes the good made their own luck.

"So you have no idea where he might be now?" Geoffrey said.

"No," Piers said.

The interview was over. I refrained from standing up and calling attention to myself, even though I really wanted to. Carew, if he knew about it, would have been beside me in a flash, whispering wise and calming words in my ear. I let my own sense guide me, however, and didn't move or say anything. If Geoffrey concluded this conversation successfully, without me giving the game away, he could continue to be a spy for me to the French. I wasn't going to blow his cover.

Instead, he blew his own by turning to look at me. "Is there anything else you would like to ask them?"

I'd been watching my feet, and it took a moment for me to realize Geoffrey was talking to me. I looked up, saw his questioning glance, and stood to approach the cell. Geoffrey must have decided there was no danger to himself in revealing who I was and the false pretenses under which he'd questioned the Frenchmen because their lives were forfeit. I supposed he was right. I owed him now, and strangely, I didn't mind the debt. He'd done me a considerable favor today.

"How did you know there was a traitor in the king's household in the first place?" I said.

"Who are you?" Piers said.

"Answer his question, and he will tell you," Geoffrey said in a sharp voice.

Piers gave him a wary look but then answered amicably enough, "We've been hearing rumors about it for months."

"But how did you know his identity?" I said.

"From one of the ladies-in-waiting to the queen," Piers said, and named a woman I might not know to look at, though I'd heard her name. "She befriended the man and passed word to us that he held no love for King David—and that he might be interested in speaking to others who shared his disdain."

I let out a slow breath. I would deal with the woman in due course, but for now ... "We're still talking about Lee, correct?"

Piers brows came together in puzzlement. "Was there someone else?"

That, in itself, was a huge relief. I didn't know if I could handle any more traitors today. "What about his companions, Mike and Noah?"

"They spoke little, and no French at all," Jacques said. "We can tell you nothing about them. They were Lee's companions, whom he'd brought for protection, as if we could be overpowered by any brute." He snorted his derision.

"Were you aware that all three men were from Avalon?" I said.

Jacques scoffed. "A fairy story. There's no such place."

"Isn't there?" I said.

Piers folded his arms across his chest. "I'm not saying any more until you tell me who you are."

"He's your only hope for getting out of here in one piece," Geoffrey said.

"Though I regret to say that the odds of that have become vanishingly small," I said. "Continue to cooperate, and we'll see." I turned towards the door, gesturing that Geoffrey should come with me.

"Tell me your name!" Piers said from behind me.

My hand on the frame of the door, I stopped to look back. I wasn't choosing to tell him because of his insistence, but because of the sheer joy of it, "David Llywelyn Arthur Pendragon, King of England. You may have heard of me."

21

"**I** am in your debt, as I'm sure you know," I said to Geoffrey, who was climbing the steps behind me.

"You are my king."

I stopped myself from commenting that up until today, I wouldn't necessarily have known it from Geoffrey's demeanor. Today, Geoffrey's loyalties had broken my way. It felt like the time Humphrey de Bohun, a sworn enemy, had come to me at midnight and at great danger to himself to ask me to care for his son. Given that William had eventually become my squire—and Humphrey had become an esteemed (if still not entirely trusted) member of my inner circle—that decision had turned out well for him. If Geoffrey continued as he'd started, this would probably turn out well for him too.

Not that I wanted to develop a reputation for being easily charmed. King Stephen, who in the twelfth century fought for his throne against his cousin, Maud, had been so easy-going that he'd paid the wages of the troops his eventual successor, Henry, had led against him. Henry had then gone back to France, his tail between his legs, defeated. And yet, I could see myself doing the same thing because I thought the move quite clever: by defeating Henry militarily *and* paying his men's wages, Stephen had shamed Henry completely. But Henry had become king anyway upon Stephen's death, and Stephen had been reviled by his own barons (and historians) as too chivalrous for his own good. Sometimes a king couldn't win no matter what he did.

Sir Stephen met us at the top of the stairs that led into the bailey, Carew and Ieuan beside him. Quickly, I related what we'd learned from the spies about the coming of King Philip. Stephen listened intently and then hastened away. We'd begun preparations for a possible war, but now it was really happening.

William de Bohun hovered a few feet away, and I nodded at him, indicating that it was all right for him to join us. It was better he do that than for me to have to relate the conversation to him later. The boy longed to be in the center of whatever action was going on at any given moment, and he had shown himself most times to be up to the task.

Then I laid out what Piers had said about Guillaume and their relationship with Acquasparta. When I finished, Carew looked very grave. "What do you want to do about the legate?"

"He must be contained," Geoffrey said, surprising me with his certainty. "The man is ill, but his machinations cannot be allowed to continue."

"I will send two men riding to Callum immediately," Ieuan said.

"Peckham needs to know what has been going on under his nose," Carew said. "I find it astounding that a papal legate could have been involved in a conspiracy to murder you."

"Send me with the riders." William broke into the conversation. "You need someone who can accurately relay to Lord Callum what has happened, and it is too sensitive a matter to put into writing."

I studied the boy, who was no longer a boy, for a minute, and then I nodded. "You should leave within the hour. Come see me in the moments before you go. I may have more instructions for you."

William bowed, his face lit by his new responsibility.

My mood had lifted for the first time since Canterbury Castle had fallen. "Acquasparta will deny any involvement, of course, but we can see the links in the chain now. These Frenchmen are tied to Acquasparta, Philip, and Lee."

"We have leverage against Boniface now." Carew bobbed his chin in agreement. "We will offer to suppress what Acquasparta has done if Boniface gives way on his demands."

"It's too late to stop Philip from coming, if he is coming," Ieuan said.

"So it is," I said. "If he lands successfully and we lose, it will hardly matter what Acquasparta has done. We need to not lose."

"Did you learn what has become of Lee?" Ieuan said.

I gestured to Geoffrey. "Geneville proved himself to be an exemplary questioner, but the Frenchmen do not know where Lee is now—nor Guillaume for that matter."

"They would have told you the truth about that?" Ieuan said, his eye on Geoffrey, of whom he'd always been suspicious. The man was a privileged Norman baron, and his lands in the March had been fought over by Ieuan's ancestors for centuries. I couldn't blame any Welshman for instinctively holding a grudge.

I canted my head to the older man. "I believed them. Did you, Geneville?"

Geoffrey nodded. "I did, sire. It interested me that Lee hadn't intended to sail for France with them. Does that say something about his ties with Ireland? It seems to be a part of the scheme these Frenchmen knew nothing about."

I studied Geoffrey, again regretting the four years I'd spent holding this man at arm's length. He was observant and had asked the right questions down there. He'd just hung two men out to dry who could have been his allies, and done it with skillful subterfuge. No matter how well I mastered a poker face—which probably wasn't ever going to happen, though I was going to keep trying—I was never going to be that good. "If Lee had meant to flee England, there was no better time than this morning."

"Instead, he stayed in Canterbury until he learned the outcome of the explosion," Carew said.

"Maybe he knew something they didn't, since we caught the Frenchmen," Ieuan said.

Carew looked thoughtful. "I can't see Lee having the reach to have warned the coastal patrol about the Frenchmen's existence. Nor would I have thought he'd have a reason to do so, unless his plan was to find a different way to France, one more secret, in hopes of currying favor with King Philip without the spies' interference."

"Pardon me, my lord, but I don't think that's it," William said. "My gut tells me that Lee is still here, in England, planning some new devilry. He could have followed us to Dover and be here even now, watching."

As one, our eyes went to the battlements. When we brought our heads down again, all but Geoffrey, who was looking at us with something approaching consternation, laughed at our mutual paranoia.

"Trust the boy to go right to the heart of our troubles," Carew said.

"I'm not even going to ask why Lee would choose to come here," I said. "His reasoning is beyond me."

"To finish what he started, sire," William said.

"If what Bohun says is true, you should not be standing here so exposed, sire," Geoffrey said. "If murder is Lee's aim, he could try again. Sometimes one man has more capacity to cause great harm than an entire company of soldiers."

"Thus we saw in Canterbury." Ieuan gave Geoffrey a slight bow. "Geneville is right, sire. That cannot be allowed to happen.

Besides, it's growing late. We're all dead on our feet. We must rest."

William put his heels together, preparing to depart our little circle. "If I may suggest an additional course of action, sire, the guards at all the gates and on the walls should be doubled. What's more, anyone or anything moving in or out should be carefully inspected."

Ieuan frowned. "I should have ordered it done the moment we arrived." He didn't wait for me to approve William's plan but pointed at my squire. "Leave this to me."

William bowed and departed.

I suddenly felt a little nauseous, and it wasn't only because I was tired and had spent the day with too little food and less sleep. I could easily see Lee sneaking into Dover—without even having to sneak, if he came in on the tail end of a party of workers or in a hay wagon. The man was clearly well-versed in the customs of medieval English society. He could have figured something out.

And Dover Castle was unreasonably huge. It had inner, middle, and outer wards large enough to encompass many football fields. The walls were lined with towers, and the inner ward could have fit Canterbury Castle inside it and then some. The way the stones loomed up around me gave me the feeling of being both safe and exposed at the same time, now that I knew how incredibly vulnerable we were to a single man's evil plan. Standing in the bailey, the sun warm on my back, I bent my head.

Geoffrey had been watching me, and now he frowned, emphasizing the wrinkles on his prominent forehead and reminding me again of his age and his long relationship with the Crown. "We will keep you safe, sire."

I looked at him carefully and then gestured with one hand that he should continue. Something about the way he'd spoken had me thinking that he had more to say. I didn't want to press him, but I needed to know what it was.

Geoffrey breathed in deeply through his nose. "We need more men—today. We need to be prepared beyond the doubling of the guard."

"The men of Dover have been on alert since this morning," Ieuan said, "but Sir Stephen should speak to the Portsman again. He could start marshalling every available man tonight, or at the very least, make clear to everyone the high alert and the possible threat—not only from France, but from a traitor."

"I agree, my lord," Geoffrey said. "If you wish, I will see to it."

"I would be grateful," I said, and meant it.

Geoffrey bowed. "Of course."

Ieuan looked at me. "Food and sleep for you, sire. Then we need to arrange for armor for you. You cannot go about without it for even another hour."

I rolled my shoulders, already feeling the weight of the mail Ieuan would put on me. I was used to it, but that didn't mean I missed it. "Someone else's armor, you mean," I said, resigned to at least an hour in the armory to find something that fit me. Given my height and weight, the choices would be limited. My armor had been crafted for me personally. It fit perfectly and allowed me full freedom of movement. Anything borrowed from the armory at Dover was bound to chafe.

"We will get yours back," Ieuan said. He knew about the Kevlar I wore as an extra layer of protection, and how naked I'd come to feel when I didn't wear it. Wearing it also gave Lili peace of mind and meant she was less likely to worry about my misadventures. It was easier to convince her I would come to no harm with it on. "At least you have your sword."

"I have more than my sword," I replied, shaking off my melancholy once again. I clapped Ieuan on the shoulder. "We are alive. For the moment, that is all that matters. We can worry about our possessions another day. Do with me as you wish. I won't complain."

I had to focus on what would move us forward, but I hadn't even seen my son yet. The sun had disappeared below the western horizon, meaning it might be Arthur's bedtime soon. Perhaps I could go to sleep with him, crisis or no crisis. I didn't need Ieuan to tell me that I would be no good to anyone if I didn't rest.

Then I felt a gentle hand on my shoulder and turned to see my wife looking up at me. She'd come all the way from the hall in the inner bailey to find me. "You are asleep on your feet, and I imagine you haven't eaten a bite since Canterbury. Whatever you're doing can surely wait until morning, can't it?"

I thought back over the last twelve hours and acknowledged that the bread and cheese I'd hastily consumed beside my horse in the courtyard of the Archbishop's palace was the last thing I'd eaten, though I'd drunk water on the road.

I caught the nod Ieuan directed at his sister and knew I was being managed, but honestly, I was grateful for it. Arm in arm, Lili and I crunched across the outer ward to the interior gatehouse. Gravel had been mined in southern England since Roman times, and the builders of Dover Castle had taken advantage of the proximity of the mines to cover the castle grounds with loose stones. Given all the rain that had fallen this summer, without the stones we'd have been ankle-deep in mud.

Once in the inner ward, we headed for the king's apartments, which Lili had taken for her own. We always slept in the same bed, so she generally left the queen's apartments for other nobles. Bronwen looked up as we entered our sitting room, where she was minding Catrin and Arthur. "I sent the nannies away," she said before Lili could ask. "They needed sleep, just like the rest of us. Catrin will sleep with Ieuan and me tonight." Bronwen had a fierce look on her face. As if anyone was going to argue with her about that.

I stretched. "I should find Jeeves."

"He is already preparing a bath for you," Lili said, indicating how confident she'd been that she could get me to do what she wanted. "Somewhere around here are clean clothes he rustled up for you too."

"Maybe Edward left something that will fit me." I laughed at the thought of wearing the dead king's clothes. He'd be rolling over in his grave.

"Hey." I ruffled Arthur's hair and then pulled him into my lap, where he curled up with his head on my chest. "How was the ride with Mommy?"

"He slept the whole way," Lili said before Arthur could answer.

"I did not!" Arthur sat up, all indignant. "I was keeping watch."

"I'm sure you were." I hugged him and smiled at Lili over the top of his head. He wiggled to get down to continue his game with Catrin, which appeared to involve a complicated arrangement of beads and cups, like a medieval version of mancala.

"You need to tell me everything that has happened since we left you," Bronwen said. "While I appreciate you bringing my husband back to me, I would rather not see him if it means you have neither found Lee nor managed to escape the pope's clutches."

"I've done neither," I said. "I hope we haven't simply brought danger to Dover rather than leaving it at Canterbury."

"Do you think Lee would follow you here?" Bronwen said.

"It is something to fear," Ieuan said from behind me. He entered the room and closed the door, coming towards his wife and leaning down to kiss the top of her head. They clasped hands briefly. "The castle is locked down tightly."

"One man shouldn't be able to pose such a threat," Lili said.

"Unless that man has a bag of C-4 and knows how to use it," I said.

"How much could he have left?" Bronwen said. "Canterbury Castle is in ruins. You don't do that with seven or eight pounds."

"According to Callum, twenty pounds, set in the right places, was all he needed," I said.

Bronwen pursed her lips. "The right places being the toilets on two of the levels. With those walls blown out, the upper floors were unsupported and came crashing down."

"That is how it appears," I said.

"Did he actually crawl into those latrine shafts?" Lili made a face. Regardless of latrine cleaner Tom's love of his job, cleaning the latrines was still viewed by most as the worst form of employment in a busy castle, and you didn't have to be modern to think so.

"It seems so." I sat heavily in a chair near where Arthur and Catrin were playing. A tray of fruit, cold meats, and cheese lay on the table beside me, and I began to eat, too tired to really taste the food but knowing I needed it.

Lili's hands found the knots in both of my shoulders and began to work them. My head sagged forward. I might even have fallen asleep.

A gentle knock came at the door and at Lili's 'enter', William poked his head inside. "Lord Callum sends word that he is on his way."

"Bad news?" Lili said.

William made a very French moue with his lips. "They tracked Lee to a stable where he'd paid to house a horse he bought the day we arrived at Canterbury. He told the stableman that he was returning to London at dawn today."

"Which means he was really riding east." Lili gave my shoulders a squeeze.

"Should I still go to Canterbury, sire?" William said.

"Yes. Peckham needs to know what Acquasparta has done. Hopefully, you will meet Callum on the road, and the two of you can confer before you continue on to Canterbury."

William bowed. "You can depend on me, sire."

"I know." What could be done for Canterbury was in motion, and until Lee showed his face, we could do little more for Dover. What I hadn't done was what I needed, which was to sleep, if I was to be ready for whatever King Philip of France—and possibly Lee—might throw at me tomorrow.

22

An earthshattering bang followed by screams beyond the room's windows had me leaping from the bed and striding to the window. It had been dark by the time I'd gone to sleep, and it was plain I'd slept many hours because dawn had come and gone. Our room was located on a high floor within the great keep, giving us a marvelous view of the sea, the rest of the castle—and the remains of a building in the outer ward that was wafting past on the sea air, sending choking smoke and dust into the air.

"What is it, Dafydd?" Lili sat up in bed, wiping at her eyes.

"Another explosion. Some craft huts to the right of the main gatehouse, I think." I spoke matter-of-factly, trying to orient myself and to remember the arrangement of the outer ward. The evening before, after Geoffrey had questioned the Frenchmen, we'd talked in the courtyard near the gatehouse. That cluster of huts had seen many comings and goings in that time. I seemed to recall a candle-maker working there, and perhaps the castle potter.

Now that I knew Lee was here, I felt strangely calm, and my heart rate was starting to slow from the gallop that had resulted from being woken so suddenly.

Leaving the window, I scooped up Arthur, who'd woken too, and went to the door.

It burst open before I could reach it, and Callum bounded into the room. "This has to be Lee," he said.

Setting Arthur down on the bed, I quickly gathered up my discarded clothing from last night. "I'd say so too."

"Cassie is here as well?" Lili swung her legs out of bed and grabbed a dress that had been draped over an adjacent chair. Like all of us who'd come from Canterbury, she'd had to borrow clothing from others; all her richly appointed gowns were gone. She'd slept in a plain linen long-sleeve underdress and now just had to drop the long blue tunic over her head to be dressed.

"We came here together once we knew Lee had left Canterbury." Callum tipped his head towards the window. "She's hopefully on the wall-walk above the middle ward, trying to spot Lee." He fisted one hand and pounded it into his thigh in a gesture of frustration. "I feared Lee had followed you and felt that my place was at your side."

"He did follow me, so you were right," I said. "We locked down the castle last night, but apparently it wasn't enough."

"Or it was too little too late." Bronwen brushed past Callum, Catrin in her arms. Ieuan followed, already fully dressed. Lili and I had slept through the dawn, but we looked to be the only

- 245 -

ones who had. Nobody seemed to care that we weren't dressed, but then, we were family, and this was an emergency. I loved them all the more for how little they cared about my sensibilities.

"Which would be my fault since I was here first and should have been thinking about being followed." Lili picked up Arthur, and he put his face into her neck, his small arms wrapped around her tightly. "Still, you would think that if Lee could have attacked us in here he would have."

"I had the same thought," Callum said. "That's why he blew up a few huts and not the whole keep—because he couldn't get inside the inner ward. This explosion is designed to flush you out."

I stopped in the act of tugging on my right boot. "If the movies I've watched are at all accurate, if I were the President of the United States, this kind of threat would call for my removal from the situation. The Secret Service would get me into the emergency bunker at the White House or maybe into a helicopter to take me to Air Force One. Lee would know that. Perhaps I'm better off staying put."

Justin appeared at Callum's left shoulder. "There is a passage through the catacombs that can take us out of the castle."

I looked at Callum, who pressed his lips together, thinking. Then he said, "Follow my logic: I take it as a given that the explosion was caused by Lee. Thus, he is inside the castle. If he is inside the castle, he knows that you are here."

"How?" said Bronwen.

"A question or two to a serving girl could have told him that," Callum said, "and he has proved himself adept at getting information."

"My flag isn't flying," I said, "but it's a weak attempt at secrecy at best. We didn't tell the inhabitants of the castle to keep my presence a secret, and even if we had, I rode here in broad daylight. The entire town of Dover knows by now that I am here."

Callum nodded. "Thus, if Lee came to Dover, he knows too."

Impatient with our conversation, Justin gestured to indicate I should enter the corridor. "The entrance is this way." He was practically dancing on the tips of his toes in his urgency to get us moving.

Callum overrode him. "Alternatively, rather than draw you out, Lee could be using this explosion as a distraction so he can get inside the keep. Men should be pouring towards the destruction, which might give him the opportunity he needs to go the other way."

"He could be on his way here even now," Justin said.

I took in a breath and let it out. "Okay." I still had my reservations, but I let Justin hustle us into the corridor and along it to the stairs. "I'm not sure about the catacombs, though, Justin. That's where he'd expect us to go, isn't it? We should go up."

"It's human instinct to go up," Callum said, keeping pace beside me. "Justin is right that we need to go down."

"There is no 'up' anyway." Lili touched my arm briefly before returning her hand to Arthur's back. I would have taken Arthur from her since he was so heavy, but he was wrapped around her like a four-armed octopus. "The keep isn't connected to the battlements. We'd be stuck on the roof with nowhere to run."

"Maybe it isn't Lee." Ieuan had come up behind us, Catrin on his back, piggy-back style. She'd be four years old in November and was bigger than Arthur.

"I don't know Lee well, but it's him," Bronwen said. "Two explosions within twenty-four hours at castles where David is staying can't be coincidence. It's him."

So we did as Justin suggested and went down. We did take the precaution of not exiting through the main hall on the first floor but, as when we fled Canterbury, went down another floor to the basement. There I stopped everyone again.

"Okay," I said. "Let's think. I don't want to go out there and join the throng in the inner ward without a thought about what we're walking into. What does Lee want?"

"He wants you dead, sire," Justin said without hesitation.

I shook my head, but Lili said, "That does seem to be the case." She held her hand over Arthur's exposed ear, not that he could help hearing us. He was learning a very hard lesson with every word his parents spoke.

"Lee cannot be alive at the end of the day," Justin said.

I glanced at Justin, disturbed at where his mind had gone but unable to blame him for it either. "I don't disagree, but that's getting ahead of ourselves since we have to catch him first. Given that he has only blown up a small building in the outer ward so far—"

"—I can't believe you just used the word 'only' in this context," Bronwen said.

I smirked at her, grateful for the touch of levity at this stressful moment. "I assume he's planning something specific, which he hasn't yet accomplished, and is still here. The whole purpose of this bombing has to be because he can't get to me any other way. It's either a distraction so he can get inside the inner ward, or he wants me to come out the gate and walk straight into his arms."

"He could have blown a hole through the wall here like he did at Canterbury," Ieuan said. "That would have been the fastest way to get to you."

"Only if he could then get through the hole," Lili said. "He wants to be certain he gets Dafydd this time, which means he has a plan he thinks will work."

"Because he knows me," I said.

"It's more than that." Bronwen was looking down at her feet as she thought. Then she glanced at Callum. "I'm no expert on explosives, but I saw what happened to Canterbury. This explosion was nothing compared to that. What if he *couldn't* blow a hole in the wall?"

Callum's eyes narrowed as he thought. "Are you thinking he's out of explosives, or at the very least, out of detonators?"

Ieuan looked from Callum to me. "I'm not sure I understand."

"If that's true," I said to Callum without answering Ieuan's question, "and he fails to draw me out, he could disappear in the crowds here, to appear a hundred miles away with a new plan and new way to harm us. We can't take that chance. We can't allow him to get away."

"Those of your men who guard the walls and the gatehouses know what he looks like because they've seen him," Bronwen said, "but nobody else in the castle does. A quick disguise, slipping out in all the commotion, and he could disappear with nobody the wiser."

Lili's face was paler than usual. "He has a gun, too, don't you think?"

"Yes." Callum's hand made a reflexive jerk to the small of his back. "We should assume it. I have one too, as does Jeffries, but—"

"We don't want to go there," I said, "not unless we have to."

"It does make the need to hide you all the more urgent," Bronwen said.

"The Welsh guards have taken over one of the towers near the Fitzwilliam gate," Lili said. "David and I could go there."

"You just want to get your hands on a bow," I said.

"It's the only counter to a gun that I know, other than another gun," Lili said.

"It isn't safe, Dafydd," Ieuan said. "We have no way to get you there without being seen."

I put up a hand to Ieuan. Lili was his little sister, so he'd spent all of her life telling her what to do, but I needed to hear what she had to say. "If he really has blown up those buildings to draw me out, he must have a plan as to what to do with me once he has me. Any public harm to me and he ends up dead too. He is inside Dover Castle, surrounded by soldiers."

"I know," Lili said.

"I can see from your eyes that there's more to this than you've said so far," I said. "What's the rest of your thought, Lili?"

She lifted her eyes to the ceiling and took in a breath. "At worst, you can escape Dover by going back to Avalon."

"What?" Ieuan said.

"What are you saying, Lili?" Bronwen said.

"Dover doesn't have moats so much as dry ditches," Lili said, "dug deep to increase the height of the wall above. I asked Sir Stephen how water could remain in a ditch that was so high up a cliff, and he explained that in all the years he's been Dover's constable, he's never seen more than an ankle-deep amount of water in the wettest of them. But we've had so much rain this summer, many aren't draining as they usually do."

If I went back in time, it affected everyone, and our son especially. That she still held Arthur, knowing that he was listening to every word, meant to me that she was not only serious, but perhaps even right. "The particular spot I'm thinking of is right next to the tower where the archers are staying, and it's slightly deeper than the rest of the ditch. Yesterday there was three feet of water in it. It rained all night, so there's probably more now. Beneath that is the same mud and grass that's everywhere else. It isn't the Wye River, but the wall is only twenty feet high along that section. Dafydd could use it, if he had to."

I put a hand on Arthur's back and leaned close. "Show me."

Lili passed Arthur to Bronwen, who took him in her arms. He wrapped his legs around her waist and his arms around her neck in the same position as he'd been holding onto his mother.

I kissed Arthur's cheek. "We'll be back. Stay with your auntie." There was no talk this time about being brave or behaving like a man. What was important was that my three-year-old son knew he was loved by everyone in his life, and that he was safe. Except for a few brief interludes, Ieuan, Bronwen, and Catrin had lived with us since his birth. Bronwen was like a second mother to him, and Catrin more like a sister than a cousin.

Arthur nodded into Bronwen's shoulder. Ieuan still held Catrin, and the four of them stood stricken, looking after us as we left the basement for the inner ward. Justin hurried to take his place beside me. "I can't let you expose yourself like this, my lord."

"You can, and you will," I said.

Callum's silence I took to be approval—neither enthusiastic nor grudging, but with the same sentiment that was passing through my head: if Lili was right, than getting to the tower where the archers had stored their gear was a better place than any other to hide me. Her idea was good enough to try, even if none of us were happy about the Avalon part of it.

Justin made a choking sound. "Sire—" But at my calm look, he subsided and bowed his head. "I will keep you safe, if it's possible to do so."

"I know," I said. "That's why I'm willing to risk this."

Dover Castle was a busy place—a town in and of itself—and between the normal state of affairs and the explosion near the gatehouse, nobody took any notice when the four of us emerged from the basement into the inner ward. As had been the case since I arrived, I was dressed inconspicuously in clothes that were clean this time, but not my usual wardrobe. As it turned out, King Edward hadn't left any finery at Dover, and we'd had to borrow from a member of the garrison yet again.

We were well into mid-morning now, as Lili and I really had slept quite late. While it wasn't raining at the moment, the day was overcast, and many puddles several feet across remained in the courtyard from rain during the night. As Sir Stephen had implied to Lili, it had rained so often this summer the ground was saturated.

"I need to see what's what first," I said.

"Sire—" Justin was set to protest again, but I ignored him and mounted the stairs to the battlement on the inner curtain wall and looked out. The dust was settling and something had caught fire again, near the main gate where the two Frenchmen were being housed. The curtain wall which abutted the destroyed buildings had been damaged too, though it was still standing in parts.

Justin gave a snort of disgust. "I see now. The explosion was a diversion so Lee could free those French spies."

"You could be right," Lili said, "or we could be meant to think so. Maybe, like Bronwen suggested, the explosion didn't go off quite as Lee had hoped. Maybe he meant to blow a hole in the wall."

"He came close enough that it might not matter." I looked at her carefully. She was unusually determined today, which was saying something for her. "Is there anything else I should know?"

"It's going to be okay," she said without looking at me.

She didn't often talk about the premonitions she had—she was self-conscious about not being believed—but what other people called gut instinct came out as something akin to the *sight* in Lili. I'd learned to trust the few occasions when she'd made clear that a certain course of action should be followed.

Cassie waved to us from the tower above the gatehouse. Callum put up a hand to her. She seemed to want to talk, and I could see him warring with himself because of his obligation to me. I pushed at Callum's shoulder. "Go. Find out what she knows." Callum dashed away along the wall-walk.

"Where's this tower?" Justin said.

"I'll show you," Lili said.

We had to leave the inner ward, which had Justin grumbling again as he jogged down the stairs to the ground and then across the inner ward to the southern gate. We had to go through it to reach the middle ward. The outer ward was an enclosed area beyond that one, and its walls went all the way to the edge of the cliff above the beach, a full quarter-mile from the keep.

The gate wasn't closed, but the drawbridge had been lifted a few feet up from the ground to prevent anyone from entering. People were streaming out of the northern gate that led to the main entrance to the castle (and the northern part of the outer ward). They might be gawking, but they also wanted to help put out the fire. It *had* to be put out as quickly as possible, for the same reason we'd put so much effort into putting out the fire at Canterbury Castle. Fire could spread, and without sophisticated fire-fighting equipment, it could destroy a castle nearly as easily as Lee's C-4.

The guards were preventing anyone from returning to the keep, however, even though I could see several people gesticulating to them about how important it was that they do so. The security measures we'd instituted before I'd gone to sleep were still being followed. With the outer ward on fire, it should have been obvious that the measures needed to remain in place, but I acknowledged that what was obvious to me might not be to a medieval person who'd never before dealt with a terrorist such as Lee.

We skirted a crate that had been discarded on the ground in someone's haste, and then we reached the southern gatehouse. "Let us out," I said to the guard.

"My orders are clear." His eyes flicked to Justin's face. "Nobody in or out of this gate."

Justin stepped closer. "I was the one who gave you that order, wasn't I?"

The guard put his heels together. "Yes, sir!"

If I wasn't in such a hurry, I would have found this funny. The guard thought Justin was testing him.

"I honor your commitment to duty, Osmond," Justin said, "but I didn't mean that you shouldn't obey the king."

23

The guard's expression turned to horror. He sputtered, gaping at me, and I clapped him on the shoulder to reassure him. Justin, for all his reservations about this plan, didn't wait for the guard to act. He grabbed the wheel, around which was wound the chain that held the wooden drawbridge, and released it. The drawbridge dropped to the ground with a sudden bang, and we ran across the bridge into the middle ward. I turned back and made a winding motion with my hand. "Bring it up!"

The guard, still wide-eyed, hastened to obey. Callum hadn't caught up yet, but I knew he could talk his way past the guard, or simply exit by the other gate and come around the long way. Then I ran after Lili, who was making for a tower that lay kitty corner to the gatehouse and southeast of the Fitzwilliam gate, which was the northeastern exit from the castle. Here the curtain wall made an inward jag before heading south to the white cliffs above the sea.

All told, the outer walls of Dover Castle encompassed so many acres that nearly four football fields laid end to end could fit between the inner curtain wall and the sea. Watch towers, which gave shelter to the guards and access to the wall-walk, were placed every fifty yards or so along the curtain wall. Many ladders were also propped up against the edge of the walkway for easy access to the battlement.

As agile as ever, even though she was pregnant, Lili took a ladder up to the wall-walk, and I followed. Once I reached the top, however, I pulled up, a tendril of unease curling in my belly. The distance to the ground might be twenty feet on the inside of the wall to the bailey, but it was higher than that to the bottom of the ditch outside the wall. Very few people could survive a fall from that height unless they fell into a body of water. For distances greater than a hundred feet, water acted like concrete—you'd hit the surface with an almighty *splat* and break every bone in your body.

"This way," Lili said, pretending she didn't see my dour expression and turning to run along the wall-walk. After a few steps, however, she halted with a gasp.

Lee himself stepped out of the doorway to the tower we'd been aiming for, his ever-present duffel bag strung over his shoulder. Whatever vision she'd had of the way events were going to go, Lee's sudden appearance apparently wasn't a part of it. Shock crossed Lee's face too, and since my breath had caught in my throat, I doubted I had been able to control the surprise in mine.

Then Lee dropped the duffel back to the wall-walk, reached behind him to the small of his back, and pulled out a gun.

He pointed it at me. "Tell everyone to get off the wall." Then, as if the gun wasn't bad enough, he raised his left hand to show me the trigger remote he held.

I spoke to Lili in Welsh. "Get away, *cariad*. Find Callum. Find the explosives. I will stall him as long as I can. I love you. Go."

She obeyed instantly, backing up and ducking under my arm. I glanced back to see her shooing Justin back down the ladder. In a moment Lee and I were alone on the wall-walk.

I turned back to Lee. "Hello. You've been busy." Now that the worst-case scenario was underway, I felt calm. It was almost a relief to face it rather than waiting around as we had been for the other shoe to drop.

The shock on Lee's face had turned to a sneer. It was a look I'd seen before, but not often and never directed at me. I'd been blind to his faults, taking his cynicism and snide comments as a sign of intelligence and wit. He'd amused me, and I'd enjoyed his company. But in that look, I saw him for who and what he really was.

"I have done what was necessary."

My son would have called him a bad man, with the clarity that only a three-year-old child can muster. Perhaps ardent Irish nationalists would have excused his behavior, but he'd tried to kill several hundred people. He was a terrorist. It would be wrong to sugarcoat the truth, even if he thought of himself as a freedom fighter.

He also didn't look good. In fact, he looked terrible. His face was flushed, but at the same time a bit greenish, and he was definitely limping. I'd have to ask Rachel, but my guess was that he was suffering from blood poisoning from his infected toe.

"What happened to you?" I said.

"Nothing." Lee's eyes flicked this way and that, looking for a way out that wasn't there. He sidled sideways, putting his back to the parapet, so he could see both me and the entrance to the tower. He kept the gun trained on my chest. Callum would have known the type and caliber of the gun. All I knew was that it was big.

I was honestly more interested in what was in his other hand. Lee saw my eyes go to the remote, and a gruesome smile appeared on his face. He held the thing up to show me. "Yes, you see that right. If someone tries to stab me in the back or shoot me with an arrow, I release the trigger and the whole tower goes up."

Except for a few flicks of my eyes, I kept my gaze steady on Lee's face, resolutely ignoring the activity developing in the bailey. A crowd had formed in the ward below us. Even if the guard at the gate out of the inner ward hadn't recognized me at first, I was the King of England, and it was midmorning.

"Come here." Lee motioned with the gun.

I didn't move.

Lee fired a round at my feet. The bullet sparked off the stones and ricocheted past me. I was really glad nobody was behind me to get hit.

"The next one will be in your leg. You don't have to be healthy to take me home."

So it was Avalon he wanted now, not surprisingly since he had to know that without modern medical treatment, he would die. I didn't want to go to Avalon and so decided to stall. "I thought you didn't want to go home."

"Are you saying you'll give me free passage out of Dover?"

He correctly read the denial on my face.

"Right. Come here. I won't ask a third time."

I took a single step towards him. I hoped that Lili had found Callum, and that even now he was tearing apart the tower, looking for the C-4. It would have been helpful if the gift of time travel had included telepathy. "Why are you doing this?"

Lee's lip curled. "Did you actually expect me to be *grateful*? Do you know what it has been like for me, listening to those fools at court every day, self-righteous and sanctimonious blowhards, pontificating about this policy or that policy, right and wrong, your vision for England. It just about killed me. My God, if they would just *shut up*! How could you stand to listen to them when you have the power to do anything you want? You could change the world!"

"I am changing the world."

He laughed. "Right. Just like I am."

His surety was real, that was clear. He was talking about my friends and the people I ruled. What he called sanctimonious, I called sincere. These people *cared* about England. They could be selfish and arrogant, like any of us, but this was the only world they had. And it was my job—they had given me the job—of ruling them. Lee's words made clear to me that he'd lied and manipulated his way through the Middle Ages without ever making an attempt to understand it.

"You want to free Ireland from outside rule," I said.

"You would have done the same for Wales," he said.

"I did do the same for Wales," I said, "but I am not your enemy. You should have asked if I had a plan for Ireland. It never occurred to you to ask?"

Lee scoffed. "Money from Ireland feeds your coffers. You would never have let it go. The only choice is to depose you and bring in someone else—someone who has no vested interest in Ireland."

"Who?"

He laughed. "You don't know?"

I jerked my head, impatient with his mockery. "Philip."

"Philip is coming." Lee glanced to his left.

"You wanted to blow a hole in the castle."

"Two holes, actually." His brow furrowed. "The first one didn't go off quite like I wanted, but this one ..."

I didn't follow Lee's gaze. If he succeeded in destroying the wall here, he would make Dover indefensible and give Philip an opportunity to take the castle when he came.

Lee took a step towards me, tension radiating from every line in his body. "You've been blind to what was right under your nose."

"Crowning Philip as King of England won't change anything," I said. "The barons aren't going to give up Ireland easily—not for me, and certainly not for a French king." Nor would they give up the crown of England to Philip, but Lee obviously hadn't considered that. I worried again about the loyalty of my barons.

"Philip promised me he'd force your barons out of Ireland," Lee said.

"And you believed him?" I couldn't keep the incredulity out of my voice. I'd spent the last ten years playing politics in the Middle Ages, and I'd learned a thing or two in that time.

Lee's expression turned fierce. "After Canterbury, you think I couldn't make him? Do you think any king would be foolish enough to not keep his promises to me?"

I thought threatening the King of France, especially Philip, was a good recipe for ending up dead. It surprised me how much Lee didn't understand. The rules he blithely violated in the modern world didn't exist here. Philip would think nothing of having him murdered. Lee had taken my way of doing things as the way things were done, instead of seeing me for the outlier I was.

He'd allowed his single-minded hatred of all things English to blind him to what was right in front of him. And with that, I wasn't angry with him anymore. I had no interest in anything so pedestrian as revenge because he wasn't worth the emotion. He needed to be stopped, and I would stop him if I could, but I didn't feel anything for him but pity.

I didn't allow a hint of what I was thinking to appear on my face, however. The tension in my chest was almost unbearable. I couldn't talk him out of blowing up this wall, not with the disdain he held for me and everyone I cared about. I had kept him talking to give Callum and the others time to find the C-4, but Lee motioned with his gun one more time, and I couldn't put him off any longer. Another two steps, and I reached him.

But now he had a problem. He knew the story of how Marty had fallen to his death at Rhuddlan Castle, trying to force my mom and my sister to take him back to Avalon. Lee needed to hold onto me, but his hands were full. Then, to my horror, with his teeth he ripped off the safety ring for the trigger and thrust the remote into my hand. "You'd better hold on to this."

Wide-eyed, I clutched it, hardly noticing that he'd grabbed me around the shoulders and pressed the gun into the small of my back.

"You will jump now, or you will die. The only way to stop the bomb from going off is for you to take the trigger to Avalon."

"My men have probably already found the C-4."

"All of it?" Lee nudged me in the back with the gun, and I was truly out of time.

I eyed the crenellation beside me. No wooden catwalk extended out over the ditch here, which is why Lili had thought this might be the ideal place to do exactly what Lee wanted me to do. I edged to the left and took a quick look down. The wall itself was a good twenty feet up, plus another fifteen at least to the water in the ditch. I'd jumped a far greater distance off the rooftop of the hospital in Cardiff when I'd come home without Cassie and Callum. That didn't make me feel any better about doing it again. Or more convinced that the time travel thing would work one more time.

I really didn't want to go back to Avalon today. I had too much to do.

It was some comfort that Lee didn't know my history with going back and forth to Avalon. A *flash* accompanied every entry and exit. If someone was paying attention, we'd be caught quickly. Lee wouldn't face justice for the murder of Noah and Mike and for the destruction of two castles, but he might face justice for the bombings in Cardiff.

What's more, he would no longer be screwing up my life in the Middle Ages. I would face some music too, but I'd been there before and would figure it out, even without Callum and Cassie as allies.

And then it occurred to me that Lee might just shoot me once we arrived safely.

Thinking of Marty, Mom, and Anna, I put my free hand on the battlement and hoisted myself up into a crenellation. Lee was right that if I went to Avalon, the signal from the remote would cut out before it instigated the explosion. I could save all of us in one go. It didn't mean I had to take him with me, however, and in my head I ran through some possible one-handed moves that would shake him off me. Unfortunately, the gun constituted something of a problem. I didn't want to get shot—either here or in Avalon. And I didn't want Lee to shoot someone else if I went and he stayed behind.

And if I didn't make it to Avalon ... well, I'd cross that bridge when I got to it. I would have the whole way down to the ditch to think about it. In other words, I'd have one second. I gripped the remote even more tightly.

Lee looped his fingers through the belt at my waist, having switched the gun from his right hand to his left so he could hold on to me with his stronger hand. I leaned outward over the ditch, drawing him closer to the parapet. Lee put one booted foot up in the crenellation and then heaved himself into it. It was time. I was heftier than he was, and all I had to do was step off to bring him with me.

Which I did.

The instant I let go of the stones, however, I twisted in midair, so that my right elbow drove into the barrel of the gun at my back. My elbow hit his wrist, dislodging the gun, and I reached with my free hand to grapple with him for both the gun and for my freedom. I couldn't see anything, however, because within a millisecond of jumping, we'd entered the great yawning blackness.

It lasted forever, as it always did. Somewhere in the blackness, I dropped the remote I'd been holding and used that hand to grasp Lee's wrist while my other hand clutched at the gun itself, struggling to keep it pointed upward and away from me.

Then, still falling, we came out of the blackness into broad sunshine. Lee's face was inches from mine. He held the gun double-handed, a finger on the trigger.

The gun went off.

Pain surged through my left hand where the fingers held the barrel, and I let go. I heard a second shot, echoing around me almost like an afterthought, and then I must have blacked out for a second.

Time stood still. Right before it speeded up.

24

I hit the water feet first, thudded down to the bottom of the ditch a half-second later, and fell sideways with a splash into the murky water. My head went under. Happy to be alive, I was glad for the cushioning effect of the water. Still, I hadn't actually hit that hard, and my feet found purchase on the solid ground beneath the mud and grass. I came up with a surge of strength. The only physical effect of my fall seemed to be that the wind had been knocked out of me a bit. That and I was soaked in muddy ditch water from head to foot.

I put a hand to my chest, feeling an ache there as I coughed and sputtered. Water streamed from my hair into my eyes, and I brushed it away, along with some blades of grass that had adhered to my forehead. I couldn't have blacked out for more than a few seconds, if that.

I stared up to where the tower still showed against the sky.

The tower still showed against the sky.

I was still in the Middle Ages.

The wall hadn't blown up.

I hadn't time traveled.

I was both relieved by the thought and completely terrified. It hadn't worked. Just when I thought I had the whole world-shifting thing figured out, it went and threw a wrench into the works.

Whatever 'it' was.

Memory came rushing back. "Lee." I began to move through the water, searching underneath the surface with my hands and feet for a sign of him. It was impossible to see anything in the turbid water. If he'd fallen harder than I had, he could have passed out and be drowning. While that end might be better than the hanging he was going to get if he was alive, I still didn't want him to end his life in a muddy ditch.

A crowd of people, led by Justin and Lili, burst through the nearby Fitzwilliam gate and ran along the rampart above the ditch to where I stood waist deep in the water. Lili came slipping and sliding down the embankment and flung herself into my arms. "You're all right! Thanks be to God, you're all right!"

I hugged her, throwing off the anxiety that had briefly consumed me, and laughed. "That so totally didn't work like I planned." I glanced upwards again to the tower. "I'm lucky to be alive."

Lili looked to the top of the battlement too and took in an audible breath. It had been a long way to fall, especially looking at it from down here. "Justin and I were watching from the top of the gatehouse. I never want to see anything like that again."

"My lord!" Ieuan elbowed his way through the crowd to stand at the top of the rampart beside Justin. "I saw it all—" His eyes were wide and staring.

"I'm okay, Ieuan," I said. "I'm okay."

"How did you do that?" he said.

"Do what?"

Following his sister down the embankment, somewhat less gracefully in his heavy boots, Ieuan slipped and slid until he came to rest in a squat just above the level of the water. Lili and I were sopping wet, of course, but he managed to keep all but the toes of his boots dry. "I'd never seen the traveling from the afar before."

"What do you mean?" I said. "I didn't travel. It didn't work."

"Dafydd," Lili said. "It did work. You disappeared and came back."

"I did?"

"You disappeared halfway down and then reappeared about a foot above the water," Ieuan said.

Lili looked stricken and gestured helplessly with one hand. "Lee didn't return with you."

It was like I'd been punched in the gut. I believed her because she couldn't be mistaken about something like that. I hadn't been able to find Lee because he wasn't here. I finally noticed the great welts across the end of my left thumb and two fingers. They'd been burned by the barrel of the gun when it had fired.

"He fired the gun at me, and instead of dying, I came home." I could hear the wonder in my own voice. "Coming back here saved my life."

I'd jumped from the roof of the hospital in Cardiff in complete belief that I would end up back in the Middle Ages. It wasn't that I took my own importance for granted or that the power behind my family's ability to time travel had been resolved. We had a lot of theories, but I'd come to the conclusion that we possessed a quirk in our genetics that opened a wormhole in time at moments when our lives were in danger, and usually in a time of abject terror as well.

To that end, in the space of a few seconds, I'd gone to the modern world, *dropped Lee off*, and returned.

Lili put a hand to my cheek, and I pulled her closer, renewing my tight embrace. It had been a very near thing. Then I looked at her brother over the top of her head. "How many people were watching, do you think?"

"Many," Ieuan said.

"More people than at Rhuddlan?" I said. "We managed to keep that situation contained."

"We won't be able to contain this," Ieuan said. "You're the king, and people who haven't had the privilege of meeting you before witnessed a miracle just now."

I made a move to run a hand through my hair and stopped myself, since my hand was wet and covered in muck from the moat. The very idea of miracles made me uncomfortable, never mind that I might be part of one myself.

"Did Callum find the C-4?" I said.

"Yes. You kept him busy long enough to disarm three of them," Lili said. "Lee put the bombs in the latrine shafts in the tower, just like at Canterbury."

I looked down at Lili, hearing the *but* in her voice.

"He was working on a fourth when you jumped," Lili said.

Ieuan stuck out a hand to me. "Let's get you out of there."

I grasped his hand and allowed him to help me out of the water, and then we both pulled Lili up the embankment. It was only when we were at the top of the turf wall that I really took notice of the hundreds of people silently watching our progress. They lined not only the wall-walk on the battlement above the ditch but also the pathway that led back to the gate. I raised a hand in acknowledgement of their presence, and then fisted it, as if in triumph. As one, they bowed to me, which gave me a moment to gather my thoughts. I had nothing to say to them, no words that could explain what had happened, but I was their king, and I had to say something.

"All is well." I gestured that they should rise.

Several men, led by Sir Stephen, hustled out of the castle. Jeeves was among them and he was carrying blankets. In a moment, both Lili and I were warmly wrapped.

I put Lili's hand in the crook of my arm and started walking towards the gatehouse, as if being soaked from head to foot was a normal occurrence and we were out for a Sunday stroll. The crowd of onlookers parted to let us through, many falling to their knees as I passed. I couldn't blame them, really. I was still in awe of what had happened to me too.

I wondered what the explanation was going to be this time: had Avalon accepted Lee and spit me out? Or could I spin it in such a way as to say that the journey had saved my life while at the same time taking Lee off my hands? That certainly was the way I was choosing to see it.

We reached the stairway to the Fitzwilliam gatehouse. Geoffrey de Geneville met us on the bottom step leading up to the entrance. "Sire."

"Geneville," I said. We started up the steps—and not two at a time.

Bronwen met us at the top. "How did you do that?" she said as she hugged Lili and then me, heedless of the fact that we were both soaking wet.

"We'll talk about it later," I said. "Right now we have bigger problems."

"Bigger problems than Lee?" Bronwen said.

I barked a laugh, filled suddenly with a feeling of exhilaration. "It isn't as if he's a problem anymore, is he?"

Her brow furrowed. "I suppose not."

Lee was gone. I hadn't had to arrest him and see him hanged. His fate was out of my hands. Even with all I'd learned about him—everyone he'd hurt and what he'd destroyed—it would have been hard to do what had to be done with him. Medieval justice, as my mother would have put it, would have been his fate. And it would have been I who would have had to mete it out. I'd have done it out of a sense of justice, and justified it to myself for that reason. But I wouldn't have liked it.

"Lee told me the King of France is coming," I said.

Concern entered Bronwen's eyes. "That's what everyone is saying."

"Lee was going to blow a hole in the outer ward so Philip would have an easier time taking the castle," I said. "He wasn't here for me."

Bronwen patted me on the shoulder in a consoling way, half-serious and half-joking. Being the King of England meant that I tended to assume most things that happened in my vicinity were about me. It was a bad habit to get into, except that it had developed because I had been accused of being an insensitive jerk for *not* realizing the effect I had on other people.

"Preparations have begun to counter him," Ieuan said. "It would be good to know where the fleet intends to land—and we still need more men."

Many soldiers lined the battlement above the outer ward, and one leaned through a crenellation to look down at us, waving a hand to get my attention. "It's Clare, sire!" He pointed northwest. "He comes!"

I looked at the soldier for a beat or two as I processed what he'd said. And then all of us took the steps up to where he stood.

An army was coming towards us. It was the very thing I needed. Valence may have been fooled by my citizen army back at Windsor, resulting in his capture and hanging, but I needed real soldiers if I was going to repel an invasion army.

"Clare to the rescue," Bronwen said. "Again."

Lili slipped her hand into mine. "He relishes that role. Admittedly, he's also very good at it."

25

It took the rest of the morning for Clare and his men to reach Dover Castle. By the time the company passed underneath the gatehouse and Clare had made his way to my receiving room, I'd had time for a quick bath and had dressed in yet another set of borrowed clothes—these somewhat finer than the ones I'd acquired either from the Archbishop's palace or from Jeeves the night before. I decided not to ask who was going shirtless at my behest.

I'd made good use of the time too, calling all my advisers currently at Dover in to talk to me. Geoffrey had become a veritable font of good information about how to repel the King of France with efficiency and the least loss of life. As I'd said to Bronwen, the aftermath of Lee's disappearance was still before us—uncovering his allies sprang to mind—but if I'd really taken him to Avalon, he himself was no longer our problem.

"Sire." Clare stopped fifteen feet from me and bowed. He was of average height, but that was the only thing about him that was ordinary. He had graying red hair, piercing blue eyes, and a way of looking at you that made you think he could see right through you. His line was as noble (though not royal) as any man's in England (more so than mine), and he dressed the part in silk and linen. He was also sporting a newly trimmed mustache and, fascinatingly, a goatee. Like the hair on the top of his head, the red goatee was liberally salted with white, reminding me of my father. I rubbed my still unshaven chin. If I grew one of those, Lili might never kiss me again.

I waved a hand for him to rise and moved forward to embrace him the French way, with a kiss on each cheek. "You came."

"You summoned me, sire." His brow furrowed. "I hear there's been some trouble."

I was glad to laugh. "You could say that."

Trouble was Clare's middle name, and he would probably be the first to admit it. For all that he had vacillated between loyalties in his younger years, I had no doubt about his loyalty to me now. He had a magnetism and sincerity about him—and no claim to the throne himself—that had convinced me, as it had convinced Edward, that he could be trusted.

"Carew met me on my way in and related some of the recent events that have occurred, though he didn't have time to go into detail. Are we sailing for France?"

"We might have been, if the last day had not happened. I know you are concerned about your lands there," I said. "But no— France is coming to us."

Clare raised one eyebrow. "That is bold of Philip." The nonchalance was typical of the man.

"He thinks me weak," I said.

"He is wrong."

"Perhaps so, but I was certainly foolish," I said. "For the last three months, I have harbored a traitor in my court and allowed him to connive unimpeded. I have seen the error of my ways, but only because my loyal followers intervened. They were almost too late, and we almost died. It was Lee, as I'm sure Carew told you."

Clare's lips twisted in a grimace.

"I see you didn't like him either," I said.

"I didn't know him for a traitor," Clare said.

"I was arrogant and didn't listen."

"It is the other side of the coin we all store in our purse, my lord," Clare said. "You make decisions every day that would bring a lesser man to his knees, and you must know your own mind in order to do that."

"I wish I'd been wiser."

He gave a rueful smile. "I imagine you already are."

I nodded, unsurprised that he, of all my advisers, understood how events had fallen out as they had.

"I have sent for the leader of the port authority and the commander of the navy," I said, relieved to put the *mea culpa* part of our conversation behind me. "The Dover Portsman is inappropriately named Jack Butcher. The latter is an old friend of yours, I believe."

"Henry de Lacy, Earl of Lincoln." Clare nodded. "I was the one who counseled you to put him in charge of your navy."

"Well, either he's really that good, was very lucky, or has better spies than I do, but he sent word yesterday that he believes the King of France is on his way." I settled a hand on Clare's shoulder. "His report has been confirmed twice over from unrelated sources."

"Including Lee, I hear."

"Yes," I said.

"Does Lacy know where Philip intends to land?"

"No," I said. "Nor did Philip's spies."

Clare smoothed the goatee he was sporting into a perfect 'v'. "Would it do any good for someone else to speak to them?"

"Geoffrey de Geneville believed them when they claimed not to know," I said. "I was witness. More extreme measures of questioning might only reveal what we want to hear, rather than the truth."

"That Philip moves now is incomprehensible to me," Clare said. "I can't understand what he's thinking."

I'd heard an earful of what Philip was thinking from Lee, of course. "He thinks he has all the advantages and we are set back on our heels."

"He's wrong, sire," Clare said.

"You bet he is."

26

"Hythe! He's landing at Hythe!" These words shouted in the corridor followed by a pounding at the door woke me.

Goddamn it!

I'd been standing in an ice cream store, gazing at the various choices, with the server waiting to select my favorite flavor. The dream winked out, superseded by the threat of a French invasion, and I rolled out of bed. I wondered why I even bothered sleeping these days, since some new disaster was going to waken me before I was ready.

Lili rubbed her eyes. "What is the hour?"

"I don't know." I turned back to her and leaned heavily on the feather bed, my hands forming fists to support my weight. I bent close to her and kissed her temple. "I'll find out what's happening. Stay here for now, and I'll return when I know more."

"Send word at the very least," she said, knowing that sometimes these events got out of control very quickly, and I might not have even a moment to speak to her myself. She snuggled back down under the covers, yawning. "Don't forget."

"I won't."

I pulled on my breeches and wrapped my cloak around myself before going to the door. It was William de Bohun who'd woken me. He'd returned from Canterbury, it seemed. I stepped into the corridor and pulled the door almost closed, so we could speak without keeping Lili awake. Her pregnancy meant she needed sleep, even in the middle of a war. Short of joining the archers on the walls (which I wouldn't have put past her), she couldn't do anything about the preparations at this point anyway.

Arthur slept in the adjacent room with his nanny. Though having him in bed with us was often comforting—to all three of us—he was a very active sleeper, and Lili and I slept better without him.

I looked at William. "How do we know they're landing at Hythe?" It was a town of roughly two thousand, southwest of Dover.

"A fisherman spotted the sails in the channel and turned for shore to warn the town. He says the boats must carry hundreds of men and horses, sire." William's face was pale in the torchlight. I was impressed with the way my other advisers were continuing to ensure that it was William who brought me news, rather than any of them, and I wondered at what point he would figure out that it wasn't the honor he thought it was.

"The Portsman of Hythe himself sent a rider to Dover to tell us of it."

Some, who didn't know the intricacies of England's maritime alert system, might call it luck—and we seemed to be getting our share of it—but the fishermen of Kent had been sent out from every port and village to watch for the French, so it was no coincidence that one of them had reported back as soon as he'd spied the fleet. As with Dover, the men of Hythe constituted a Cinque Port: owing service to the crown to defend England from invasion. Since yesterday, the word had been sent up and down the coastline, from Weymouth all the way up to Yarmouth, that the French were coming.

Some of my advisers had questioned my decision to retain the Cinque Ports as a semi-military unit once I established the royal navy. They saw the ports as independent to a fault and difficult to control. I couldn't disagree with their assessment—the portsmen *were* difficult to control. Sometimes trying to get them to agree on anything was like herding cats. It was worse than Parliament. But as I was a red-blooded American, my sympathies lay with them. I understood their drive for self-governance. In the long run, England would be better off with more of it, not less.

As it turned out, after a somewhat rocky start, the two halves of our defense fleet had been rubbing shoulders without an excess of rivalry or conflict, once the Cinque Ports understood I wasn't planning on closing them down or restricting their privileges. This threat from the French was lighting a fire under both organizations.

The Navy had never been called upon to fight and wanted to prove itself in battle. Since Lacy had been the first to warn me that the French might be coming, the initial bragging rights had gone to them. The Cinque Ports would want to even things out by being the first to take on the French, and the Portsman of Hythe would want to prove to me that his people were capable of defending England and were still relevant.

I didn't care who took on the French first, as long as they were stopped. It would be better if nobody decided to be a hero and go it alone, but we might not have a choice about that. Though all the fleets were on alert, it would take time for word to reach each town and for the boats to sail to Hythe, which meant that the men of that town had to hold out until reinforcements arrived.

I could see why the French had chosen Hythe as the best place to land their fleet. It had a good flat beach, and it was one of the few beaches along the Kent coast that didn't have massive cliffs overlooking it. When Julius Caesar had attempted to land at Dover, the sight of the opposing army of Britons standing on the cliffs above the port, brandishing their weapons and screaming at him, had sent him scurrying north to Walmer to find a better place to land. Such was the Roman war machine that Caesar had managed not only to land his ships, unload men and horses, and form up, but he'd done it while under constant fire from above, since the Britons had followed him up the coast. I could see them now in my mind's eye, taunting him the whole way.

I had no idea if Philip knew his history, but Walmer had certainly been a possible landing spot for him, particularly if he knew about the army I had standing on the cliffs of Dover. My men, like their long-dead brethren, were ready to repel an invasion. Also like the ancient Britons, my army was mobile, but I didn't exactly have a convoy of trucks by which to move them. Caesar had come across the English Channel at its narrowest point, not knowing what lay on the other side. Philip knew that the center of my fleet was at Dover, and wisely had chosen to land at a spot fifteen miles away. I could be grateful that he hadn't decided to go fifteen miles farther to Dungeness.

William recognized the expression on my face. "Sir Stephen says the men of Hythe will be crushed."

"And what does Jack Butcher say?"

William cleared his throat and looked down at the ground. "I cannot repeat it in your presence, sire, other than to say that he respectfully disagreed."

I laughed. "I bet you can't. Let me put on my boots and you can help me into my armor."

"Yes, my lord."

"We'll need every archer," I said, with a glance at the door through which Lili lay sleeping. My archers accompanied me everywhere, but we didn't have two hundred horses available for them. They had nearly fifteen miles to march to reach Hythe beach.

"Lord Ieuan already has them moving."

"How late are we going to be?" Whether because she couldn't lie there and wait for the news or because she could hear me through the door, Lili had risen and now stood in the doorway. She'd lit the candles in our room. Branwen, her maid, and Jeeves, my manservant, had entered the room through a side door and were bustling about, choosing clothing. William and I returned to the room. Jeeves would help me dress, but William was my squire and would arm me. He began laying out my gear while I put on a pair of socks.

"Dawn is less than hour away, my lady, and it seems the French intend to make the beach before the sun rises," William said.

I exchanged a look with Lili, and her expression showed worry. We couldn't reach Hythe in an hour, not with the kind of force we needed to repel an invasion. Our need to organize ourselves was going to give the French precious time on the beach at Hythe. Both successful invasions of England by the French—the first in 1066 and the second in 1215—had succeeded in part because the landings had been unopposed.

If I were invading the beaches of France, I would have chosen the gray light before dawn too. At that hour, the white beach would stand out, and sometimes you could see all around you more clearly than a few minutes later when the sun was shining behind you. Not that we'd had a plethora of sunny days recently.

I wasn't going to second-guess Dover's Portsman about the doughtiness of the men of Hythe, but unless they'd been practicing their archery such that they were better than my Welshmen, they didn't stand a chance against the French fleet and would be better off waiting for our reinforcements. The best I could hope for now was containment.

"What do you want from me?" Lili said.

Jeeves had polished my boots until they shone, and he handed the right one to me. I paused before putting it on, surprised she'd asked the question in front of everyone else. And then I realized she'd done so because she knew what my answer was going to be and was going to accept it. "I want you to help defend Dover, which will need defending if we're wrong about where the French are landing. I can think of a scenario where Philip sends an expeditionary force to Hythe to distract us, while the main body of the fleet lands right underneath us here."

Lili nodded, looking down at her feet. I leaned sideways a bit to see into her face, but when she looked up, it showed simple concern, not the intensity of yesterday.

"Do you have a further thought?" I said hopefully.

She shook her head. She couldn't force the *sight* to come to her; we just had to be grateful when it did. I consoled myself that at least she wasn't having foresight of my death.

"All the Cinque Ports are on alert, my lord," William said. "The men of Dover are moving into position now. Ships have put to sea and are sailing for Hythe as we speak."

"From what direction comes the wind?" Jeeves said. He might not be a warrior himself, but he knew a thing or two about warfare.

"The southwest, as usual," William said.

I grunted my disappointment. "Our ships won't beat those of us on horseback there—and maybe not even those on foot, not sailing into the wind like that."

"No, sire." William bowed his head.

"I don't suppose a storm is coming?" Lili asked.

"Portsman Jack cursed the absence, my lady," William said. "We can't count on such luck today."

I sighed, accepting the fickleness of the weather without too much resentment. The rainy summer had put water in the ditches at Dover, which had allowed me to dispense with Lee, so I could hardly complain that it wasn't going to come through for me on all occasions. Besides, before I'd been crowned King of England, a storm had saved Wales from domination by a rogue alliance of Norman barons, led by William de Valence. It would be unfair to expect divine intervention twice.

"Where's Edmund Mortimer?" I said.

"The riders who went in search of him have not yet returned, sire," William said. "If he was in Herefordshire like my father, as last we heard, it will take days to reach him there, and more time for them to return."

I nodded, accepting the truth of William's words. It would do no good to curse the fact that an earthquake hadn't brought

Mortimer's castle a hundred and fifty miles closer to Dover overnight.

Within another few minutes, William had armed me. Lili walked with me to the door, and I kissed her goodbye. "Be safe," she said.

"Always," I said.

We didn't discuss the fact that we spoke the same words to each other every time I left, but no king could lead his men into battle and remain safe. That was the reality of war in the Middle Ages. I was facing death for the fourth time in four days.

27

A force of two thousand men, including my two hundred archers, marched towards Hythe. While my cavalry and I could reach it in two or three hours at worst, fewer than five hours was probably pushing it for those on foot. At least in this case, we had no baggage—it was a straight shot down the road as quickly as we could travel. We would worry about food and supplies once we knew what we were facing.

The Archdeacon of Canterbury, one Richard de Ferings, had a castle and church at Lympne, two miles to the northwest of Hythe. He might find himself descended upon tonight by me and more men than he thought he could feed. Given how things had gone back in Canterbury, however, I assumed he wouldn't complain about it or feel he had anyone he could complain to, barring Pope Boniface himself.

Since the incident with Lee, I'd almost forgotten about my dispute with the pope. It was odd to think that two days ago I thought I could—and needed to—put my concerns about Lee on the back burner. At least, with the French spies locked in the basement, I had their testimony to fall back on when it came time for negotiations with Philip and the pope. I had every intention of putting both Archbishop Romeyn and Geoffrey de Geneville to good use as my ambassadors. For once, I'd have gravitas on my side.

The sun was well up by the time we rode from the cliffs at Dover, keeping to the high ground more than three hundred feet above sea level. The sick pit of tension in my stomach drove me forward, and all of us kept our eyes on the sea to the southeast, straining to see the sails of the French fleet and praying we would reach Hythe before the French did.

We didn't.

And what's more, it didn't matter.

We approached the town, still on the high ground, and came to a complete halt. At the top of the ridge, with still a half-mile to go to the beach, we could see sails in the distance off shore, but they weren't coming inland to join the handful of ships that had already landed. I pulled out my binoculars and stared through them until the men around me grew impatient with my sudden stillness and silence.

Finally, Clare said, "What is it? What's happening?"

I scanned up and down the beach. All along it, men, women, and even children mingled, while others worked to lay out dead men in rows. There must have been at least a hundred dead on one section of the beach, while a smaller number—perhaps two dozen—had been laid together fifty yards closer to the town.

As I watched, one man stabbed a flagpole, with a French flag flying from it, into the sand and set it alight—to match the three others that were already burning farther down the beach. The people seemed completely unconcerned about the French ships that remained in the Channel.

At first I gaped, speechless, and couldn't answer the men, and then I laughed. "See for yourself." I handed the binoculars to Clare. "The army we brought appears surplus to requirements. Portsman Jack Butcher of Dover is going to be very, very happy that he was right."

I spurred my horse. Clare was slow to respond, since he'd been looking through my binoculars. I would have thought he'd have acquired his own by now, but maybe they were in the bottom of his saddle bags. Regardless, he and my other companions caught up to me quickly.

I led the cavalry down the hill and through the town of Hythe. Not a single person came out to greet us, not surprising since the entire village was on the beach. Five minutes later, we spilled out onto the wide sand—flags flying, armor glinting in the sunlight—into a fight that had already been won.

Three French galleys—large, well-built, and empty—had been pulled up onto the sands. Englishmen swarmed over them, some passing items to other men and women who'd made a path through the shallow water from the ships to a stash of goods that was piling up a few yards above the high water mark.

At first nobody noticed us, and then a man in a hat with a flamboyant white feather raised his hand above his head and waved. "The king! The king is here!"

As one, the people on the beach stopped what they were doing, turned to look at us, and sent up an enormous cheer, complete with hats tossed into the air in jubilation. I shook my head in wonder. The dead men on the beach weren't English fisher folk. Uniforms tended to be haphazardly worn in the Middle Ages, but I could tell the difference between the villagers' attire and that of the dead French soldiers.

The man in the white-feathered hat was surrounded by a half-dozen sweaty but grinning men, all of whom stepped forward to greet me. "Sire, I am Portsman Tom Gurney, baron of Hythe Cinque Port."

I leaned forward, crossing my forearms and resting them on my thigh. "What has happened here, Portsman?" I could figure out for myself that they'd defeated the French, of course, as unlikely as it seemed, but the man had a story to tell and deserved the right to tell it.

Tom's eyes lit from within. "The French came, sire, and we slaughtered them."

I gazed at him for a second and then lifted my head to look to where the French fleet was still visible offshore. The ships seemed farther away than they'd been when my army had been standing on the hills above Hythe. It could have been the result of the change in perspective, but it also could be that the French army had seen what had happened to the men they'd sent in first, noticed my army's arrival, and thought better of the whole endeavor.

Then a horn call echoed across the water. I sat up straighter, my eyes searching to see who'd blown it and afraid I'd been wrong about the French. It wasn't until I stood in the stirrups that I could see beyond the curve of the land into the eastern Channel: our ships—both Cinque Port and Royal Navy—were moving into position.

Then an answering call came from the west, and my heart lifted again. Portsman Tom whooped, finally tossing his hat into the air in his exuberance. Our fleet was sailing towards Hythe from both directions, hemming the French fleet in. Philip had two choices now: land and fight or retreat back to France.

Even as I watched, multiple flashes followed by the boom of cannon fire came from several of my ships that were closest to the French fleet. Cannons were new to medieval warfare (thanks to the technology I'd brought from Avalon), and I didn't know how effective they were really going to be, but their very existence could put the finishing touches on the French defeat.

I found myself grinning. Dismounting, I moved towards Tom, who'd retrieved his hat and now swept it off his head again in a bow. I waved aside his obeisance and clasped his forearm man to man.

"I think you'd better tell your story from the beginning," I said.

Tom relished the telling of the tale, first on the beach to me, in the company of the men (and women) who'd fought beside him, and then again in the assembly building for the Cinque Port where they put on a feast, one like I hadn't seen outside of Westminster Castle, to celebrate the victory.

"We had word, of course," Tom began, "that the French were coming. Me and my boys got together right there and then in this hall last night to decide what to do about it. Some of the men put to sea immediately, and others went up on the bluff to watch and wait. The rain held off, with clear skies, which we took to be a sign of God's blessing on our endeavor. Though there was no moon, the stars were bright."

"We were there too, Tom!" A young woman spoke up from the left of the dais where Tom was telling his story. She looked to be in her early twenties, tall and slender, with her blonde hair wound into a knot at the back of her head. She wore breeches, as did half the women in the room. Lili and Bronwen would have been pleased to see it.

Tom pointed at her. "You were, Rosalind, and I was remiss not to mention it. Times have changed."

"And for the better!" An older woman, who wore a dress and apron, cupped her hands around her mouth and shouted up to the front.

"I can't argue with that, can I?" Tom said. "Seeing as how my own wife skewered a Frenchie all on her own." He turned to look at the woman in question, who'd been sitting on the dais beside him. She, along with many in the room, both men and women, nodded their heads. Now I really wished Lili and Bronwen were here.

Tom cleared his throat. "If I could continue without any more interruptions—"

"—they're just setting you straight, Tom." This time it was a middle-aged man who spoke. He had a paunch and a self-satisfied look on his bearded face.

Tom flapped a hand at him before launching into the rest of his story. "When John Goodbody came flying back to port with news that the French were headed across the Channel, we knew it was us they was coming to see, not Dover, Folkstone, or Dungeness. We were ready, glad it was us and not them."

Again, there were nods all around, and I couldn't blame them for being proud. They'd done a great deed and deserved all the accolades that would be heaped upon them in the coming days and weeks. The Hythe casualties—mostly men but a few women too—had been laid in state in the nave of the Hythe Church. Earlier, before the dinner, the entire town and all of my men had filed past the dead in a long, solemn column to pay our respects.

"We got ourselves set—men hidden in the sands—" Tom held up a hand to forestall the protests before they could start, "I'm callin' 'em men but there were women among them too. When you're a soldier, you're all my men."

The various women in the audience subsided, evidently mollified.

"—more on the bluff above. We've archers too, some good boys and girls among them, and we watched and waited for them Frenchies to hit the beach. We were lucky they sent only a few boats to start, to scout out the situation—"

"Don't call it luck, Tom." The same middle-aged man spoke and then stood up. "It was good policy on the French's part. They didn't know what they were walking into, and they were smart enough not to commit their whole fleet without knowing what they were up against." He looked at me. "Our king knows a thing or two about fighting. We could have lined that beach with munitions like's been done along the Severn."

I nodded my head gravely. "They were offered to you."

"We didn't want them going off accidently," the man said. What he didn't say was that *maybe* they hadn't quite trusted their new upstart king as yet.

"I understood that even at the time, and as it turned out, your own defenses were more than adequate."

The man nodded his head gravely at me. "Will Thompson, at your service, sire. I'm the chief watchman for Hythe."

"I'm glad you know your business, Will," I said.

Will bowed again before gesturing to Tom that he should continue.

"Well, the Frenchies landed," Tom said somewhat huffily at having been interrupted yet again. "Only twenty men disembarked first. We let them set up a perimeter, knowing that our archers were going to take them out first. Then the rest decided they could follow. We hid in the sand until nearly all two hundred were on the beach. They lit two torches to let the rest of the fleet know they could come in. We let them, though we were worried about how big their army was."

More nods all around. None interrupted now, however. They were reliving the scene, breaths held. I could tell how touch-and-go the victory had been. The people of Hythe had had only a short timeframe in which to attack the advance party before they would have had to deal with the whole fleet.

"The light ruined their night vision, o' course. We could see them, and they couldn't see us," Tom said. "The archers on the bluff shot one volley to disable the outer sentries, and then we moved."

Silence fell in the hall. It would have been the first time many—if not most—of them had seen battle or killed a man. It wasn't something any of them would ever forget, and the story of the victory at Hythe would live on, perhaps for centuries.

I rose to my feet and said gently, "How many men did you have on the beach, Tom?"

"Everyone we could muster. We had two hundred on the bluff, and five hundred on the beach," he said.

"Enough." I lifted my cup of beer. "To the people of Hythe."

"To us!" came the answering toast.

"To those who fell in sacrifice to our way of life." I raised my cup again.

The answer this time was a silent lifting of cups, grave nods, and a draining of drink.

Then Tom raised his cup one more time and called out. "We taught them Frenchies a lesson!"

"Hear! Hear!"

I drank with my new friends, happy to celebrate tonight's victory, even if I'd played no role in it.

Tomorrow I would return to Canterbury. There was one more thing I had to do.

28

As at our previous meeting, Archbishop Romeyn ushered me into the receiving room at Canterbury Palace. I'd wanted to come every day for the last week, but Cardinal Acquasparta had taken a turn for the worse and hadn't been able to receive me. It was just as well. My time had been spent seeing to the aftermath of the battle at Hythe and the destruction of Canterbury—as well as conferring with my advisers.

They'd spent the whole of this week counseling me against one course of action or another in my dealings with the Church. I had leverage, now, to use against Acquasparta, Philip, and the pope. We had the testimony of the French spies, which gave us all the evidence we needed of a broad conspiracy stretching from Ireland to Italy. There was no need for a confrontation when all I had to do was suggest to Acquasparta that I knew of his involvement. At worst, I could send Romeyn to Italy and have him threaten to reveal to the world who was really behind the destruction of Canterbury Castle and the attack on Hythe. Lee may have destroyed Canterbury, and the French king had attacked my shores, but all these events could be laid at Acquasparta's feet.

If I did that, the pope would back off. He'd have no choice.

I could simply let it happen. It was the medieval way of doing things.

After the incident with the heretic, I'd controlled my anger in front of my subjects because I hadn't wanted to expend it on the innocent. I'd been busy this last week, so I hadn't been cooling my heels, exactly, but it was probably for the best that I'd cooled my temper. After the castle had fallen, it was in Peckham's own courtyard that I'd been reduced to a trembling wreck by the attack on my family, and it was better to have that memory less fresh in my mind now that it was time to talk to Acquasparta.

And though Acquasparta was far from innocent, he was ill with abdominal cancer. Rachel couldn't diagnose the type more specifically without surgery, but his end would be far more painful and severe than any punishment I could devise for him.

"Sire!" Peckham bent his head gracefully and rose to his feet, more steadily than when I'd last seen him.

Acquasparta, who'd been standing by the fire with a cup in his hand, turned to me too. I'd confirmed by back channels (i.e. Aaron) before I came that he was out of bed and had been assured that today was one of his better days. I don't know what I would have done if he'd been too ill to see me. It would have been frustrating to be all fired up with nowhere to go, like at Hythe, for all that I was happy we'd won that battle with little loss of English life.

"King David." Acquasparta inclined his head. "I trust you are well."

"Yes, thank you. I am pleased to see you on your feet."

"Today is a good day," Acquasparta said. "We've had so few of them recently."

"Hopefully the coming days and weeks will see only improvement," I said.

Acquasparta smiled in that superior and self-satisfied way he had. "I understand that plans are already underway to rebuild Canterbury Castle."

"Indeed." I just managed not to gape at him. I couldn't believe he could so calmly mention that which he'd had a hand in destroying.

"And I believe congratulations are in order as well," Acquasparta said. "All applaud that you managed to defeat King Philip's fleet with so little loss of life."

"The people of Hythe are to be credited with that achievement," I said, "but I accept your compliments on their behalf."

Acquasparta moved to one of the ornate chairs and sat with a sigh. It was rude of him, actually, to sit before me. Peckham hastily gestured that I should take the chair opposite. I waved him off, moving instead to the side table to refill my cup of wine. It didn't actually need a refill, since I'd taken only a few sips, but I was giving myself time to think. I couldn't believe that

Acquasparta could speak of Canterbury Castle and Hythe with such aplomb.

I looked over at the cardinal, studying his drawn face. Despite his illness, he still managed to look at me with superiority and a hint of disdain.

The legate lifted one hand and dropped it. "Have you considered what we discussed during our last visit?"

"I have."

"It is my hope that you will consent to all three items I put to you."

What a shocker. "Even after the invasion attempt, Pope Boniface would continue to support Philip's claim to the Duchy of Aquitaine?" I said.

Acquasparta waved a hand dismissively. "The two issues are unrelated."

I kept my voice mild. "So your position on the matter of prosecuting heretics in England has not changed either?"

Acquasparta's eyes turned steely. "These are matters over which the Church has complete jurisdiction. It must be allowed to oversee the spiritual needs of the people as it sees fit."

As I considered him, I was glad to realize—just as when I'd encountered Lee on Dover's wall-walk—that it wasn't anger I felt, even though I had every right to be angry. I didn't desire revenge or retribution. I didn't feel the need to one-up the pope. Those emotions were for my enemies and opponents. I was reminded of the time when I was fourteen, back at Castell y Bere before I knew

I was my father's son. He explained to me then that a leader had to control himself—to be cold, not hot—to mete out true justice. As this understanding renewed itself in me, resolve crystalized in my belly.

I wanted to do what was right. Threatening the pope might get me what I wanted in the short term, but it wouldn't address the real issue—and it wasn't *me*. While the heretic had turned out to be a fraud planted by Acquasparta to challenge me and allow him to meet with one of King Philip's spies, that fact didn't change the truth of what I'd declared to my own men in this very palace.

"Cardinal Acquasparta," I said, "you should know that I have made Geoffrey de Geneville my ambassador to the French court. His commission is to inquire of King Philip as to the timing of the withdrawal of his claim to Aquitaine in favor of my own."

I didn't mention the possibility of going to war if Philip didn't comply. Again, I wasn't interested in threatening anyone. I was done playing games.

Puzzlement entered Acquasparta's expression, and he gave me an oily smile. "Sire, I'm not sure—"

"I am," I said. "As regards to the return of the funds from the *taxatio*, I would appreciate it if you could explain to Pope Boniface about my new and urgent need to expend those funds for the defense of England. I'm sure he will understand how the unprovoked attack on our shores by France only served to emphasize the impossibility of complying with His Holiness's request."

Peckham was staring at me now, his mouth open. I had Acquasparta's attention, too. My serenity and surety felt like an extra layer of armor, and I took a sip from my goblet.

I had one last issue to address. "As to the matter of heresy, England will continue to welcome people of every faith, religion, and creed to our shores." I gave him a slight bow. "It is the foundation of my rule, and it is thanks to you, in fact, that I am now able to articulate it."

"How is that?" Acquasparta said, perhaps despite himself. He was looking much less contented than when I'd arrived.

"'Give me the liberty to know, to utter, and to argue freely according to conscience, above all liberties,'" I quoted again, and as Acquasparta blinked at me, I added, "As I told my men in the aftermath of the heretic's arrest, that right has always been inherent in their souls and in the souls of every human being on this planet, whether they knew it or not. I will not take it from them, and I will not allow anyone else to do so either. Not in any England that I rule."

Acquasparta's brow furrowed. "His Holiness is the head of the Church. He is the steward of Christ on earth. You cannot change that with a snap of your fingers."

"I don't intend to," I said, "but in my England, every man may worship God according to his conscience."

Peckham was staring at me, aghast.

I didn't look at him but kept my eyes fixed on Acquasparta, whose face had paled. Then he gave a little laugh. "This is absurd—"

I inclined my head, to the exact degree Acquasparta had done when he greeted me. "I must attend to my other duties. I pray your health continues to improve, and you have my best wishes for your upcoming travels home to Italy." I spun on my heel and headed for the door. Before I reached it, however, I turned back. "I almost forgot. If you happen to see him, please convey my regards to Martin the heretic." I snapped my fingers. "Oh, I forgot. His friends informed me recently that his real name is Guillaume."

SARAH WOODBURY

Epilogue

Westminster Palace

David

—Two months later

I sat on my throne in my receiving room, waiting for the Archbishop of Canterbury to come to me. He'd appeared at the gate three minutes ago, having crossed the Thames River from Lambeth Palace, his residence in London. Carew, who'd arrived only that morning from his estates in Somerset, was even now escorting the Archbishop here. He'd sent a runner at top speed to give me fair warning first, probably more miffed than I that Peckham had shown up unannounced. I didn't begrudge the Archbishop his little ploys. It was only fair after what I'd sprung on him at our last meeting.

I'd been receiving guests anyway, so I already wore my crown and was dressed in an ornate robe as befitted the King of England. Lili insisted that silver and dark green suited my coloring as much as blue and gold did, and she wore a gown that was the feminine twin of mine.

Her blue eyes glinted with a tinge of defiance, an emotion that I myself had been feeling ever since the victory at Hythe. King Philip had crossed the Channel to test my strength and been defeated by a motley crew of villagers. Cardinal Acquasparta had thought to test my strength by inciting the people of Canterbury to riot and been defeated by my resolve. Pope Boniface should know by now not to test me again.

But I was ready to stand my ground if he did. In fact, I couldn't wait. The defeat of King Philip's fleet because of the determination and will of my subjects cast a rosy glow on every act I shepherded through Parliament and every decision I made. It was the common folk who'd sent the French fleeing for their own harbors—common folk who hadn't even done it for me. They'd done it for England—for the *idea* of England, which I represented, but which would exist long after I was gone.

I was prepared, in fact, to declare the Protestant Reformation right here and now. Even not knowing what Archbishop Peckham had to say to me that might inspire an impromptu trip across the Thames, I'd chosen not to clear the room. Maybe it was unwarranted bravado, but as I'd told Acquasparta back in Canterbury, I didn't fear the pope or what he might do to me.

Callum, who'd taken up a place to my right for the audience, took a half-step closer to me. "Are you ready?" He'd just returned from his lands too.

Tomorrow would be my twenty-fourth birthday, and Thanksgiving was a week after that. My whole family was coming, in fact, and would be gathered for the first time since last year's disastrous holiday when we lost Anna, Mom, and Marty to Avalon. I gave an inward laugh. On second thought, maybe we ought to have gathered for Christmas instead.

Smiling, I reached out to take Lili's hand and squeezed it in reassurance before letting go again. She rarely sat beside me during these receptions, but I was glad she'd chosen to do so today. Nearly six months pregnant, she had piled her throne with cushions. Now she shifted in her seat to adjust them more comfortably.

"He's here, Dafydd," she said.

Sure enough, a moment later the Archbishop of Canterbury came through the archway. He hesitated on the threshold, perhaps surprised to see how many people were in the room. Archbishop Romeyn held his elbow, and I met Romeyn's eyes for a moment. He gave me an infinitesimal nod, and a bit of the tension in my shoulders eased. After my conversation with Acquasparta, I'd sent Romeyn to Italy anyway, just to make sure Boniface knew I was serious about what I'd said.

Peckham advanced towards me. He wore white and gold robes and his chain of office around his neck. He was dressed as formally for this occasion as I'd ever seen him, down to the funny peaked hat on his head. I was glad I'd worn my crown today. We would face each other in our official capacities, which was the only proper way to discuss a momentous missive from the pope, especially if it put my throne in jeopardy.

But then, to my surprise, Peckham's face split into a smile, wider than the one I'd directed at Lili. I hastily rearranged my own face to one of interest, rather than the benign amusement that I'd been affecting, the better to absorb whatever was in the letter Peckham held that had made him happy. I was almost more worried now, because I couldn't remember the last time I'd seen Peckham smile.

Callum gestured with one hand that Peckham should come closer. He had walked down the red carpet on Romeyn's arm, but now he released it and came the last few paces alone—a little more slowly than the last time I'd seen him. At least his color was good. The Archbishop came to halt at the foot of my throne, down three steps from where Lili and I sat.

"Sire."

"Archbishop," I said, "how good of you to come today. To what do I owe the pleasure?"

Peckham pressed his lips together, restraining his smile, though a hint of it remained around his lips. Then he said, "I have received a letter from Pope Boniface addressed to you. Romeyn carried it all the way from Italy. His Holiness asked that I present it, with his best wishes, and his surety that God will guide your decisions along the straight path."

The second part was somewhat alarming, but best wishes sounded promising. Beside me, Lili let out the breath she'd been holding.

"Is the letter something that all might care to hear," I said, "or would it be better to read it in private?"

I wanted it to be his choice. If he thought the contents of the letter might humiliate me, I had the sense that he cared enough about me and my future as the King of England to give me warning before cutting me off at the knees. Everything so far had indicated good news, but I wasn't going to assume that quite yet.

"That should be for you to decide, sire," Peckham held out the letter, "but please know that I asked Romeyn not to tell you of his arrival so that I could be the one to bring the letter to you."

Carew stepped forward, took the letter from Peckham, and turned to hand it to me. This was one of those strange formalities of the English royal court—no courtier gave anything—messages or gifts—directly to me. It was easier to accept the tradition than to argue with it. Better to save argument for the issues that were really important.

I held the scroll in my lap for a second before opening it. The wax seal hadn't been broken. I looked at Peckham, who was standing with his hands folded across his belly. "You have not read it?"

"It came under the cover of another letter to me," Peckham said, still serene.

"So you don't know what it says," I said, not as a question.

For the first time, Peckham's expression faltered. "His Holiness conveyed to me his warm regard for you and for the people of England."

I looked at Romeyn, but his eyes were downcast, focused somewhere in the vicinity of my boots. I wasn't getting any help from him, not this time.

Lili was back to being tense beside me. Callum leaned in to whisper to me, his face turned away from the audience room. "He can't be that innocent, can he?"

"I wouldn't have said so," I said. "Well, no time like the present."

Callum stepped back, and everyone in the room watched me intently—even Romeyn, who'd looked up now that it was too late to answer my unspoken query—as I broke the seal on the letter. Unrolling it, I was happy to see it was written in Latin. The pope's English was nonexistent, but he could easily have written the letter in French. After the various greetings and flourishes, it turned out the letter was one sentence long and could be translated:

His Holiness Pope Boniface VIII lauds your continued protection of the Jews who have sought refuge in your kingdom and urges the end to murder and persecution of the same based on the unfounded accusation of blood libel.

That was it.

I looked at Peckham, hardly able to believe it. The letter said nothing about the conspiracy or about any of the three items Acquasparta had brought to my attention. It had focused on the one thing we hadn't even discussed.

"What does it say, sire?" Carew said.

My eyes on Peckham, I handed the letter to Carew, who took it. When he'd finished reading, I tipped my head to point with my chin to my herald. Carew gave the letter to him, and he began to read it in a sonorous voice. The educated among us understood Latin, but those who didn't wouldn't have to learn the gist of its contents from their neighbors, because the herald transitioned smoothly into English for a second reading.

When the herald finished, I gestured to Carew. "Clear the room, if you will."

Maybe it was odd of me to want privacy now, but the pope's letter brought up more questions than it answered, and I needed room to think about it. I looked at Peckham, and then beyond him to Romeyn. "Have you dined?"

Peckham canted his head. "We would be happy to share your table, my king."

"In his letter to me, His Holiness asked me to convey to you his confidence that your rule of Aquitaine as its Duke will result in peace and prosperity for its people," Peckham said.

I took a sip of wine. "How kind of him to say so."

Peckham either didn't hear the ironic cast to my voice or chose to ignore it. "I endeavored to impress upon His Holiness the manner in which you have taken the admonition of our Lord and Savior to heart in your dealings with those who have strayed from the Church's teachings: that no man is without sin, and thus no man should judge what is in another man's heart."

"*He that is without sin among you, let him first cast a stone,* you mean?" I said, quoting John.

Peckham nodded. "He wrote to me that he understands now that your wish to shelter those whose beliefs diverge from the right path is out of a desire to extend Christian charity to all. In this case, he believes that desire to be misplaced, but he would prefer you be guided gently to the straight path over time. That is my task." Peckham paused a moment, before adding, "Perhaps my last one."

I leaned forward, suddenly more concerned about him than what the pope had said. "Archbishop, you are not well?"

"My time is nearing an end," he said. "Perhaps you could humor an old man by speaking with him on matters of the spirit every once in a while between now and then."

He was talking to me like a son, or a grandson. It shamed me a little to realize he had such regard for me, when I had given little thought to him beyond his role as the pope's errand boy. "It would be an honor, your grace."

Peckham rose to his feet. Carew escorted him from the room, leaving me momentarily alone with Romeyn, since Callum had gone off to see to other duties.

"The letter Boniface sent was a masterly display of obfuscation and deflection, and a far cry from his earlier demands." I felt that I could talk to Romeyn in a way I couldn't speak to Archbishop Peckham.

"I read it similarly, sire." Romeyn took a sip of wine, watching me over the rim.

"It implies that Acquasparta's entire mission has been abandoned," I said. "Has the pope, in fact, given way on the issues of heretics, the *taxatio,* and Aquitaine?"

Romeyn put down his goblet. "My lord, I believe you are meant to take the letter as it is written."

"So Boniface is sidestepping the issues—for now, or forever?" I pushed my half-eaten food away.

Romeyn spread his hands. "It is not for me to say, sire."

"Was Acquasparta acting for the pope, or did he overstep his mandate?"

"Again, sire, His Holiness didn't see fit to convey his opinion on these matters to me."

I supposed I shouldn't have expected more. "Thank you for trying."

"It was my honor, sire," he said, "though you laid all the groundwork yourself. I did little."

"I am not displeased with the results," I said. "Perhaps you made a better impression than you think."

"Perhaps, sire."

I nodded and indicated that Romeyn was dismissed. I planned to talk to him again later—probably tomorrow or the next day, to get a better sense of what had gone on in Italy. I would have to speak to Peckham after that, but I was looking forward to it. I didn't plan to argue with him. Just because Peckham and I disagreed about some things didn't mean we disagreed about everything, and I was pretty sure we could find common ground that would ease some of his concerns about my spiritual health.

After Romeyn left, I sat a while at the table, trying not to feel melancholy and to enjoy the brief moment alone. I shouldn't have felt downcast. The pope's answer was the best outcome I could have hoped for, but it was as if I'd charged myself up for a battle only to find my opponent had left the field.

Then someone knocked on the door. "Come," I said, channeling my inner Star Trek because I could.

It was Bevyn. He shut the door behind him, though not before having a quick look up and down the corridor to make sure it was empty. Then he turned to me and bowed. "Sire." He stood stiffly by the door, his hands clasped behind his back.

I looked at him warily. He was nervous about something. "Is everything all right?"

He came forward. The room was narrow, warmed by a broad fireplace on my left. A dozen candles shone from the mantelpiece above it, and the long, polished table at which I was sitting took up the whole of the middle of it. Upright chairs lined both sides. The wooden table was large enough to seat twenty, though only five of us had eaten at it this afternoon. Bevyn's stocky body filled all the space between the wall and the row of chairs to my right, and he halted two paces away from me.

"I have a confession to make," he said. "I'd like you to hear me out before you respond."

I nodded, my heart beating a little faster. "Go on."

"It has to do with the letter Peckham just brought you from Pope Boniface." Bevyn had unclasped his hands from his back, but now they clenched and unclenched at his sides.

"Just tell me what this is about, Bevyn. It can't be worse than my imagination."

"I can't speak to that, my lord."

I waited, my elbows on the arms of my chair and my hands folded in front of my chin.

Bevyn drew in a breath, glanced up at the ceiling briefly to find his courage, and then looked me straight in the eye. "Sire, six months ago, when it appeared that Pope Boniface was the frontrunner to be ordained pope, the Order of the Pendragon secretly arranged to buy up all his loans from his Italian creditors."

I pressed my folded hands to my lips and looked at Bevyn over the top of them. I'd managed not to gasp or exclaim, though my eyebrows had to be in my hairline.

"As you know, our paramount concern has always been your wellbeing, sire. What we knew about Boniface indicated that he might not view the world as you do. It was a precaution only. At first."

"And now? You threatened to call in his loans if he didn't back off, is that it?" I said. Though he hadn't owned the loans himself, King Edward had done the same to both Peckham's and Boniface's predecessors—to get them to excommunicate my father.

"No, sire, we didn't."

Now I was confused. "So ... you're confessing this to me—why?"

"To alleviate your concerns that the Order has lost its ability to protect you, or—if you feared it—that the pope's actions were in any way influenced by your allies. I assure you that we had nothing to do with the letter he sent. It was your righteous action alone that forced his hand."

"Why are you telling me this?"

"We felt you needed to know," he said.

"The others threw you before me as the sacrificial lamb, did they?"

"I volunteered."

I studied him. Bevyn's demeanor had prepared me for bad news, but this was almost worse. I had refused to use the leverage I had against Boniface, and so had they. "So what you're saying is that you had the chance to influence him, to ensure that this letter contained what I wanted, and yet you didn't act? Why? Don't try to tell me it was what I would have wanted, because you don't think that way."

Bevyn had the grace to look briefly abashed, but then he said, "We had word that Boniface hasn't given up, sire. He believes he still has moves to make."

I felt a growl forming deep in my chest. "What moves?"

The grim lines on Bevyn's face deepened. "He is planning a new Crusade to take back the Holy Land, and he wants your support for it."

I gave a gasping laugh. "A new Crusade? Does he want me to go on it?"

"He wants you to lead it. You and King Philip of France are the same age, sire. Young enough to endure the hardships, and powerful enough in your own countries, both of you, to lead an army to take back Jerusalem."

I sat back in my chair. I hadn't seen that coming. "So what exactly is his play now?"

"Pope Boniface is still drafting the missive. He hopes to release it in the new year," Bevyn said, "but if he calls upon you publicly to Crusade and you refuse, you will look very bad indeed. Any complaints you have against Acquasparta will appear to be a false accusation to distract from your refusal."

I gave a laughing scoff. "So, if I crusade, he leaves me alone to do as I wish in my own country. And if I don't ..."

"That is still many months away, sire. Best not to borrow trouble."

"How did you hear of this?" Then my eyes narrowed. "I thought you didn't have a spy in Boniface's court?"

"We didn't—"

I overrode him. "Don't deny that you know about this because of the Order. It's written all over your face, and I can tell you're quite proud that you had the foresight not to call in Boniface's debts now, to give you influence and leverage over him later. Who is it?"

"Sire—"

I leaned forward. "Tell me who it is."

Bevyn swallowed hard, knowing better than to deny me this one thing I asked. "Acquasparta's secretary."

"Why would he report to you?"

"He has an English mother. Acquasparta doesn't know."

"Who found that out? Whose idea was it to recruit him?"

The door opened behind Bevyn, and Lili entered the room. "It was mine." She hesitated on the threshold. Her chin was up and her gaze steady, but she had her hands clasped in front of her in such a way that told me she was a little nervous too.

I studied her. "Did you fear I'd be angry?"

"It was a possibility," she said.

I shook my head, caught between disbelief, gratitude, and awe. "I don't know what I've done to deserve such loyalty, but I can't be angry when you were looking out for my interests in a way that I could not."

"We love you," Lili said.

"I know." Then I bit my lip. "I'm not exactly looking forward to crusading with Philip of France, however."

"You can't predict the future, my love," Lili said, advancing towards me. "Not even you know what it holds anymore."

"No, I don't. I suspect that's a good thing." Smiling, I rose to take her hand.

The End

SARAH WOODBURY

Historical Background

"In king Edward I.'s reign, anno 1293, the French shewed themselves with a great fleet before Hythe, and one of their ships, having two hundred soldiers on board, landed their men in the haven, which they had no sooner done, but the townsmen came upon them and slew every one of them; upon which the rest of the fleet hoisted sail, and made no further attempt." –Edward Hasted (*The Town and Parish of Hythe*, 1799)

Isn't that awesome? As my eldest son says, "you can't help but feel there has to be more to the story!"

The townspeople's ability to repel a French invasion is rooted in the formation of the Cinque Ports: "In the centuries before the Tudor Kings of England first developed a standing navy, the men and ships of the Cinque Ports provided a fleet to meet the military and transportation needs of their Royal masters. With good reason, these small ports have been dubbed the Cradle of the Royal Navy." http://cinqueports.org/

Men of the Cinque Ports, the five initial ones being Dover, Hythe, Sandwich, New Romney, and Hastings, were given freedom from a wide range of taxes and the ability to be tried in their own courts rather than royal courts. In return, they were expected to defend England from invasion. Which the men of Hythe seemed to do with efficiency, in our history as well as David's.

As the *After Cilmeri* series has continued, I have tried to adhere to the history and culture of the Middle Ages, even as David's story has strayed further from 'real' history. The descriptions of the towns in England, England's political structure and issues of the time, and its conflict with the Church that David faces, all evolve out of the people and events of the late thirteenth century. Disputes with King Philip of France were ongoing during this era, and Pope Boniface's view of the Church's role in secular affairs conflicted with the philosophies of both France and England. The Medieval Inquisition was also in full swing, much as I've described in *Warden of Time*.

As always, a difficulty with writing historical fiction—even when it's fantasy—is to tell the story without getting bogged down in historical explanations or politics. Suffice to say that the number of players in the English court and the intricacies of English politics can be both deadly dull and endlessly fascinating, and I try to walk the line between the two.

Acknowledgments

First and foremost, I'd like to thank my lovely readers for encouraging me to continue the *After Cilmeri* Series. I have always been passionate about these books, and it's wonderful to be able to share my stories with readers who love them too.

Thank you to my husband, without whose love and support I would never have tried to make a living as a writer. Thank to my family who has been nothing but encouraging of my writing, despite the fact that I spend half my life in medieval Wales. And thank you to my beta readers: Darlene, Anna, Jolie, Melissa, Cassandra, Brynne, Gareth, Taran, Dan, and Venkata. I couldn't do this without you.

About the Author

With two historian parents, Sarah couldn't help but develop an interest in the past. She went on to get more than enough education herself (in anthropology) and began writing fiction when the stories in her head overflowed and demanded she let them out. While her ancestry is Welsh, she only visited Wales for the first time while in college. She has been in love with the country, language, and people ever since. She even convinced her husband to give all four of their children Welsh names.

She makes her home in Oregon.

www.sarahwoodbury.com

10192494R00184

Made in the USA
Lexington, KY
19 September 2018